Young-Minded
Hustler

Young-Minded Hustler

Tysha

www.urbanbooks.net

Urban Books, LLC
78 East Industry Court
Deer Park, NY 11729

Young-Minded Hustler Copyright © 2012 Tysha

ISBN 13: 978-1-60162-516-8
ISBN 10: 1-60162-516-2

First Printing August 2012
Printed in the United States of America

10 9 8 7 6 5 4 3 2

This is a work of fiction. Any references or similarities to actual events, real people, living or dead, or to real locales are intended to give the novel a sense of reality. Any similarity in other names, characters, places, and incidents is entirely coincidental.

Distributed by Kensington Publishing Corp.
Submit Wholesale Orders to:
Kensington Publishing Corp.
C/O Penguin Group (USA) Inc.
Attention: Order Processing
405 Murray Hill Parkway
East Rutherford, NJ 07073-2316
Phone: 1-800-526-0275
Fax: 1-800-227-9604

Young-Minded Hustler

by

Tysha

Dedication

Young-Minded Hustler is dedicated to my first true love, my oldest son, Je'Vohn M. Hill. I'm so very proud of the man you have become. You are headed for celebrity, success, and greatness. There are no words strong enough to describe how I feel about you and your life. It is a pleasure to call you my friend, my son, my life. Thank you for the honor of writing this story. I only pray it reads exactly the way you imagined. The world is yours, forever.

Mommy loves you, dearly.

Acknowledgment

My youngest son, Je'Ronn M. Hill (a.k.a. Reese). God blessed me with two of the strongest, independent souls to call my own. You are not only my son, you are one of my best friends. Others may never understand our bond and it doesn't matter because we do. I'll always have your back as I know you will always have mine. My world is incomplete if my baby boy isn't with me. We will be three against the world forever.

Mommy loves you, always.

Prelude

Boom!

Boom!

The pounding on the door sent a deafening vibration throughout the townhouse.

"What the fuck?" Melvin yelled. His frame lay resting on the living room couch when he heard the banging. Melvin jumped up and ran into the bathroom to flush the bags of rock cocaine in his pants pocket. He knew this day would eventually come and had prepared for it years before. Melvin never kept any significant amount of weight in the place where he and his family rested their heads. As Melvin flushed the toilet, he remembered his son, Prince, was in the house with him.

"Prince, run to your bedroom, little man, and stay there. Run, Prince, run!"

There was urgency in his voice that startled his son. Something in his father's words told the ten-year-old that his life would never be the same.

Prince was in the kitchen, planted in front of the open refrigerator. He heard the banging followed by his father's orders for him to run to his room. Unfortunately, his body would not move. Determined not to give the police reason to pump holes in him, he stood frozen. With the refrigerator door in one hand and a pitcher of red Kool-Aid in the other, Prince began shaking uncontrollably.

Boom!

"Police!"

"Freeze!"

"Daddy, where are you? Daddy!"

He knew his father would protect him. Prince's heart pumped so hard he thought it would jump right out of his chest.

"Get down! Now," Roberts demanded. This bust was going to catapult his career. Taking down the man known as Legend on the streets was certain to get the police Commisioner's attention. A promotion was sure to be in the near future. "Get down and don't move or I'll put lead in you."

"Daddy!"

"My son is here. Do *not* hurt him." Melvin caught sight of the narc with a gun pointed to his head. For a split second, Melvin wanted to spit in the crooked cop's face, but the thought of his son being hurt stopped him. "Prince, it will be okay, son, just stay where you are."

"Shut the hell up," commanded a young white officer.

The cop's words pissed Melvin off and it took all he had inside not to haul off and backhand the rookie. "Go straight to hell, man, and y'all better not hurt my son," Melvin responded.

"It doesn't look like you're in much of a position to be giving orders. This is the end of the road for you, McGee. Time's up." Roberts and a few uniformed officers laughed.

"Man, fuck you! What, you think you got something on me? You think I'm not smart enough to have a protective shield of my own? Man, suck my dick, Officer Bitch Ass," barked Melvin.

Discovering that his new drug connection was an undercover cop infuriated Melvin. His instincts had told him from the beginning that the man was untrustworthy. The only reason Melvin dealt with Roberts was because a loyal worker had vouched for the narc. After a year of drug deals between the two men, Roberts had power over his target and all was well in his world. Melvin realized he had thrown his last brick at prison walls. Melvin knew the situation could only end in one of two ways: life in prison or six feet under. He was going to take the narc Roberts down with him one way or another.

"Does the department know about your little habit? They know what you snorting up your nose, Detective? Do the higher-ups at the precinct know about the dope you dealing? Do they know about your five hundred-thousand dollar house out in the suburbs?"

As Melvin put his business out on Front Street for his peers to hear, Roberts made a split-second decision that would change his life forever.

"Shut the fuck up, I said," Roberts barked through clenched teeth. He punched Melvin in his stomach. "Don't make me say it again!"

Melvin doubled over in pain as he spat more obscenities at the men invading his family home.

Within minutes, the apartment was flooded with officers yelling commands and turning over furniture. Tears began to stream down Prince's pecan-shaded cheeks. As he stood trembling, a SWAT officer grabbed the young boy by his left arm, snatching him away from the open refrigerator. Prince immediately dropped the pitcher of Kool-Aid he was holding and screamed out in pain. His shoulder popped out of its socket and the pain was unbearable.

Despite multiple guns being pointed at him, Melvin rushed to protect his son.

"Leave my son alone. Let him go!"

Melvin ran toward the officer holding on to his eldest son.

"Freeze," various voices yelled.

Melvin ignored the command. His son needed him.

Blast!

The shot came out of nowhere. Melvin saw the flame before he felt the pain sear through his chest. The loud thud caused everyone to pause and take notice of the man sprawled out on the tiled floor.

"Daddy! No, no, no, Daddy, get up! Please, Daddy, please *get up!*" Prince broke free from the rookie's hold. The officer was green and just as shocked as some of the others in the room, so he offered no resistance when the young boy pulled away from his grip. He looked on as Prince rushed to his father's side and kneeled over his father's still body.

Melvin lay whispering and moaning as the sounds of men running in different directions became fainter with each passing second. Melvin struggled against the urge to give up his time here on this earth. Prince's cries made him fight for each breath.

"Daddy, be strong. Be strong like you always tell me to be," Prince begged.

One tear escaped Melvin's eye. Melvin struggled to whisper his last words to Prince as he continued to fight, knowing he would die. "I love you, Prince, and I'll always be with you, son."

The last thing Melvin heard was his son crying for him not to go. Police officers stood frozen at the sight before them. Not one of the spectators attempted to save the life of their now victim. Rigor mortis would soon find the body of a man deemed a menace to society by law enforcement but stood larger than life to his family.

Still in physical pain from his dislocated shoulder, Prince fell on top of his father's body as screams from deep inside escaped his heart. Prince looked up at the officer who fired the fatal shot and asked, "Why y'all have to take my daddy from me like that? He didn't do anything for you to shoot him," Prince cried. "I swear that I'm going to get you back for this, one day."

His experience on the streets told Roberts that the grieving ten-year-old boy meant what he'd just said. Though he didn't show it, Roberts took heed to the threat.

"Yeah, boy, whatever. We'll be arresting you soon enough. I'm sure you'll follow in Legend's path one day." Roberts laughed.

"I'm going to get you for this," Prince promised through clenched teeth and a tear-stained face. "You remember me, because I'm going to be coming for you one day."

Part 1

Of This Urban Tale:

Dynamics of a Relationship

Chapter 1

Flashback, 1987—The Meeting

Cherise Rihanna Peters knew she was a dime piece, with a golden complexion, light brown eyes, and shoulder-length hair. If it weren't for her short stature she could have been a model. Her petite frame and small voice were in vast contrast to her will and presence. She was conniving and hard-core to the bone. When Cherise put her mind to something, she went after it full force, no matter what the cost to others.

Shy stood five inches taller than her best friend. Her honey-bronze skin and hazel eyes gave her an exotic look. With her hair pulled back into a ponytail and her lips glossed with a shimmer of glitter, Shy was indeed turning heads as she walked next to Cherise. Cherise and Shy were both blessed with firm, perky C cups, flat stomachs, tiny waists, and perfect-sized hips and behinds.

The best friends were dressed alike in white biker shorts with form-fitting cropped tops that read: I Love My Boyfriend. Despite the declaration, neither girl had a special friend. Boyfriends meant drama, something they tried to steer clear of.

"Where did he go that fast?" asked Cherise. She tried to search the crowds for B-Boy without looking obvious. Word had gotten back to her that a baller from the north side wanted to get to know her. He was everything Cherise liked in a boy: tall, fine, confident, and interested in her. Cherise had played hard to get for two weeks and was finally ready to put her mark on B-Boy, literally.

"There he go right there." Shy pointed him out.

"Don't point. Let's walk over that way. It's time for me to get his pager number and see what's up with that fine specimen of a man," Cherise smiled.

"You mean a fine specimen of a boy, right?" Shy laughed.

The two walked slowly toward the group of boys as if they owned the sidewalk. Cherise smiled when she made eye contact with her target and instantly picked up her pace.

"Do fries come with those shakes?" B-Boy asked.

"They just might if you can answer one thing for me," Cherise replied.

"Oh yeah? What you want to know, baby?"

"Nigga, what is your name?"

"Come on, let's take a ride and I'll tell you whatever it is you want to know," B-Boy invited.

Cherise looked at Shy with pleading eyes. There was no way she was going to leave her best friend standing alone in the projects. Shy could read the look on Cherise's face and quickly let her know she had no interest in being a third wheel.

"No, Cherise, I am not trying to ride with you like you're babysitting me or something," Shy whined with crossed arms.

"Don't sweat it, baby girl, here come one of my boys now. Y'all can hook up and keep each other company while me and your girl get to know each other." B-Boy smirked, eyeing Cherise from head to toe, licking his lips.

"I don't know, because my aunt will kill me if something happens to her car," Shy stalled. She had to see what this friend looked like before making a decision.

"Don't worry about the car. Just let Aisha know we're leaving it parked outside of her apartment for an hour or so," Cherise suggested.

Before Shy could think of another reason to stall, the sexiest baritone voice erupted behind her. His words sounded like Bootsy Collins playing the bass.

"'I love my boyfriend'? How could you love me and we haven't even met yet?"

Shy turned around and found herself face to chest with a body that should have been against the law. The voice belonged to a fine, tall, sun-kissed brown athletic type. Shy looked up into the prettiest eyes she had ever seen on a boy. She was at a loss for words. Her mind alerted her to introduce herself before he thought she was an airhead but Shy could not find her voice.

"Hey, what's up with you, boy?" B-Boy greeted his friend with a handshake. "This right here is Cherise and this is her friend, whose name I do not know."

Once it became clear that her best friend was in a trance, Cherise interjected, "Shy. Her name is Shy." Cherise elbowed Shy in an attempt to snap her back to reality.

Shy blinked her eyes rapidly from the pain of Cherise's elbow in her side. She was a little embarrassed and focused her attention on a crack in the sidewalk. *Oh my God, I hope he does not think something is wrong with me,* thought Shy. *I have to get it together before I scare him away.*

"Oh, I'm sorry, I'm Shy."

"Nice to meet you, Shy. I'm Melvin and before the night is over, I will be your boyfriend."

From that moment on, Melvin Shane McGee and Shayla Evette Wilson became inseparable.

Chapter 2

June, 1988—The Relationships

Commencement ceremonies for both South High School and The Rayen High School were held on the same day. High school graduation was finally over and the parties were off and jumping across the city of Youngstown, Ohio. Finally, Shy, Cherise, Melvin, and B-Boy were free at last. The friends had decided to celebrate by getting motel rooms. The adjoining rooms were nice, clean, and out of the way. Melvin dove onto the king-sized bed like a little kid playing Superman in his parents' bedroom. Shy laughed and jumped on top of Melvin, giving him a wet kiss as soon as their bodies connected.

"You just don't know how happy I am that we are finally out of school." Shy sighed.

"I feel you. You know what we should—"

Melvin's statement was interrupted by a knock on the door connecting the couples' rooms. Shy put a little switch in her hips because she knew Melvin was watching her ass as she went to answer the door. If it were up to Shy, she would lock Melvin in the room with her until checkout time, but no one asked her how she wanted to celebrate their accomplishment. Shy was never asked what she wanted to do when the four friends got together. The plans always seemed written in stone by the time she found out about them.

"What up? You ready to get this shit over and done with?" B-Boy asked. He stood with his pelvis stuck out and his shoulders slouched over. His naturally wavy faded haircut matched his six o'clock shadow beard. Michael 'B-Boy' Jackson was known for being a stick-up-kid. So far he'd been lucky enough to avoid arrest, so far. No one in the city trusted him and B-Boy would not have it any other way. Rumor had it that the only reason B-Boy never tried to double-cross his best friend was because he knew Melvin wouldn't hesitate to put a bullet in his kneecaps twenty minutes before finishing him off.

"Yes, let's go get this shit over with so we can enjoy the rest of the night," Melvin said as he looked at Shy. Shy sat on the bed, looking at Melvin with a puzzled look on her face. She had no idea what Melvin and B-Boy were talking about, but she had a strange feeling that it was not good. Melvin tried to relax Shy with a smile to let her know he would be fine, but his nonverbal communication was not getting through to her.

"Chill, baby girl, everything's going to be cool. Just take a shower and relax. I'll be back before you know it; then I'm all yours until checkout tomorrow afternoon."

"What do you mean, just relax? Why the fuck she never has to play chauffeur when you and B-Boy doing shit like this? This isn't right. If I got to go, she should have to go," Cherise whined to Melvin.

"Man, shut the fuck up! What I tell you about questioning shit we do?" B-Boy spoke in a threatening tone.

"Look, this is the last time I'm going to tell y'all this. I take care of Shy; Shy don't take care of me. There is no way in hell I'm putting her freedom in jeopardy. Whatever's going on between the two of you, leave my girl out of it," warned Melvin as he grabbed his cigar and headed out the door. He stepped outside to light up and wait for his partners in crime to join him.

"Get your ass in the fucking car. See what the fuck I mean? You always questioning shit instead of going along with the game plan," B-Boy fumed.

"Do this seem right to you, B-Boy? Melvin got love for Shy and he don't put her out there like you do me," Cherise challenged. She knew she was pushing her luck but felt it had to be said.

Slap!

Cherise saw stars and felt the floor rise up to meet her. She lay with her hands over her left cheek as B-Boy hovered, daring another word to come out of her mouth.

"You did not have to hit her!" Shy screamed. "Melvin, come in here and get your boy."

Shy rushed over to her friend to see if she was okay. Cherise felt dazed and lay still to keep B-Boy from putting hands on her in anger anymore. This was not the first time B-Boy hit Cherise; however, it was the first time Shy was witness to it. Shy was infuriated with B-Boy and wanted him to know it. For a year Shy had become a sounding board for Cherise's complaints about B-Boy and his abuse of her. Shy sat through countless late-night phone conversations listening to Cherise cry and complain about her juvenile-minded boyfriend cheating on her. There were times when Shy found herself in fights with girls who targeted Cherise because of B-Boy. The first few times B-Boy mistreated Cherise, Shy told her to break up with him. The advice only caused a strain in the best friends' relationship. Cherise's crying about B-Boy became routine after a couple of months and Shy learned to keep her opinion to herself.

"Man up, nigga! What's wrong with you? Since when do you feel cool popping off in front of my girl like that? I told you about this shit," Melvin fumed.

"You ain't got to come out-of-pocket on me like that." B-Boy threatened, "You need to be checking your girl and that bullshit she spitting."

"Who the fuck you talking strong to?" Melvin asked. He walked up on his friend and stared him down, waiting for his response.

The look in Melvin's eyes told B-Boy that giving the wrong answer would result in something he did not want to happen. B-Boy grabbed hold of his senses and calmed down before things got out of hand.

"Man, it's not even like that. My girl in here trying to disrespect me in front of her friend and shit. You know I ain't got no problem with Shy," B-Boy explained.

"Melvin, this shit isn't right, he didn't have any reason to put his hands on her," Shy fumed. "Come on, Reese, let me help you into the bathroom and put some ice on your lip."

Shy helped Cherise to her feet and led her into the bathroom before leaving the room in search of some ice. After filling the ice bucket, Shy returned to find Cherise alone in the room, and helped her nurse her bruised cheek.

"Thank you, Shy. I don't know what I'd do without you."

"You don't have to thank me. I'm not doing anything different than what you would do for me. But, Reese, why do you put up with his laying hands on you?"

"He doesn't mean to hurt me. He really does love me and he'd do anything for me."

Shy looked into Cherise's eyes, trying to find some sign that her friend believed what she'd just said. All Shy found was an empty spirit looking back at her.

"Cherise, you can't possibly believe that. If he loved you so much he wouldn't cheat on you, lie to you, or ask you to put your life and freedom on the line just so he can do whatever his heart desires," Shy preached.

"It's not even like that. I have to hustle in order to eat. My parents don't give a fuck about me and you know it. Besides you, B-Boy is all I have, and doing a few things for him is a small price to pay," Cherise explained. "You don't know how it feels to fall asleep at night to the sounds of your mother getting her head beat in by her flavor of the month. After my father left to be with his new family, he never looked back to see if I was still breathing. I don't have a mother with a good job or an older sister to borrow clothes and money from like your spoiled ass do. I love B-Boy and he loves me too, that much I know for sure. I know he's not as perfect as Melvin but he's mine, and nothing and nobody is going to change that," Cherise spat angrily, "including you."

Shy's jaw hit the floor as she stood in disbelief listening to Cherise rationalize getting the shit slapped out of her. Her feelings were hurt by the tone Cherise used to spew such hateful words.

"You know what, Cherise? I have been your friend my entire life and I love you dearly, but from this day forward, don't call me crying when his sorry ass goes upside your head with a closed fist. And don't look for me to have your back when some chick rolls up on you because B-Boy has been fucking her too. I mean damn, if you like it, I love it!"

Shy stormed out of the bathroom, leaving Cherise standing alone with a busted lip. She was hurt and beside herself with anger. In all the years she and Cherise had been friends, they never had a serious argument. Since Cherise hooked up with B-Boy, she had become a completely different person, and Shy did not like it.

Cherise felt bad for her choice of words as soon as they escaped her mouth, but after they were gone, there was no pulling them back. She treasured the relationship she had with Shy and would not trade it for the world. Cherise knew that Shy loved her unconditionally, and that was more than she could say for B-Boy. As much as her friendship with Shy meant to her, it just was not enough. She had chased the love missing from her life for so long that when those three little words, "I love you," were uttered from the opposite sex, it was like a crack head hitting the pipe for the first time and Cherise was addicted.

She stood staring at her reflection in the mirror, and felt as if a stranger was looking back at her. *Why did I just say that to Shy? She is the closest thing to family I have and I know what I said hurt her.* As the pressure behind her eyes fought to burst through, Cherise was unable to fight back the tears. *What is wrong with me? Why can't I have Shy's life?*

"Cherise, come on, let's get this shit over so we can get back here," B-Boy yelled.

Cherise opened the bathroom door to find Shy sitting on the bed with her arms crossed, and B-Boy standing inside the doorframe with his back facing her. Cherise's first instinct was to run over to Shy, apologize, and wrap her arms around her friend, but embarrassment, shame, and B-Boy wouldn't allow her to. All Cherise could hope for was that any damage done to their friendship was reversible. Shy put her head down without acknowledging Cherise or B-Boy being in the room. Cherise did as she was told and followed B-Boy with her eyes focused on the ground.

Three hours later, Melvin, Cherise, and B-Boy returned to room 1227 to find a sleeping Shy.

"Shy, baby, we're back," Melvin whispered as he gently shook her awake.

"Let her sleep, Melvin. We can get our drink on in our room," Cherise suggested. She tried to sound concerned when, in reality, Cherise knew Shy would still be mad at her and she was too embarrassed by their argument to face her. Since the threesome left the hotel room to take care of some business, the swelling in Cherise's upper lip and cheek got worse, and two of her teeth felt loose.

"No, I'm spending time with my queen and she's not going to miss out on the fun of graduation night. We're about to kick it up in this bitch. She's getting up." Melvin laughed.

"Yeah, wake your girl up and let's get this party started," B-Boy said loudly.

Melvin sat next to a sleeping Shy, who seemed to be having a dream. She awoke after Melvin began kissing her earlobe and running his fingers through her shoulder-length hair. A smile crossed her lips as she opened her eyes to find Melvin looking down at her.

"Hey, how long y'all been back? What time is it?" Shy yawned.

"It's time to kick it up in here. Get up, girl," B-Boy joked while doing a little dance.

Cherise sat on the edge of a chair with her attention focused on her new white and blue British Knights tennis shoes. She continued to chastise herself for the way she spoke to Shy. Admitting being wrong about anything was out of character for Cherise, but she knew she owed her best friend an apology. Either Shy forgave her and wanted to move on or she didn't. As far as Cherise was concerned, the ball was in Shy's court.

Shy stretched, looked over at the clock, and headed for the bathroom to brush her teeth and wash her face. She had been asleep for two hours but it felt more like eight. Between studying for finals, getting ready to vacation with her family, and shopping for the right graduation outfit, Shy was exhausted.

B-Boy sparked a blunt and cracked a cold bottle of Thunderbird to get the party going. Melvin poured Shy a cup of White Mountain berry wine cooler because he knew that even a drop of what they were drinking was out of the question for her.

"Hey, baby girl, turn on the radio. Or better yet, do you feel like going to grab those DJ Quik and Too Short cassettes out the front seat of the car?"

"Anything for you, Bookey." Shy smiled. She held out her hand to retrieve the keys from Melvin. Before walking away, Melvin grabbed her around the waist, pulled her to him, and gave her a long, passionate kiss. The display of intimacy immediately annoyed Cherise and jealousy reared its ugly head. She rolled her eyes and smacked her lips at the sight the lovebirds were putting on. B-Boy looked on and subconsciously stroked and repositioned his member through his pants as he stared at Shy's perfect behind. Cherise saw B-Boy checking out Shy and her anger started to rise.

Shy put Too Short in the portable tape player and the party began. After playing a round of Spades, smoking two nice-sized joints, and drinking three bottles of Thunderbird, the high school graduates had a good buzz going on.

"Man, it's not even midnight and y'all suckers look like its past bedtime," B-Boy griped.

"Yeah, I could go to bed right now," Melvin flirted as he stroked Shy's hair. "What about you, baby girl? You ready for bed?"

Shy blushed and giggled at how obvious it was that Melvin was horny. She was too, but she was also hungry.

"Let's order a pizza or something because all this smoking has made me hungry," Shy said.

"Yeah, I'm hungry too. Do you want to run to Bellaria before they close?" Cherise asked Shy in an attempt to break the tension between them.

Shy ignored her friend as if she had not heard a word she said, and never took her eyes off Melvin. He was not sure what was going on between Shy and Cherise but Melvin could tell that something was wrong. Whenever the four of them got together, Cherise and Shy were always giggling and whispering to each other, but they had barely said two words to one another. Melvin decided to hold off asking Shy about it until morning. He did not want to chance not getting any sex because of their beef.

It was obvious to Shy that Cherise was trying to smooth things over by acting as if nothing had happened. Shy would not be so easily forgiving this time. Cherise had really hurt her feelings with that jealous outburst.

"Yeah, go on and order a couple of pizzas, and I'm going to run across the street and pick up a twelve pack. After we eat, we going to get a nice game of Zoom going," B-Boy announced.

Everyone agreed, and an hour later a shot glass filled with Thunderbird and a beer mug full of St. Ives sat in the middle of the table. The loser would have a choice of poison to drink. If they failed to drink the alcohol straight down, they had to drink them both.

"Zoom."

"Zoom."

"Irk!" Shy said to the right of her when she should have said it to the person sitting to the left of her.

"Drink up, baby girl, drink up," Melvin teased.

Shy laughed at her third error and took the cup of beer to the head. Her head was beginning to spin and she regretted eating. The pizza was fighting its way back up. Shy jumped from her seat and ran into the bathroom to answer the call from Earl.

"All right, game over. Y'all got my baby sick fucking around with this stupid game," Melvin announced.

"Yeah, man, you go on and take care of your girl, and I'm going to our room and take care of mine." B-Boy smirked as he motioned for Cherise to follow him toward the adjoining door.

Cherise stood up and felt the room spin. She held on to the wall for support as she walked. She had a nice buzz going, but she knew her limit and she was nowhere near being sick. *I may not have as much as Shy does but at least I know how to handle my liquor.*

Melvin went into the bathroom where Shy remained kneeled on the floor with her head against the wall. She was too sick to be embarrassed as she forced a smile.

"Come on, baby girl; let me take care of you."

Melvin helped Shy over to the bathroom sink, and assisted her with brushing her teeth and washing her face with a cold rag.

"Melvin, I want to be with you more than anything but not like this. I drank too much and I can't even stand up straight." Shy slurred her words.

"It's okay, baby girl. I'm just going to take care of you and get you into bed."

Melvin tucked Shy in bed where she immediately passed out, asleep for the night.

Melvin relaxed on the bed next to Shy, watching her sleep for what felt like forever. He knew Shy was out cold and cursed himself for not putting a stop to the drinking game. After surfing the channels for an hour or so, Melvin found himself unable to fall asleep. He noticed that the sounds of sex coming from next door had stopped and Melvin wondered if B-Boy was still awake. Melvin wanted to blaze a joint but forgot to get a bag of weed from his boy. *Shit, if he is asleep, he won't hear me knocking on the door. The only way I'm going to find out is to try.*

In spite of Cherise's complaints, B-Boy got out of bed to answer the tapping on the door.

"They don't want anything. Just ignore it."

"Shut up, bitch. You don't know what the fuck could be going on with them. For all you know your girl is sick and need help."

Cherise smacked her lips and pulled the covers up to her chin. She couldn't care less about Shy being sick; all she wanted was B-Boy's undivided attention.

Wearing nothing but his boxers, B-Boy slowly opened the door and took a drag on the Newport dangling between his lips. "What's up, boy?"

Melvin looked at B-Boy's attire, glanced over his shoulder, and saw Cherise trying to hide herself under the thin white sheet.

"Ah, man, I'm sorry I interrupted," Melvin said.

"It's cool. I mean, it's not like I'm hitting something I ain't ever had before," B-Boy said arrogantly.

"Shit, you don't have to get it again since you want to be all disrespectful. You standing there talking shit like I'm not even here," Cherise whined.

She looked at Melvin for the umpteenth time that night, and regretted ending up with B-Boy. Cherise tried as hard as she could to fight her attraction to Melvin, but the moisture between her legs couldn't care less about her conscience. Cherise found more than just Melvin's looks attractive. It was the confidence he displayed and the way he carried himself. Unlike B-Boy, Melvin did not have to force people to respect him. Melvin earned respect just by being himself. The way he walked, talked, stood, and spoke made men want to know him and women want to be with him.

Cherise noticed Melvin taking quick glances at her and took full advantage of the situation. She eased the sheet down just enough to show her left breast and slowly eased her right leg from under the sheet. Melvin grabbed his dick while watching Cherise's peepshow. B-Boy saw Melvin checking Cherise out and decided the time was right for him to fulfill a fantasy.

"Come on in here, boy. Let's get another party started," B-Boy invited.

Cherise folded the sheet down to her waist, fully exposing her plump breast to her best friend's man. *Shy thinks she's better than I am because everything has been handed to her. She wants to act all uppity and superior with her prissy ass; let's see just how much love Melvin has for her after tonight,* Cherise thought.

"Yeah, Melvin, why don't you come and party with us?" Cherise asked with the sexiest voice she could muster.

Melvin looked at his boy, over at Cherise, and back at B-Boy before checking to make sure Shy was still asleep. He was sure to lock and chain the door behind him before stepping farther into the room. Melvin pulled his T-shirt over his head to kick off the night's real festivities. He would feel an immense amount of guilt in the morning, but not enough to keep him from betraying Shy's trust again in the future.

Chapter 3

Reality, 1991—This Ain't Love

"What da fuck you mean no? Bitch, do what I said before I beat ya dumb ass," B-Boy threatened.

"We're having a baby. Nigga, I'm pregnant and not that young bitch no more. I ain't doin' it," Cherise argued defiantly.

"See that's that bullshit right there. I own you and I said run that shit. My connect waiting."

"This baby needs me because his sorry-ass daddy ain't gonna step up to the plate if I'm on lockdown behind his ignorant ass," Cherise spat truthfully.

Over the years, Cherise had put herself into some dangerous situations, all in the name of love. She ran more drugs up and down highway I-71 than B-Boy. Their relationship was one of convenience for him and one of addiction for her. Cherise didn't love B-Boy; she craved him. As long as he gave her the attention she desperately needed, Cherise was happy. Even if the attention resulted in a visit to the emergency room, it was better than nothing.

"Bitch, did I ask you to carry my seed? I told ya ass to pay the clinic a visit. Every time I turn around you whining about being pregnant. That's ya problem. Back pain, foot pain, pussy pain. Bitch, so the fuck what? You 'bout to have my foot in dat ass if you don't head over to PA," B-Boy threatened angrily.

It was obvious that B-Boy was high and Cherise knew her next statement would ignite the fireworks, but so be it. More often than not, she had homicidal thoughts when she thought about B-Boy seeing EVERLAST printed across her forehead. She was going to plant her feet firmly and say what she wanted.

"Nigga, kiss my ass," Cherise spat and braced herself for impact.

As expected, B-Boy reacted by sucker-punching Cherise square in the face. He kept punching and she started swinging. Cherise had become a middleweight-class boxer in the five years she'd known B-Boy. Even he noticed she was no easy win for him anymore. It was obvious B-Boy had snorted or smoked something. His buzz gave him the blind courage to take the fight to a place of no return.

B-Boy had Cherise cornered. He wrapped his hand around her neck and slammed her on the hardwood floor. As soon as Cherise's body made a thud, B-Boy began stomping her, aiming directly for her stomach.

"Bitch, I told you not to have a fuckin' baby."

"Boy, stop, stop!" Cherise screamed. The screeching in her voice snapped B-Boy out of the black. Cherise lay in a puddle of blood. The pain was immeasurable. Before she could catch her breath, Cherise felt drenching wetness between her legs. She instinctively knew what had happened.

B-Boy stood over Cherise, watching as she miscarried his baby. He responded to her cry for help with an evil smirk. He walked away from her, only to return a few minutes later with the telephone.

"Here, it looks like you better call 911 before your ass bleeds out," he said callously.

B-Boy left the house, leaving Cherise where she lay.

***

Emergency services were very familiar with the Jackson/Peters home. The police warned Cherise repeatedly that her boyfriend would kill her one day. The domestic violence had been going on for years. Cherise was never the one to call for a squad. Neighbors always called when her toe-curling screams became too much. That night had the most serious injuries the medical transporters had witnessed. They were amazed she was still alive after the amount of blood loss suffered.

"Ma'am, where's your boyfriend?" a voice asked.

"Did Michael Jackson do this to you again? Miss Peters, where is B-Boy?" The officer on duty had responded to countless calls made on Cherise's behalf. He prayed she pulled through one more time and it would be her wake-up call to leave.

Cherise was in shock and unable to talk. They had to get her to the hospital as soon as possible, if she had any chance of survival.

After three pints of blood and a D & C, Cherise was in stable condition. As expected, she'd lost the baby. Her body needed rest and she slept through the night. She finally opened her eyes midmorning the following day to find Shy sitting on the side of her hospital bed. Shy offered her best friend a weak smile.

"How do you feel?" Shy spoke softly.

"Shy, he didn't want me to have the baby. He stomped me; he made me lose my baby," Cherise cried hysterically. The hurt, anger, and rage erupted. She began to hyperventilate, scaring Shy half to death.

"Nurse, help me please!" Shy yelled into the hallway.

The nurse injected Cherise with a sedative to calm her down. Her heart was broken right along with her spirit. She kept asking herself why B-Boy couldn't love her right. Nothing she said or did ever seem to be right. B-Boy found fault with every aspect of their life togeth-

er and it always fell on her shoulders. Cherise had little
self-esteem and thought B-Boy was the only man she
was meant to be with. Time after time, B-Boy called her
names and swore if she ever left him he would kill her.
He threatened to torture her forever if another man
tried to step into his spot.

Cherise noticed Shy and Melvin hugged up together
in the hallway, talking. They appeared to be having a
serious conversation but Cherise could not hear what
it was about. Based on the current circumstances, she
was sure it had to do with her and B-Boy. Shy had tried
to help Cherise reverse the emotional abuse she endured. That moment her self-esteem improved, B-Boy
always wooed his way back in. Cherise didn't believe
Shy could possibly understand her life.

The caliber of man Melvin aspired to be was appeal-
ing to Cherise.

Melvin and B-Boy were totally different.

She understood why Shy stayed by Melvin's side.
Their type of love was one in a million. From Cherise's
point of view, Shy had the perfect life. At times, she
hated her best friend for having all the things a woman
deserved. Melvin took care of her in every way possible. Cherise would trade places with Shy in a split
second. Maybe if Shy got beat a few times she wouldn't
be so quick to judge.

Cherise wanted to have a baby to fill a huge void in
her life. That's why her pregnancy was so important.
B-Boy had once again swooped in and destroyed her
dream. Just once in her life, Cherise wanted to experience unconditional love. She knew a baby would love
her no matter what. Cherise felt she'd suffered enough
being raised by an irresponsible mother who couldn't
care less if she ate or had clothes on her back. Tears

began streaming down her face as she thought about all the heartache and difficulties of life.

"Hey, girl, it's about time you woke up," Shy smiled sweetly.

"How long was I asleep?" Cherise asked as she wiped the tears from her face.

"Over eight hours now. The doctor said your body needed the rest but your vital signs are good. They had to give you a blood transfusion. You're lucky to be here," Shy explained.

"When can I go home?"

"I'm not sure, but the police want to talk to you. Cherise, you have to stop this madness before he kills you," Shy said with sincerity.

Cherise was quiet. Shy was right but Cherise didn't want to hear it, not from a woman who couldn't possibly understand her plight. Shy wondered if her advice would've been better received from a counselor.

"That girl knows I didn't mean to do that shit. She just don't know when to shut her mouth. I didn't mean to make her lose the baby," B-Boy arrogantly said. He startled Shy and Cherise. B-Boy was the last person they expected to show up at the hospital.

"What? Did you come to make sure she didn't put a warrant out for your punk ass?" Shy spat.

"Don't start no shit. I'm here to see my girl and make sure everything's okay," B-Boy lied.

"Bullshit!" Shy hollered.

Cherise was too weak to intervene. Though envy had her head twisted, Cherise knew Shy always had her back and was only looking out for her. Shy often stood up for Cherise against B-Boy. Shy stood firm when Cherise wouldn't stand up for herself. B-Boy never disrespected Shy because of Melvin. B-Boy knew not to cross that line.

"You beat that baby out of her. There's no way you give a damn about Cherise. You never have," Shy continued.

"I ain't tryin'a hear dat bullshit. You need to mind your own business." B-Boy took a step toward her as he spoke.

"She almost died because of you. Black eye, busted lip, and a miscarriage; you went too far," Shy voiced.

"Bitch, who da fuck you think you talkin' to?" B-Boy's voice raised two octaves.

"No, bitch, who da fuck you calling a bitch?" Melvin stormed into the room, taking B-Boy by surprise. He wrapped his hands around his friend's neck and slammed him into the wall. "Nigga, I will snap your weak-ass neck. Don't ever step to my wife like that again. You understand me?" Melvin's grip tightened around B-Boy's neck, cutting off his air supply. Melvin was furious.

B-Boy struggled to breathe, though his efforts were in vain.

Shy and Cherise looked on in shock. B-Boy had stepped too far across the line. Melvin would not stand for that level of disrespect. He was willing to sacrifice his life and freedom for Shy.

"Mel, babe, stop, let him go," instructed Shy.

"Nigga, you're a bitch. What type of man beats on a woman? You've never gone toe-to-toe with a man but you beat on her like she's some random nigga off the street. I should end your miserable life right now." Melvin seethed.

"Come on, babe, let him go. He's not worth it." Shy spoke slowly in attempt to calm Melvin and grab his attention. She knew him better than he knew himself and if he wasn't reeled in soon, life would never be the same.

Melvin heard Shy but didn't respond to her request.

Cherise's nerves were on edge and she didn't know how much more she could take. Even as she lay in the hospital bed B-Boy put her in, jealousy washed over her heart. Melvin had B-Boy in check; she just wished it was her he was protecting.

"Melvin, I'm okay, baby, let go of him," Shy repeated.

The police were headed for Cherise's hospital room in search of B-Boy when they heard a ruckus. They stepped into the room with weapons drawn. Cherise screamed at the sight of the guns.

Shy's concern quickly turned into frustration. Melvin rarely allowed Shy to see that side of him. It would've been nothing for Melvin to kill B-Boy. Melvin was well versed in the killing of men and B-Boy knew it.

B-Boy continued to struggle against Melvin's strength.

"Freeze!"

"Let him go, sir, and step out of the way. We're here to pick him up," a young officer stated.

"Listen to me, Melvin, please. Let him go," Shy angrily instructed.

Melvin gave in and released his hold. B-Boy was on the verge of passing out. He fought to catch his breath as the police handcuffed him. The officers knew B-Boy well. They'd had the pleasure of arresting him multiple times; plus, B-Boy often worked as an informant.

Shy stood in front of Melvin, fearful he would also be arrested. The police had witnessed the assault. In the grand scheme of things, they did not care, nor did they want the extra paperwork.

"Reese, tell them it wasn't me," B-Boy told Cherise. "I wasn't even in town."

"Miss Peters, is this the man who beat you?" the first officer asked.

Cherise was silent. She looked around the room at the assuming glares her visitors were giving her.

"Cherise, please press charges against him. You almost died this time. He is going to kill you one day." Shy felt helpless.

Again, Cherise was quiet. Her hands touched her stomach in search of a baby. Tears filled her eyes. She felt as if she were being judged.

"Miss Peters, did this man do this to you?" the second officer asked.

"No, it wasn't him. It was a masked intruder," Cherise lied as tears streamed down her face.

Melvin shook his head and walked out of the room. Shy could not believe her ears. Cherise had become a stranger to her. She looked into her best friend's eyes and saw nothing but emptiness. Shy couldn't even feel sorry for Cherise. *This bitch must enjoy getting her ass beat.*

"We're still arresting him for an outstanding warrant," the first officer told Cherise before pushing B-Boy out of the room.

Shy was outdone, disappointed, and angry with Cherise. She had tried her best to save her friend. It was now out of her hands.

"Do me a favor, the next time he beats the shit out of you, don't call me. You obviously love the drama. You take care of yourself, Cherise, and get well soon. Maybe B-Boy will be back to take care of you."

Cherise knew Shy's words were an empty threat. Just like she kept returning to her abuser, Shy remained friends with Cherise.

Chapter 4

Actually, I Love You More

Melvin sat on the couch with Shy's swollen feet resting in his lap. They were bringing in the New Year together. Shy was close to her delivery date and the doctor had her on bed rest. Carrying twins was playing havoc on her back. Boredom and isolation were getting the best of her. She wanted Melvin around her all time. She craved his attention.

"I can't wait for the babies to get here. I want my body back," Shy pouted.

"Baby, you look beautiful. You're sexy to me," Melvin assured Shy while rubbing her stomach.

"You're just saying that. I've gained eighty pounds and can't see my own feet."

"Stop that. You're giving me two sons. I don't care if you tip the scales at three hundred pounds, I love you, always."

Melvin was consistent with his compliments. He sincerely loved how Shy wore her pregnancy. Melvin had spent a fortune on her maternity clothes but they were worth every penny. She still kept her hair done, eyebrows arched, and feet soft. Shy had always been fine to him; carrying twins to term didn't change that.

"Which one of your girls stopped by the crib today, Bossy?"

A nurse Melvin hired took care of Shy, and her friends checked in on her every day.

"Terry and Cherise came by too. Cherise brought the baby to see me. I can't believe he's walking already." Shy smiled thinking about her godson.

"Yeah, little man is getting big," Melvin commented.

"Cherise is taking good care of him. She's lucky to have had a baby after that miscarriage. I doubt if she'll have any more kids. Raequan is lucky he doesn't have his sorry-ass daddy around. I hope B-Boy rots in prison."

"That nigga was always reckless. I'm still tripping on how bad he fucked up."

"Pulling a home invasion." Shy shook her head. "Pitiful but typical."

"All the houses in the world and his ass kick in the door of the DA. He deserves that twenty-five to life sentence"

"For Cherise's and the baby's sakes, I pray he does the life. Twenty-five years isn't long enough," Shy remarked.

"You know your girl's still running shit for him, right?"

"What do you mean?" Shy asked, confused. She didn't understand how or why Cherise was still risking her freedom with B-Boy locked up. Cherise needed to get a grip on her life for her son's sake.

"I don't know how, but she's been sneaking drugs into the prison for him. Cherise never stopped running drugs for B-Boy's supplier. That's how she's been eating."

"I thought she was doing well at the catering thing. She just leased a building and said business was soaring," Shy said, confused.

"Come on, baby, you know better than to believe some bull like that. I know she's your girl but Cherise lies when it suits her. She's not going to tell you that the business is for money laundering and dope cooking," Melvin pointed out while still massaging his wife's swollen feet.

Shy had heard enough. Cherise never ceased to amaze her but Shy assumed having a baby would change her best friend's mentality.

"Enough about them. Baby, do you love me?"

"With everything inside of me," Melvin assured his wife.

"It's countdown time. Eight, seven, six . . ."

"Happy New Year, baby girl," Melvin said, leaning over to kiss Shy.

"Happy New Year, baby." Shy returned Melvin's kiss. "Don't stop now; you done got me moist, boy," flirted Shy.

Melvin laughed at Shy. Her sexual appetite had increased during the pregnancy. Though they enjoyed a healthy and frequent sex life, Melvin had no complaint.

"I heard that having a strong, intense orgasm will send a woman into labor. Let's test out that old wives' tale."

Melvin helped Shy into the bathroom. After showering together, they climbed into bed. Melvin waited patiently for Shy to get comfortable. Various-sized pillows enveloped her once she got settled. She was too big to lie flat on her back. Melvin massaged cocoa and Shea butter over her body, paying close attention to her stomach, hips, and behind. The feel of his sons kicking when he touched Shy's stomach felt empowering. He fell in love all over again.

Shy enjoyed the feel of his touch. No one did for her like Melvin. He took very good care of her in every possible way. His love made Shy feel like the most beautiful woman in the world. Shy placed her hand over

Melvin's, guiding it up to her tender breast. He gently fondled her extra plump breast before wrapping his thick lips over the nipple. He suckled like a baby, causing Shy to moan in pleasure.

"You like that?" Melvin asked.

"You know I do, boy." Shy giggled.

"Let me make you feel even better."

Melvin slid down on the bed and positioned himself between Shy's thick, silky, soft thighs. He slowly planted wet kisses on the inside of Shy's legs, slowly building up the anticipation of what she knew was to come. The warm, wet sensation of her lover's tongue on her clit relaxed Shy's entire body. She smiled at the way he was making her feel.

"Oh, boy, you're so nasty," Shy moaned.

He sucked Shy's clit and put a finger inside of her. Her legs tightened around his head. She grabbed the back of his head and said, "Baby, eat all you can. This is your buffet."

Melvin did just that. He ravished Shy like he hadn't had a meal in days. It was like a game of hockey with her pearl tongue. He played until her juices flowed like a tropical spring. Melvin's pole was hard as a steel rod. Shy rolled onto her side as Melvin lifted her leg, giving him access to her guilty pleasure. The sensation of becoming one with the love of his life felt like heaven. Melvin was slow, methodic, and careful with his woman. Knowing it might be their last time together for at least six weeks, he paced himself. Shy's pussy was like a drug to Melvin. The only thing on his mind while he was inside of her was staying there. He knew that after he withdrew, all he'd think about was getting back in it.

The walls of Shy's pussy tightened. She gripped the bed sheets and held her breath for as long as she could. When she let go, her juices drowned Melvin's dick, forcing him to shoot his essence inside of her treasure. They lay panting, drenched in each other's bodily fluids, feeling fulfilled and exhausted.

After his heart rate returned to its normal pace, Melvin washed Shy up and then himself. He crawled into bed and spooned with the woman he loved more than life itself.

"I love the way you take care of me," Shy said softly.

"Good night, baby girl, I love you."

The expectant parents-to-be slept peacefully for a few hours. Shy was awakened by horrible lower back pains.

"Melvin!" Shy screamed.

"What's wrong?" Melvin jumped up, instinctively reaching for his gun.

"Get me to the hospital. It hurts," Shy cried.

Twelve hours of hard labor produced two healthy baby boys. Prince Jayden McGee came into the world at 12:05 A.M. on January 2, 1993, weighing in at five pounds, three ounces. His identical twin brother arrived sixteen minutes later. Jayden Prince McGee weighed four pounds, seven ounce.

Chapter 5

Our Private Time

Melvin stepped through the door when the clock read 11:56 P.M. Lucky for him the police didn't catch him speeding. He'd rather deal with a speeding ticket than an angry and disappointed wife. Melvin was curious as to what Shy had planned for them. Bedtime was his favorite time of day. The way he was feeling, Melvin hoped his wife wasn't in the mood for romance because he planned to give it to her aggressively. Melvin had to fulfill the urge to ravish his wife.

Shy knew how to pleasure Melvin. They hadn't lasted year after year by chance. It took a lot of hard work on both their parts. The intimacy they shared outside of the bedroom remained strong. Stealing kisses and copping feels was a daily occurrence. Communication and intimacy helped them withstand the test of time.

A smile spread across Melvin's face when he walked into their bedroom. Shy was in a freaky mood. Melvin couldn't have been happier. Shy had her toys laid out and was dressed in Melvin's favorite play clothes.

"Get in here, boy," Shy ordered.

"Let the fun begin," Melvin said as he undressed.

Melvin loved the pink thigh-high fishnet stockings Shy had on. The lace garter belt and matching bra made his dick stand at attention every time. After carrying twins, Shy's body had changed but Melvin loved her un-

conditionally, flaws and all. After he finished undress-
ing, Shy pushed Melvin onto their bed. She jumped up,
kneeled between his legs, and immediately took him
into her mouth. The warmth and wetness of her mouth
drove Melvin crazy. She ran her hand up and down his
shaft as she sucked, licked, and French kissed the tip
of his dick. The thick vein lining the length of his shaft
began to pulsate, causing Shy to stop. She planned on
taking her time teasing him. They had all night together.

Melvin grabbed Shy's arms and slammed her onto her
back. He rolled her over and pulled her hips back toward
him. With the right amount of force to make Shy smile,
Melvin entered her from behind and wrapped her hair
around his hand. Shy threw it right back at him. She
was going to give as good as she got. Melvin released
her hair, bending over to grab her bouncing breast while
never slowing the gyration of his thrust.

"Can I give it to you?" Melvin grunted.

"Give it to me, nigga," Shy directed.

With her permission, Melvin burst his first nut of
the night. The night wasn't over. That was just the first
round. Melvin and Shy would be ready for round two
after a quick water break.

The couple lay across the bed, talking and joking.
Shy picked up her feather and ran in across Melvin's
left side, tickling him. He laughed and grabbed her in a
bear hug. They wrestled for the handcuffs. Melvin won
and hooked Shy up to the bed railing. Shy lay on her
side, begging for her freedom.

"Relax," Melvin told his wife. "I'm going to take care
of you." He proceeded to rub cocoa butter body oil all
over her body. Melvin inhaled Shy's scent, giving him
butterflies in his stomach. At times he wondered what

he'd done to have such a strong, devoted woman in his life. Her love had gotten him through some difficult times. The support she gave him was immeasurable. Melvin lived to make Shy happy. She completed him in every way.

Melvin couldn't stop running his fingers along the contours of his wife's body. She kept her skin baby soft and glowing. He kissed every inch of her body as their souls made an intimate connection that only they understood. Melvin went from wanting it hard and fast to taking his time. Melvin released Shy from the handcuffs. He needed to feel her touch, press her body against his, and enjoy his wife from head to toe.

Shy kissed her husband passionately. She saw a touch of sadness in his eyes that made her uncomfortable.

"Are you okay?"

"Baby, do you know how much you mean to me?" Melvin spoke softly as he ran his fingers through her hair.

Shy loved for Melvin to play in her hair. It turned her on when he verbally expressed his feelings for her. Melvin rarely said the words "I love you." He preferred to show his woman how much she meant to him.

"Tell me what's wrong." Shy began to worry. Melvin's head seemed to be elsewhere.

"Nothing's wrong. I just need you to know how much I love you. I take my responsibility as your husband seriously. I know I don't say it as often as you might need me to but I love you deep down in my soul, girl," Melvin expressed freely. He held Shy in his arms, taking in the warmth of her body. Their hearts beat in unison.

"I love you, always. It's like loving you was my destiny. I couldn't make it without you. You're my soul," Shy proclaimed gently.

They kissed passionately, lovingly, exchanging breaths as their bodies became one. Shy wrapped her legs around Melvin's waist tightly. He lifted her up effortlessly and he carried her across the room. Melvin pressed Shy's back against the wall, never losing his grip or releasing himself from her throbbing lips. Her walls felt built for only him. His fit inside her love was perfect. Melvin knew he was the one and only owner of Shy's perfect tunnel.

Hours later, the couple had visited every position possible from the book of *Kama Sutra*. They showered together before finally getting into bed for a good night's sleep. Shy curled up in Melvin's arms and he held her tightly against his chest.

"Damn, boy, you worked it out like it was the last time," Shy said jokingly.

"Girl, it's never the last time with us. I love you, baby girl."

"I love you, baby."

Chapter 6

Summer Nights—The Beginning of the End

Melvin took a long drag from the Newport 100 dangling between his lips as his dark eyes stared a hole through the small man standing before him.

For Silk, each passing second felt like an eternity. He had no idea how much longer he would be able to control his bladder. Silk knew all Melvin had to do was reach out his long arm, grab hold of his neck, and squeeze the life out of him. Melvin gave Silk a free pass the first time he came up short. That pass came with a warning never to deal Melvin another dirty hand. Silk's good luck ran out thirty minutes after that narrow escape.

Silk was pulled stopped by an unmarked police car driven by Detective Keith Roberts. The veteran narcotics officer pulled Silk over and found the three kilos of cocaine taped to the car's undercarriage. Silk was taking his last few breaths on earth as a direct result of being in an interrogation room for six hours with the detective. When the undercover cop approached Silk about wearing a wire to his meetings with his drug connection, Detective Keith Roberts said nothing about the money supplied by the department being short of his outstanding payments. As beads of sweat slowly rolled down his dark skin, Silk silently said a prayer.

"You must take me for some kind of bitch," Melvin said in almost a whisper. His tone put more fear in Silk's heart.

Silk's knees began shaking uncontrollably, causing him to lose control of his bladder. His head dropped along with his shoulders as Silk prepared to meet his Maker. The only thing that could save him was for Roberts to make his arrest.

"I warned your punk ass not to fuck me over again, didn't I?" barked Melvin. He grabbed Silk by his neck, and slammed him against his own car.

"Come on, man, you ain't got to kill him. Give him a second chance." Roberts made a weak attempt to defuse the situation. He could not have cared less what became of the weak man who was struggling to breathe. As long as he could get the DA's office to issue a warrant for the city's most dangerous drug dealer, Roberts would be satisfied. *Shit, if it comes down to it, I will add murder to the long list of charges,* thought the detective. *With the life being choked out of him, Silk cannot blow my cover as a consolation prize.*

"Stay the fuck up off me, man. This don't have shit to do with our business," grunted Melvin through clinched teeth. Silk's eye's started to bug out of his head as Melvin tightened his grip. "This little fuck must think he can keep getting away with dipping into what belongs to me. I warned him. Didn't I, you bitch-ass prick?" Melvin grimaced as he watched the life drain from Silk. He hated weak men and everything about them.

Melvin, with the help of his evasive partner, now ran the city and no one dared to challenge them. Over the years, Melvin had risen to the top of the drug chain while B-Boy was sucked into the belly of the Ohio prison system. It was not clear who Melvin's partner was but whispers from the street said the mystery kingpin was powerful enough to keep Melvin protected from betrayal, arrest, and death.

Two minutes later, Melvin released his hold and took a step back as the lifeless body fell to the ground. Melvin turned his back on his handy work and strolled off toward his car. Roberts walked behind his target and considered making the arrest but soon thought better of it. Knowing he now had enough to secure an arrest warrant and put Melvin McGee behind bars for the rest of his life almost made the detective aroused. He wanted all of the bells and whistles when the career making arrest was made.

"Look, man, I'll holler at you later. That cocksucker done fucked up my schedule for the night. I'll hit you up in a week to deliver the last ten you ordered but those few bricks lifted off Silk should hold you over 'til then," explained Melvin.

The two men clasped hands, pulled each other forward, patted the other's back, and simultaneously said, "One," before parting ways.

Chapter 7

Never Can Say Good-bye

Shy sat in the first row of the funeral home with a heavy heart and stream of tears. She was sandwiched between her ten-year-old twin boys. Through her own broken heart and grief, Shy found the strength to hold it together for her sons. She felt as if every ticking minute was like a time bomb slowly releasing pellets of sorrow into her spirit.

The teenage sweethearts had become a happily married couple. All of their free time was spent together. Shy had no idea what she would do without the love of her life. Any time the two spent apart was miserable for them both. Whether it was a fifteen-minute trip to the corner store or a five-day girls-only trip to Vegas, their time away from each other was torture.

"Mommy, are you okay?" asked Jayden. After drying his own tears, he noticed the tears streaming down his mother's face.

Terrified that she would lose all control of her emotions, Shy simply shook her head yes in response to her son's question. It was the first time the twins saw their mother cry. For Jayden, it made him feel helpless because he knew nothing would take his mother's pain away. Jayden scooted closer to his mother and wrapped his arm around hers as he stared at his father's lifeless body.

The tragic event forever changed the McGee family. His presence would be missed in his sons' lives. Melvin coached little league football and basketball games at the local Boys & Girls Club. Jayden and Prince looked forward to their annual fishing trips with their dad.

From the day he became a father, Melvin was determined to offer his children better childhoods than the one he endured. Melvin raised himself while both his parents dealt with being drug addicts. With both parents often pulling disappearing acts, waking up in the mornings to complete emptiness became a way of life for the young boy. Melvin was nine years old the last time it happened. It was the dead of winter and the heat was off at the McGee household. The cold forced Melvin to seek help at a neighbor's house. Mahoning County Department of Child Services placed Melvin in the custody of his paternal grandmother. Before he could get comfortable at his new home, Melvin's parents were killed during an armed robbery at a local pharmacy. Jamie and Patty McGee were missed by their only child. Though his grandmother showered Melvin with love, he often felt alone as a child. Melvin's parents may have been neglectful but he loved them all the same.

Shy looked to her left to find Prince sitting in a daze. His heart was filled with sorrow and his body was consumed with anger and hate. From the day they were born, Prince was a daddy's boy and Jayden was a momma's boy. Prince knew his life would never be the same again. His hero, his best friend, and, most importantly, his father was gone, never to return. Prince knew in his heart that he would one day return the favor on the trigger-happy officer who murdered his father in cold blood. The feeling of emptiness and sorrow washed over Prince like a wave during a hurricane. He lowered his head and cried for the first time since he stood over his father's warm body.

Jayden immediately jumped from his seat at the sound of his other half cries. He rushed over to comfort his brother by embracing him. The twins cried together for what their father's absence would mean. Prince and Jayden wailed for the pain their mother was forced to endure.

Shy knew the twins were sharing a moment and let them be. Cherise rushed to the front pew to comfort her two godsons but Shy put up her hand to stop her. Shy looked up at Cherise and shook her head no. Cherise understood and sat in Jayden's empty seat and held her best friend's hand. Shy was holding it together for her boys in an attempt to be strong for them. The tears that fell from her eyes were more for her boys than for herself. She sat, rocking back and forth as her heart broke into a million pieces.

Just minutes into the funeral service it was time to close the casket as Lela Boyd sang Shy's favorite gospel tune, "Too Close to the Mirror." Prince let out a scream that startled everyone in attendance, and everyone began to cry. Prince yelled out, "Don't close that door in my father's face." Unable to deal with his grief, Prince punched the funeral director, knocking him out cold. Jayden tried to restrain his brother but was not strong enough.

Jayden and Prince' cousin, Quincy, sat heartbroken and feeling helpless to assist his family through their pain. When Prince began his assault on the poor funeral director, Quincy knew he had to do something. Raequan and Quincy raced to grab Prince before things got completely out of control. They were able to drag Prince outside and calm him down.

Shy was in shock and sat helpless to take away her sons' pain. *Lord, please watch over my boys and help them through this tragedy. I beg you, Lord Jesus, get Prince through this and help deliver him from his grief and anger. Forgive him, for he knows not what he does,* cried Shy.

As time went on, Shy would pray that exact prayer for many years. Prince was never able to let go of his anger, his grief, or his thirst for revenge.

Chapter 8

Can't Stomp with the Real Hustlers

"Thirty-two-year-old Melvin McGee, an alleged drug kingpin, was laid to rest today following a ceremony fit for a king. The family and friends said their final good-byes just one week after a secret indictment came down on McGee, who was believed to be one of the most powerful drug dealers in northeast Ohio. The narcotics division of the Youngstown Police Department was attempting to serve an arrest warrant on McGee at the home he shared with his wife and twin sons, when McGee was shot and killed," explained news anchor Lori Findley. "Police are not saying what happened but it is alleged that McGee resisted arrest during the raid. Community leaders and family members are calling for a complete and unbiased investigation into the incident. It seems that McGee's ten-year-old son witnessed the shooting. A spokesperson for the family promised that both community leaders and the family will meet with the press after McGee's loved ones have had proper time to grieve," concluded Findley.

Officer Roberts's heart raced while he listened to the brief report the news anchor offered to their dedicated viewers.

"In other news . . ."

Shit, that was a waste of airtime, fumed Roberts to himself. *The news' focus on that piece of shit McGee is not going to help me make this shit go away.* Roberts jumped up from his worn couch in search of his car keys and three-year-old Air Nikes. He went to the corner store for a copy of the day's newspaper and a carton of cigarettes. The Vindicator would offer more information.

Roberts was disappointed after reading the article covering Melvin McGee's funeral. The report pretty much read like the news coverage except for insinuating he was a trigger-happy detective looking to make a name for himself. Roberts made no apologies for taking the life of any man, woman, or child who sold drugs on the same city streets he vowed to protect. His only regret was not connecting with Melvin's unidentified partner in crime.

Negative attention hovered over the city like a helicopter. The mayor had demanded a full investigation be conducted. Roberts doubted his fellow officers would say anything to drown his career but the victim's son was another matter. With his future on the line, Roberts found solace in alcohol and self-pity. A detailed report had been delivered to the police commissioner and as a result, Roberts would be meeting with him early the next morning.

Roberts arrived at the Commisioner's office at exactly seven-thirty. Roberts sat across from the oversized leather chair embroidered with the Commisioner's initials. Booker Thomas Martin III was as strong as his name suggested. The Commisioner's frame was a massive six foot, four inches, and he was 280 pounds. His skin was the color of a macadamia nut and his scalp was as smooth as a baby's bottom, which helped him sport his bald head with both dignity and authority.

Manila file folders, a desk calendar, and pictures of his wife and four children covered the mahogany desk. Roberts noticed the bright red flashes of light coming from the Commisioner's telephone, signaling voice messages.

Roberts drank a gulp of his warm black coffee in attempt to wet his palate. Nerves always made his mouth as dry as the Sahara Desert. His eyes continued to study the corner office and for the first time since entering the space, Roberts noticed the forty-two-inch flat screen hanging on the wall to his far right. *I am going to get me one of those before football season rolls around.*

Commissioner Martin walked into his office, thirty minutes after Roberts's arrival, without acknowledging the detective's presence. He set his coffee mug on its electric coaster, removed his tailor-made suit jacket, and immediately began pacing the floor. Roberts noticed the worn carpet where the Commissioner paced. *He must do that often,* Roberts thought. After what felt like an eternity to Roberts, Commissioner Martin stopped in front of the window and broke his silence.

"It's going to be another hot one today," said Commissioner Martin.

"Yes, sir, it looks like it," responded Roberts in a cracked voice.

"I wasn't talking to you. It was just an utterance on my part, so shut up," the Commissioner spoke without looking at his subordinate.

Roberts shifted in his seat, offended, but he kept his mouth shut. He swallowed another gulp of his now lukewarm coffee and waited for the pat on the back he believed was coming.

"Detective Roberts, thanks to you the city is in an uproar and the mayor has his steel toe right in the crack of my ass. To top that off, there was a message from the governor's office waiting for me yesterday morning. Would you like to tell me just what in the hell went wrong executing the warrant on McGee?"

Roberts let three seconds pass before responding to be certain Commissioner Martin was finished with his question.

"Well, sir, a rookie went to handcuff our suspect when McGee suddenly jumped at him. To protect my fellow brother, I gave him two taps of my side arm and he dropped." Roberts's response was matter-of-fact and emotionless.

"Bullshit! No man, drug dealer or not, would risk his life in the presence of his own son, especially not with sixteen firearms pointed at his ass," barked Commissioner Martin. He walked behind his desk and sat across from Roberts. "Now, I do not want the story you feed Internal Affairs." He paused briefly for effect before continuing, "I want the truth and nothing but the damn truth."

The angry tone of his superior stunned Roberts. The meeting was far left of where Roberts believed it would be.

"If I may speak," began Roberts. "Melvin McGee was a lowlife drug dealer with a natural appetite for money, power, and street credibility. I watched him choke the life out of a man with his bare hands and I cannot believe this case is getting national attention. The entire situation is a travesty and Youngstown is better off with McGee six feet under."

"You shot the man dead, Roberts, right before his ten-year-old son. What did you think would happen? Were you expecting a commendation from the mayor?" Commissioner Martin sarcastically asked.

"It was unfortunate that the boy was home but, damn, he'll work that shit out in counseling," spat Roberts. He had not meant to say it aloud but once the words left his lips, there was no forcing them back. Roberts would be damned if he apologized for doing nothing wrong.

"Are you serious?" hollered Commissioner Martin with a pound of his fist on the desk. "Are you serious? You're sitting there, lying to me in my face; are you kidding me?"

Roberts swallowed hard and tried the best he could to keep control of his anger. Roberts could not understand why he was being treated like a common criminal.

"I'm lost, sir. What am I lying to you about?" Roberts sat more perplexed than ever.

Instead of getting a sore throat, Commissioner Martin aimed the remote at the flat screen television. Roberts followed the Commisioner's eyes and focused on the screen. It did not take long for Roberts to recognize the people, the place, and the incident replaying for him. *Oh, shit! How in the hell did the department get their hands on this? I am fucked.*

Only five minutes had gone by but it felt like forever to Roberts. There he was, standing by, doing nothing when Melvin McGee snubbed the life out of Silk. Roberts knew he should have intervened and arrested McGee the minute he wrapped his hands around Silk's neck. Roberts knew he had more than probable cause at that point but he had become just as addicted to the money and power as his mark had. When the time came for Roberts to arrest Melvin, he wanted lights, cameras, and plenty of action.

"Sir, I can—" began Roberts.

Commissioner Martin raised his right palm and spewed an order at Roberts, "Shut up!" His eyes remained fixed on the television.

Roberts returned his attention to the screen and dropped the paper coffee cup he had been holding. His eyes bugged from their sockets and for the first time since his wife packed up and took off with their three children. Roberts wanted to cry. He now understood why the Commissioner, Mayor, and probably every living soul in the city wanted his head on a stick.

McGee had hidden cameras inside his cars, in each one of his drug houses, and anywhere he conducted business. Meeting Silk in the empty parking lot was no coincidence; McGee knew what he was doing when he scheduled the meeting there. The initial meeting between Roberts and McGee now played on the clear flat screen.

Roberts was on tape doing drugs and pocketing some of the drug money the department fronted him for stings.

Undercover officers were expected to melt into the melting pot of drugs and money but only to a point. No one is ever given a free ride for taking the life of another human being. With all of the police-related killings in the news lately, McGee's action threw the steel mill city into the national limelight. Killing a man in front of his son was a horrible mistake. Roberts had been undercover for so long, he'd begun to feel untouchable.

"From my view, it looks as if you provoked McGee to make a move. You have kids and you know damn well you would lay down your life for them," said irritated Commisioner Martin.

Roberts clinched his jaw at the mention of his children. It had been almost six years since he last saw them. He did not know how Brenda pulled it off, but it seemed as though his wife had disappeared off the face of the earth.

"Sir, you know I had to do certain things in order to protect my identity. McGee had the power to make me disappear if he ever discovered I was a cop. Everything you saw on that tape was unavoidable. We had to get McGee off the streets," said Roberts angrily.

Commissioner Martin aimed the remote at the screen and pushed play. There, in high definition, appeared Roberts at home alone snorting cocaine and drinking. The edited tape showed him stepping over the line from undercover officer to common criminal. Roberts sat speechless as his life played out before him.

"Detective, you became an accessory to murder when you stood by and did nothing to help the snitch *you* put in harm's way. You not only stole money from the department, you're a drug addict. Did you see all of the coke you were snorting up your nose? What the fuck is wrong with you?"

"Again, sir, I was undercover. I had to get deep into McGee's operation in order to bring him down. Thanks to me, one of the city's biggest drug dealers is permanently off the streets. With just a little more time, I could've discovered the identity of his partner."

"There is no way for you to double talk your way out of this, Roberts. You killed your career the exact moment you pulled that trigger on an unarmed man. This video can give the district attorney's office more than enough ammunition to charge you with this man's homicide. Detective Roberts, as far as the department is concerned, you are nothing more than a drug-dealing addict with a trigger-happy finger. You are hereby relieved of your duties. Please, turn in your badge and weapon," Commissioner Martin sternly ordered. He was furious with the insubordinate detective. The department had been on notice for years of Roberts taking the law into his own hands. Roberts had been involved in four shootings during the past eight years. His psychological exams had alerted to trouble ahead but the department chose to overlook each instance. Being a trigger happy, gun totting hot-head translated into career ambition until it went terribly wrong. It was an election year and the mayor couldn't afford to have a scandal ruin his chances for re-election. Roberts had to go, immediately.

Roberts stood on his weak legs, placed his badge and gun on the desk, and turned to leave the office with his head hung low and tail tucked between his legs.

Damn, what am I going to do now? Roberts asked himself. *What am I going to do?*

Part 2:

Calm Before the Storm

Chapter 9

High School Years—This Is Who I Am . . . Right?

Jayden stood in line with the other fifth-period lunch students who were paying the short, white-haired lady manning the cash register. He could only hope the forty-year school employee, was off her game. For the third day in a row, Jayden had forgotten to turn in his free or reduced lunch application and would be forced to use a number assigned to an absent classmate. He and every student at South High School knew what fate awaited them if lunch lady Betty was in true form.

Standing just over six foot tall with smooth skin, slanted hazel eyes, and broad shoulders, Jayden's quiet spirit always drew attention, but he was no match for the petite, seventy-something lunch lady.

"Number please," stated Betty while eyeing the food on the brown lunch tray.

"Twenty-one twelve," replied Jayden. He held his breath in fear of Betty's response. Betty gave no indication that she knew the lunch number Jayden had given her wasn't his. Relieved, Jayden grabbed the tray and walked off toward his regular lunch table where his cousin Quincy was seated.

As usual, the cheese pizza was lukewarm, the kernel corn was cold, and the two peanut butter cookies were golden brown. After being joined by Quincy's girlfriend, Caron Jefferson, the group sat, comparing grades received on their honors English writing assignment Miss Stevens had just given back.

"She gave us all a B, as usual," said Caron.

"Not all," corrected Jayden, "because I got an A." Jayden opened his milk and drew it up to his lips when the room grew silent.

"That's not your number!" screamed lunch lady Betty.

Caught! Jayden's nightmare had come true. A wrinkled, pale hand reached over his left shoulder and snatched the lunch tray from in front of him. Betty was notorious for calling out those who attempted to deceive her by using another student's lunch number. Today, Jayden Prince McGee, high school senior, was added to her list. No one could ever figure out how Betty was able to memorize the lunch numbers of over 800 students each and every school year. Most students heard stories about the little old lady from their parents and never believed the tales, until they entered South High School and witnessed Betty in action for themselves.

Betty turned on her heels and quickly returned to her station. The lunchroom erupted with laughter as Jayden sat embarrassed and hungry. As quickly as it happened, it was over.

"Man, you got played." Q began clowning his cousin and best friend. Jayden had to laugh at his own outing. He knew sooner or later his time would come, especially since the students were not allowed to leave school premises during their lunch hour. The old days of Red Barn hamburgers and Sammy Quick Stop subs for lunch were over before most of the current high school students had even been born.

Before the lunch bell rang, Jayden had searched the crowded hallways for his twin brother, Prince. He wanted to ask him for a couple of dollars for lunch to avoid the situation he now found himself in, but Jayden had no luck locating Prince. Knowing his brother, Prince had probably skipped school in search of the almighty dollar or was laid up someplace with one of the women so eager to get with him.

Jayden and Prince were identical twins physically but their personality traits were like night and day. Where Jayden was responsible, goal oriented, and shy, Prince was restless, impulsive, and outgoing. Jayden loved to read books and play basketball, and worked out daily. Prince's hobbies included hanging out with his friends, making fast money, and sleeping with as many girls as he possibly could. The only thing the twins seemed to have in common was the love they shared for their mother and baby sister, Lilac Princess. Though they did it in different ways, Prince and Jayden both took care of their mother and sister. As with most siblings, looking out for each other was an unspoken rule, even more so with identical twins.

As always, Jayden stood at the bottom of the school stairs, waiting for his girlfriend, Brianna. Being dedicated to sports, weight training, and studies didn't leave room for much free time, so Jayden made sure he spent at least a few minutes each day with his first love.

"Hey sexy, are you looking for me?" Jayden flirted.

"Boo, you know I am," replied Brianna.

The young couple held hands and walked out the front doors together. After school, Jayden always walked Brianna halfway home before turning around and running back to the school's field house for sports conditioning.

"So how was honors English today?" asked Jayden.

"It was cool. I got an A on that assignment and a B on a pop quiz this morning," said Brianna. Her bright smile always made Jayden feel special to be with her. Unlike Jayden, Brianna was brought up in a two-parent, middle-class family. Their family history and upbringing were the only differences the two had. Jayden and Brianna loved learning and had goals for their future. The number one goal was to leave the poverty-stricken city as soon as possible. Brianna was one year behind Jayden in school, but if fate would have it, they both planned to attend college in Atlanta. Jayden planned on attending Morehouse College and Brianna was set on attending Spelman College. They were both planning on majoring in English with minors in business management. Their dream was to one day own a successful book and music publishing company.

Jayden and Brianna walked hand in hand toward the corner of Dewey Avenue and Market Street as they discussed their day.

"Do you think we can catch a movie this weekend? We can rent one if you have a couple of hours to spend with me," Brianna said innocently.

"We have a double session of conditioning on Saturday, but if your mom will let me come over after nine, we can rent movies. I mean, you know I love your mom and all but she be cutting into my 'fill you up' time the way she be popping in and out the room. It seems like she don't trust me," said Jayden snidely.

"You know she loves you." Brianna laughed. "She just thinks you're out to steal my heart and get in between my legs."

"No, I'm not even like that." Jayden smiled. "I'm trying to get up in your tight, virgin coochie."

"Boo, you are so bad. Come here and give me my kiss."

Brianna grabbed Jayden around his waist and pulled him close to her. She stood eight inches shorter than Jayden and always stood on her tiptoes to meet his full lips for their daily French kiss good-bye. Moments later, Jayden began his five-block jog back toward the home of the Warriors. Jayden was less than a block from his destination when he saw a crowd of boys and instantly knew something was wrong with his brother.

Damn, Prince, not today. I don't need this today. Their entire lives, a shiver up his spine meant his twin brother was involved in something he had no business being in. It is said that identical twins experience some type of phenomenal experience whenever one encounters pain or danger. This was true with Prince and Jayden.

Jayden ran toward the crowd just in time to see his brother being handcuffed and thrown in the back of a police cruiser.

"What did he do? Prince, what is going on?" yelled Jayden over the ruckus.

Prince could only look at his mirror image through the raised car window and shake his head. Jayden didn't know if he should be angry at Prince or at the unfair prejudices of the world in which they lived. He had no idea what had gotten his brother arrested, but Jayden could guess it had something to do with their shiesty god brother, Raequan.

One of the boys Prince was with stepped to Jayden to provide a brief explanation of what had happened. "Hey, man, your brotha ain't done anything wrong. These racist-ass cops just don't wanna listen," explained T-Lee. "Prince and Raequan been chilling' wit' us all day and you know how we do. These cops are just mad that the average street hustler make more in one week than they do all year." T-Lee took a long drag off his Newport and pointed to the second police car parked beside a closed-down storefront. Raequan was sitting in the back seat with a stupid smile on his face.

Raequan Lamar Jackson was Prince's best friend and partner in crime. The boys were raised together because their mothers were best friends. At the early age of eighteen, Raequan had already served three different stints in juvenile, and Jayden was surprised he hadn't graduated to the big house yet. Though his crimes were petty, Raequan could be dangerous and Jayden hated the relationship Prince had with him.

"What are they arresting him for?" a shocked Jayden inquired.

"Man, some lady rolled up on us while we were chilling at the sub shop and accused him of stealing her car. So you know Prince and that mouth of his. He started cussing da bitch out." T-Lee paused to toke on his Newport before continuing. "So, she whips out her cell phone and calls the police and here we are."

"How can they just arrest him based on her word? I mean, look around at all of us; everybody dressed in jeans and a white tee, half with braids and half fades. Hell, we all look alike out here. Our own mommas probably couldn't positively identify us."

"I know, man, but you know how it is. Young black males look suspicious to everybody, especially if more than two are chilling together." Unsure of how he would react, T-Lee purposely withheld some information from Jayden. He knew for a fact that Prince was with Raequan and they'd taken a ride in the lady's car. T-Lee knew that was enough for Prince to catch a charge.

Jayden gave T-Lee the universal black man handshake and returned his attention to his brother. *How am I going to tell Mom this? Her heart is going to break,* thought Jayden. As he stood on the sidewalk, looking at his other half. Jayden wished he could protect Prince from all harm and danger. Jayden knew that Prince acted hard and talked a good game, but deep inside were immeasurable amounts of pain, resentment, and anger. It was that pain that made Prince Jayden McGee a menace to society.

Prince sat in the back seat of the police cruiser with his head hung low and his heart beating fast. He'd been placed in a cop car before. The police always harassed him for petty things but nothing that would result in him being taken downtown, processed, and held behind bars. After a call to his mother, Prince was always released to her custody and sent on his merry way. Prince knew that this time was different and he would soon be checking into juvenile detention center for an extended stay. He could feel his heart pounding in his head as beads of sweat formed on his forehead. *I really fucked up this time. I knew I should have listened to that voice in my head instead of going along with Raequan. They didn't even need the money so mugging that lady was stupid, especially after stealing that car and selling it to that chop shop. Fuck!*

The ride down to Scott Street seemed to happen in a heartbeat, much too fast for Prince. Taking a deep breath, Prince braced himself to face the unknown like a man. He had no idea what to expect, but he figured being raised in the Victories Housing Projects had groomed him for what awaited him behind those brick walls. Prince also took heed of the fact that he would not be alone. *Shit, I'm tripping. Raequan will be here with me, so I ain't got nothing to worry about,* Prince said to himself. *I know my boy got my back.*

Chapter 10

An Honest Day's Work

Shy was at work, watching the thin second hand on the clock slowly tick by. She had another fifteen minutes to go before quitting time. It had been a long day of dealing with the public and their nasty attitudes. Shy hated being assigned to the outpatient clinic, where people were free to verbally abuse her for no reason. For the life of her, Shy could never figure out why people would be downright evil to a person who was trying to help them. The last four patients she'd drawn blood from had gotten smart with her. One elderly man even cussed her out like she'd stolen something from him. She was grateful that her rotating schedule only placed her in the clinic twice a month.

In order to avoid drawing blood from one more asshole, Shy was hiding out in one of the stalls in the ladies' room. Her feet, back, and head were aching. She just wanted to go home and relax.

Shy was the type of woman who never left the house with one strand of hair out of place. Never one for much makeup, Shy made sure her lips were always glossed, her eyebrows were always perfectly waxed, and her eyes were lined with a brown liner to enhance her beautiful light brown eyes. Thanks in part to possessing natural beauty and aging well, the thirty-eight-year-old queen always caught the eyes of men.

To help pass time, Shy reached inside her pocket to turn on her cell phone and check her messages. As soon as she received power the cell phone began ringing.

"Hello."

"Mom, it's Jayden."

"I know ya voice, boy. Why aren't you at practice or lifting weights or wherever it is you should be?"

"Mom, you need to get home as soon as possible," Jayden huffed.

Shy dropped her head in despair and felt what little energy she had left seep from her body.

"Please don't tell me it's Prince," said Shy, sighing. "It is Prince, isn't it? What has your brother done this time?"

"Mom, just come home please. I don't know how to get him out of this one." Jayden hung up the phone before his mother could demand to know what was going on. He knew she would be upset and Jayden couldn't have her driving and crying at the same time. Jayden took a deep breath and sat down on the couch to gather his thoughts. His heart broke into pieces each time he had to call his mother with bad news about his reckless and, at times, even selfish brother.

"I can't believe how stupid he can be sometimes," vented Jayden.

"You need to calm down, man," said Quincy. "I love him too, but he makes these bad choices and he just doesn't care how it affects you or Aunt Shy."

"You're right, but he is still my brother and I feel responsible for him. I just don't know how to protect him from himself. How do you protect a person from himself?"

Jayden put his face into his hands and silently asked God to give his father a message. *Lord, ask my dad to tell me what to do to save my brother, and please watch over him while he's behind bars.*

By the time Shy arrived home, all of the anger Jayden was feeling toward Prince was replaced with concern for his mother. Shy parked her car and was not pleased to see her sister, Tara, standing on the porch with Jayden and Quincy.

Just what I need on top of everything else, her know-it-all, snobby ass, thought Shy. Jayden met his mother at her 2006 white Toyota Camry and opened the driver side door for her.

"Hi, baby," Shy said before giving her son a kiss on his cheek. "What has he done this time?" Shy held her breath and waited for Jayden's response.

"Mom, Prince and Raequan have been accused of stealing a car and robbing an old lady on Market Street. The police caught up with them and arrested them both."

Shy knew this day would come, she just wished it had happened sooner. With Prince being seventeen the state could decide to treat him as an adult despite the fact that he wasn't even old enough to vote.

"Did they take him to juvenile or the county?" asked Shy.

"I don't know, Mom. The arrogant cop wouldn't answer any of my questions and Prince hasn't called yet."

"Where is Baby Girl? She wasn't home to see them carrying her brother off in handcuffs, was she?"

The same day her husband was murdered, Shy discovered she was pregnant with the little girl she and Melvin had wanted for years. Melvin did not live long enough to even find out another baby was on the way. Shy had just left her doctor's appointment and stopped by the Boys Club to get Jayden from basketball practice. After picking up a celebratory dinner for the family, Shy arrived home to find an abundance of police cars, ambulances, and spectators fixated on their apartment. What should have been a happy evening turned into the most traumatic event anyone could ever experience. Shy and Jayden kept Melvin alive by sharing stories of happy times with the beautiful little girl named Lilac Princess.

"No, Mom, the police arrested Prince on Market Street. I haven't picked her up from daycare yet because I didn't know how you were going to receive the news and I don't want to upset her. You know how she likes to ask a million questions."

"How did your Aunt Tara find out about this?" asked Shy. The last thing she needed was her older sister telling her how she was failing as a mother.

"Quincy called her, Mom."

As children, Shy looked up to her big sister and strived to be just like her. The five-year age difference made Tara appear bigger than life to her little sister. Once Shy grew up and began making decisions about her life without consulting Tara, things between them changed. With life's challenges and Shy receiving a bigger blessing in life than what she did, their relationship changed from sisters to mere acquaintances. Shy was tired of Tara always judging her and pointing out her mistakes. In Shy's eyes, Tara had gone from a cool ghetto girl to a judgmental, opinionated snob overnight. It infuriated Shy that her sister acted like she had forgotten where she came from.

"Now what are you going to do?" asked Tara without greeting her sister.

"Hi, Tara, and how are you today?" Shy rolled her eyes and walked through her front door. Tara took a deep breath and followed Shy.

"Don't just walk away from me like that. I asked you a question, Shy," responded Tara.

"First, I'm going to sit down and drink a beer. Second, I will take a quick shower, and third, I'm going to send Jayden to pick up Baby Girl for me. On second thought, maybe I'll send for Baby Girl first," answered Shy with as much sarcasm as she could muster.

"Don't get smart with me, Shy, you know what I meant. What are you going to do about Prince getting arrested?" snapped Tara.

"If you would let me finish . . ." Shy rolled her neck. "Fourth, I'll drive downtown, find out exactly where my son is being held, and find him a lawyer. Does that meet your requirements on how *I* should handle this situation with *my* son?"

"You know what, Shy?"

Shy immediately stood up and put her hands on her hips. She had a long day and would have loved to release her stress on her opinionated sister.

"You need to let him sit down there and think about what he has done. If Prince was my son, I would—"

"See, Tara, that's just it. Prince is not *your* son, he's mine. I may not be raising the perfect child, with the perfect husband, in the perfect house, but I'm doing the best that I can. If that doesn't meet your standards, then to hell with you and your opinion!"

"Shy, all I'm saying is . . ."

"Have I asked you for your opinion? You being a better *parent* than me in no way means you love your child any more than I love mine!" Shy stormed past Tara, purposely bumping into her before showing her to the door. She was not in the mood for unsolicited advice, and was tired of Tara and her brother-in-law looking down their noses at her. Shy held the screen door open for Tara.

"Now take your snobby ass back to your perfect suburban life and stay the hell out of my business," demanded Shy.

"Shy, why are you always so defensive when it's about Prince? He needs more help than you can offer him. Why can't you see that?"

"Why do you have to be the one to make decisions on what is best for my son? Ain't nobody else in his corner but me, so fuck you and your advice!" yelled Shy. Her head was throbbing and it was taking everything inside of her not to punch the hell out of her sister.

"You don't even know what happened today and you already protecting him," added Tara as she walked off the porch.

"You know why, Tara? It does not matter what he did. Prince can go out and kill an entire block and I would still have his back. Right or wrong he is still *my child, my son* and nothing and nobody will ever change that. Now, get the hell out!"

"Quincy, get in your car and come home. I don't have to put up with being spoken to this way, and until your aunt apologizes to me, you are not to be over here," Tara ranted.

Quincy did as he was told, but not before apologizing to his Aunt Shy for his mother's behavior.

"It's okay, baby. You have absolutely nothing to be apologizing for," Shy assured her favorite and only nephew. "And, Tara, I'm telling you now, don't have your *perfect husband* call my house trying to force his opinion down my throat, or so help me God, all hell will break loose. Do not test me."

Shy could not believe the nerve of her sister. She had a husband at home to help raise her son. Only a man can teach a boy how to be a man and Shy understood that. What she did not understand was how Tara and her husband, Bruce, acted as if they had been perfect teenagers and never made mistakes. *Shit, if it wasn't for our mother beating the hell out of her every other day, Tara would be locked up someplace. But I guess she can't remember all the stress and trouble she caused when we were growing up. And Bruce isn't any better. His ass was in and out of juvenile so much they probably named a wing after his punk ass,* thought Shy.

"Jayden, take my car and go pick up my baby girl. When you get back I'll go check on your brother."

"Yes, ma'am."

"And, Jayden, you tell Quincy that his mother does not need to know my business. I'm sure you'll talk to him before me. You got that?"

"Yes, ma'am, I'm sorry."

Man, this just isn't my day, thought Jayden.

Chapter 11

Mommy to the Rescue

Cherise sat in the office of her soul food restaurant and catering establishment, counting money. It was the fifteenth of the month and time for her to make a deposit into her business bank account. Frustrated that her numbers didn't match the sales receipts, Cherise opened the bottom desk drawer and grabbed the bottle of Hennessy to help calm her nerves.

She began cooking for family and friends who needed catering services more than eight years ago. Soon thereafter, she began receiving requests from strangers to cater their special events. After a while, the requests began pouring in like rain and Cherise's modest-sized kitchen became too cramped and confined. A Piece Of Soul Catering and Café was a profitable business that Cherise took pride in. Cherise decided to put the money back in the safe and go cook up the most profitable item not on her menu—cocaine. Turning her hobby into a business gave her the perfect tool to hide how she really made her money. She'd promised herself that once the catering turned a profit, the drug dealing would stop but no matter how hard she tried, Cherise was addicted to money.

Cherise walked over to her state-of-the-art sound system and turned up the tunes of Mary J. Blige. Cherise put fire to a Black & Mild before she got to work, only to be interrupted by her ringing cell phone.

"Ma, they trippin' and got me down here shackled in chains like I'm a mass murderer and shit," complained Raequan before Cherise could even greet him with a hello.

"What in the hell are you talking about, boy?" Cherise sighed.

"They arrested me and Prince for no reason, Ma. You gotta come down here and get me out. Come on, Ma," fumed Raequan impatiently.

"Where you at boy? I know them stupid-ass cops ain't got you in that fuckin' county," yelled Cherise. "Where they got you at, Raequan?"

"I'm at juvie, Ma. Please come and get me out of here."

"I'm on my way."

Cherise ended the call, grabbed her purse and car keys, and ran out the front door of her restaurant. Cherise was so intent on getting her son out of handcuffs that she forgot to lock up the establishment. She was two blocks away before it occurred to her. After quickly backtracking, she was on her way to Shy's house, who, for some reason, was not answering her cell or house phone.

Cherise hightailed it over to Shy's house to find out if she knew of their sons being arrested. When Raequan called from a strange phone number, Cherise knew something was terribly wrong.

One second after dialing the last digit of Cherise's cell phone, Shy heard tires screeching and knew it was her.

"Shy, where you at? Shy!"

"Quit screaming like that, girl; you're going to have the neighbors all in my business. Come on in here."

Cherise was short of breath and excited as she jogged into Shy's house. Shy knew without a doubt that her friend would make a federal case out of the boys being arrested before she even knew what the circumstances were. Intent on not allowing Cherise to stress her out, Shy lit a cigarette and relaxed her back against the oversized pillows thrown on her couch.

"Cherise, please calm down before we go down there. You're all hyper and I am not in the mood to get locked up because you can't control your temper."

"Fuck you! Do you know Raequan and Prince got arrested for no damn reason?"

"How do you know that?" asked Shy.

"Know what?"

"How do you know they got arrested for no reason?"

"Because when I talked to Raequan he said—" began Cherise.

"See, there you go again, jumping to conclusions before you get the whole story about what led up to them getting arrested. It took me awhile to accept it but not everything those boys tell us is gospel," explained Shy with a smirk.

"Whatever, bitch, give me one of them Newports," said Cherise.

Knowing Shy was right, Cherise decided to regain her composure before going down to the Martin P. Joyce Juvenile Justice Center. The last thing she needed was to get locked up for showing her ass and assaulting a cop.

Shy was sure that Raequan's version of the arrest would have a boatload of holes in it. That boy was born a liar. A trait inherited from his sorry-ass father.

"All right, Shy, I'm going to smoke this cancer stick, down a can of beer, and try to think logically, but should one of them pompous police officers try to keep me from seeing my baby, I cannot be held responsible for what might go down," promised Cherise.

"If they keep us from seeing our boys, I'll act a fool right along with you," said Shy, giggling.

In the thirty years Shy and Cherise had been friends, not one day passed that they hadn't spoken with each other. No matter if the weather called for sun, rain, sleet, snow, or they were happy, angry, passive, or pissed, you could put money on Shy and Cherise communicating with each other. The two were as close as any sisters from different parents could possibly be.

Shy was born five years after her sister and she was truly a spoiled little poor girl. Tara and Shy's parents were considered the working poor, only managing to earn a little over the national minimum wage, but they sacrificed and made due. The sisters shared their father with an older half-brother from his first marriage but C-Lok lived with his mother and only visited on holidays and summer breaks from school. Growing up, Shy had no idea that her family was poor because they had a nice house, clothes on their backs, and food on the table every night. As Shy grew older, she began to take notice of how hard her parents worked without complaint. Shy began working at age fourteen to help relieve some of the financial burden on her parents.

Shy and Cherise were two peas in a pod. Their pre-adolescent years were filled with jump ropes, hopscotch, tag, and roller skating in the middle of the streets, little league cheerleading, and weekend sleepovers.

Their teenage years consisted of basement parties, union hall jams, Sunday night Skate Connection, basketball games, South High School variety shows, and, most importantly, wide hips, C-cup breasts, plump, round asses, and lost virginity.

***

It was after seven o'clock when Shy and Cherise walked through the doors of the juvenile detention center to see their sons. Despite the sign notifying visitors of visiting hours, the two mothers stormed toward the front desk on a mission.

Shy and Cherise looked around at their surroundings, and memories of their own stay behind the brick walls came flooding back to them.

"Shit, they have cleaned this place up since the times we used to be arrested for fighting," said Cherise.

"Yeah, girl, I know. The updates make it look like a friendly place. Look, they even have artwork on the walls and plants all over the place," noted Shy.

The counselor manning the front desk looked up from his paperwork when he heard the sound of clicking heels growing closer and closer. One look at the women's faces and he knew they were ready to do battle. After another glance, William Beldon recognized the women and braced himself to do battle.

"Hey, William, haven't seen you in quite a few years," greeted Shy.

"Hello, Miss Shy. What's going on with you, Cherise?" replied William.

"Shit, we down here to see our sons, Prince McGee and Raequan Jackson. They were brought down here a couple of hours ago and we need to see them now," demanded Cherise.

William took a deep breath before speaking again. His shift would be over in less than a half hour and he was not in the mood to do battle with two overprotective mothers. If they'd kept a closer watch on their boys, they would not be standing in the juvenile detention center, demanding to see their pride and joy.

"Yeah, I recognized the names when they were checked in. Prince looks just like his father; even his mannerisms remind me of Melvin. Cherise your son kind of looks like Prince. Anyone ever tell you that?"

"Look, William, go get them so we can make sure they were not the victims of police brutality. You know how y'all do," spat Cherise.

"First of all, I am not a police officer. Secondly, for someone who needs something from me, you sure are getting on my bad side." William smirked.

"William, please forgive Cherise. She's just upset about what happened today and we are both stressing out right now. Look, we go way back and I know this is a huge favor to ask but please, let us see Prince and Raequan. I won't be able to get any sleep tonight unless I see for myself that Prince is all right. He has never been detained overnight before. His having to stay here is foreign to me," Shy explained.

"All right, Shy, I'll bend the rules for you," said William while rolling his eyes in Cherise's direction, "but please make it quick. I could get written up for this."

Shy sat in the stiff chair with her left leg shaking a mile a minute. Her nerves were more on edge than she wanted to let on. Sitting in the visitation room, waiting to see her son, had her stomach doing flips. When the door opened and Shy set eyes on her son, it took all she had not to burst out in tears. Shy knew that if she was strong, Prince would be too. The last thing she wanted was for him to be worried about her when all of his attention needed to be on the situation at hand.

"Hi, Mommy," said Prince with a forced smile.

"Hi, baby, are you doing okay? You all right?" Shy knew Prince was feeling afraid, slighted, or guilty whenever he addressed her as Mommy.

"Yes, Ma, I'm doing okay. You know I ain't no punk. I can get through this standing on my head. We go to court in the morning and the judge will probably send me home with you."

"Well, you know I'm going to go get you a lawyer. There is no way in hell I can send you along this path with a public defender. They get their paychecks from the same place as the prosecutor. You have to look out for yourself."

"Ma, don't go wasting money on no lawyer. I didn't even do anything so nothing's going to happen to me. I'm good," Prince arrogantly said.

"Then you really do need a lawyer if you didn't do anything. Boy, don't you know that you are guilty because of the color of your skin and the way your pants hang down off your behind? You don't know everything, Prince. If you did, you wouldn't be down here now. Enough with all of that. Tell me what happened, and what did you do today, skip class again?"

"Yes, Ma, I did. We were all hanging out at the corner store up there on Earl and Market Streets. We were just hanging out and shit."

"What?"

"Oh, I'm sorry, Ma. That was a slip of the tongue."

At that moment Prince was glad to be in a room with glass separating them, because he knew Shy wouldn't hesitate to hall off and pop him in his "filthy mouth," as she labeled it. Prince loved and admired his mother but she had no idea how the streets were. Being young, black, and male in the city of Youngstown was like being in a war zone from one day to the next. The pressure to have money, material possessions, and the strength to beat somebody down for disrespecting you was mandatory.

"Anyway, we were just chillin' and laughing and stuff when a couple of girls we knew rolled up, so me and NuNu—"

"Who? How many times do I have to tell you that if their street name isn't what their momma put on their birth certificates, I am not interested? Now who is NuNu?"

"Carlos. Me and my boy Carlos went across the street to holler at them. The next thing I know, Raequan and Mike are taunting some old white lady who was trying to get inside the store. Then all of a sudden, they mug the lady and go running off behind houses and stuff. I was not involved in all of that mess. You know that ain't me, Ma."

"Why did you get arrested instead of Mike?"

"Ma, we all sport white T-shirts, baggy jeans, and braids. That lady probably wouldn't be able to tell us apart if we had our names printed across our chest."

"Well, I do have to agree with that. Sometimes I have trouble keeping the names and faces straight," admitted Shy. "So tomorrow at court you'll let the judge know that Mike was involved and not you, so maybe I won't need to get you a private attorney."

"Naw, Ma, it can't even go down like that. I can't be labeled a snitch in here or out on those streets. That's a death wish, Ma." Prince looked deep into his mother's eyes, searching for any sign that she understood where he was coming from.

Shy knew how much the rules of the streets had changed since she was a teenager. She thanked God for each and every day her boys were blessed to see. In a recent report, the city she had always called home was listed as one of the most dangerous cities in the country. Melvin often schooled Shy on the code of the streets. Some things were non-negotiable and no snitching always topped the list.

"Ma, I know you probably don't understand where I'm coming from but please keep our conversation between us. I shouldn't have told you as much as I have."

It took all Shy tried not to burst into tears. She would be the first to admit that Prince often got himself into reckless situations and his temper could be out of control, but he was always honest with her. At times, she would have to drag the truth out of him because he wouldn't just volunteer to tell his mother something that would probably end in her knocking him to his knees, but Prince never lied to Shy.

"Prince, this is serious. The deck is already stacked against you in the justice system. You're young, black, and male and the last thing you want to do is start your life off with a possible felony on your record. There is no way I can just sit by and let that happen to you, Prince. As much as I love Raequan, he is not my responsibility, you are. You are my child, my reason for breathing, and it is my job to protect you. I'm getting you a lawyer," said a drained Shy.

"What do you want me to do, Ma? I can't run my mouth and walk out of here. The streets don't forgive snitching, Ma, don't you understand that? Don't be wasting your money on no lawyer. I can just hook up with one of those public defenders." Prince was getting frustrated because it didn't seem as if his mother completely understood him. She just didn't get it; snitching could be an automatic death sentence.

"Are you serious? You really don't want me to get you a lawyer?"

"Yes, ma'am. Ma, sometimes you're going to have to just let me fall," Prince whispered, dropping his head down to his chest.

"Prince Jayden McGee, there is a difference between me letting you fall and me leaving you for dead. If I allowed your black behind to walk into that courtroom, at age seventeen, facing at least one felony with nothing more than a public defender to fight for you, I would be leaving you for dead. Now, this is not up for debate and the matter is closed."

"Yes, ma'am," said Prince apologetically. He knew his mother was right and Prince also knew how tight money was at home. Having to see his mother appear to struggle financially because of him made Prince hurt even more for his father. Melvin always took care of Shy and their boys. Prince couldn't remember having to worry about getting new shoes or designer clothes, or what would be underneath the Christmas tree.

"Shy, I'm sorry but you're going to have to get going," interrupted William. "He's due in court tomorrow morning at nine in courtroom fifty-five B."

"Okay, William, thank you. Prince, you are strong; be safe and keep your head up. I'll do what I have to do to help you through this. I love you."

"Ma, I'm sorry about this and I will be okay," promised Prince.

Shy wiped the tear that escaped from her eye and blew her son a kiss good night. She had a feeling they had a long road ahead of them and it was imperative that Prince remained strong. Prince stood to leave, when Shy called out to him.

"Prince, you know Mommy got your back, right?"

"You always have, Mommy."

"What's good?" Raequan spoke from the other side of the glass.

"Shit, little nigga, you tell me," responded Cherise.

"Man, you know them punk-ass blues be hatin' on a playa."

"What made you stand out for them to hate on you this time?"

"Look, Ma, all of that don't matter because they got me hemmed up right now. All I want to know is how long it's going to take you to get me back out on dem streets?" asked Raequan in a demanding tone.

"I can't do anything for you until you go to court in the morning, and you better hope your probation officer doesn't decide to violate you for not completing your community service and paying restitution for your last fuck up," snapped Cherise. "Enough of this bullshit; did you mug or rob some little white woman?" Cherise knew the answer before posing the question. Her relationship with her only son was one of veteran hustler and hustler-in-training. Raequan had no idea what it felt like to have parents in his life. His mother was more of a business partner than a protective, loving parent, and his father had been locked up for the betterpart of Raequan's life.

"It all started off as a joke and it just went a little too far. We were just messing with the lady, making fun of her and shit. Everything would have been cool if her little ass wouldn't have run off at the mouth, calling me a worthless thug and shit," explained Raequan.

"What did Prince's scary ass do?"

"Nothing. He ain't have nothing to do with it but the lady couldn't tell him and Mike apart. He just got caught up and shit. Enough of that talk; you know they got these rooms equipped with recording devices to go along with the cameras. They're probably recording every word we drop."

"So what the fuck you gon' do? Are you going to let the courts know they arrested the wrong person?"

"No, I ain't snitchin'! I can't believe you'd even ask me some shit like that."

"Shit, I really don't care who the fuck they lock up behind this. You're probably going to be in here for a minute and Prince ain't the first innocent person to be locked up and he damn sure won't be the last. Fuck him" stated Cherise nonchalantly.

"Word."

Chapter 12

You Were Raised Better

Lying on the uncomfortable, cold mat assigned to him made every inch of Prince's body ache. There was only one old, smelly blanket to cover up with and Prince thought for sure if sleep found him he would freeze to death. It was the longest night of his life and Prince could not wait to get to court and released into the custody of his mother. Unfortunately for him, that day would be a long time coming.

Cherise and Shy sat in the first row, waiting to get a look at their little boys. Knowing her son the way she did, Shy knew how scared Prince must have been waking up in jail. It was an experience she prayed would send him running back to the right path. He was very intelligent and kindhearted but he always sold himself short. Witnessing his father's death was very traumatic for Prince, but he rebelled against every counselor Shy took him to.

Shy dipped into her secret emergency money to retain a lawyer for her son but he had yet to show up in court.

"I can't believe it. They have started calling cases and the lawyer hasn't arrived yet," said a nervous Shy.

"Girl, don't even trip. I don't know why you paid all of that money for a lawyer anyway. I'm sure you would qualify for a public defender. Why pay for something when you can get it for free?" asked Cherise in between popping her chewing gum.

"One, you and that gum are working my nerves. Two, my children deserve the best and a public defender will not work for Prince as an individual. Each and every boy being escorted into this courtroom so far has been black; trust me when I tell you that's not a coincidence. Prince isn't just another statistic and I'm not leaving him out there for dead."

Shy's tone was defensive and so was her stand on the situation at hand. She didn't care what people said about her baby, he was worth saving and anyone who did not believe it could kiss her ass. Cherise just looked at Shy without saying another word.

Six boys had been brought out and paraded in front of the judge, who had yet to look up from the files his clerk placed in front of him. Each boy was ordered held until their next court date, even the ones charged with misdemeanors and who had no record.

Shy looked over at Cherise, trying to figure out why she did not appear to be as nervous as she was. Cherise always seemed so detached from everything and everyone except her son and that twenty-five-to-life-serving, sorry-ass husband of hers. Knowing how her friend dealt with things, Shy figured Cherise was nervous as she was on the inside.

Sitting in the courtroom had Shy's stomach doing all kinds of flips and somersaults. Shy sat wringing her hands in an attempt to stop them from shaking. Her leg jumped a mile a minute and she was sure she was on the verge of having a nervous breakdown.

Cherise's eyes searched the crowded courtroom for any familiar faces. The crackling of her gum was getting on the nerves of everyone around her, including

Shy, but Cherise did not give a damn. Chewing gum was how she worked out troubling issues. Though she had been the stereotypical worried single mother sitting inside the courtroom before, this one felt different. With Raequan's record, he was most likely going to be serving some time in the juvenile detention center.

"Would you please stop it," voiced Shy.

"Stop what?" Cherise asked.

"Cracking that damn gum. It's getting on my last damn nerve," Shy snapped.

A few of the women sitting around Shy and Cherise agreed with nods of the head, a few "amen's," and a couple "mm huh's." Cherise rolled her eyes at the collective sea of browns, beiges, and chocolates, with a look that warned them not to say another word. She popped her gum one more time just to annoy Shy.

"Cherise, would you quit it!" The words came out louder than Shy intended, but she meant them nonetheless.

"Prince McGee and Raequan Jackson are present, Your Honor. Both boys are charged with auto theft, assault, and evading arrest," announced the court clerk before Cherise could respond to Shy.

Shy's heart raced and she broke out in a sweat. Prince made eye contact with his mother and they exchanged forced smiles, both trying to be strong for the other. Shy could not believe what she was hearing. It was clear that the boys were being thrown into the lion's den, and Prince's lawyer still had not arrived.

"How do you plead, Mr. Jackson?" asked the judge.

"Not guilty, fo' sho," replied a cocky Raequan.

"'Not guilty' will suffice; the extra Ebonics are not necessary," said the judge without looking up from the open file. "And you, Mr. McGee, how do you plead?"

"Not guilty, sir," responded Prince in a nervous voice.

"Is counsel present for each defendant?" asked Judge Alderman.

"Yes, Your Honor. Simon Priestley for both defendants," replied a young white man who looked to be the same age as his clients.

"Good. Both defendants are held over until their trial dates. Next case," said Judge Alderman as he closed the file on the boys.

"Excuse me, Your Honor, but Prince McGee has never been arrested and has no record at all. I would ask that you reconsider your decision and send him home on house arrest until a deal can be reached with the prosecution or the trial date." Mr. Priestley spoke with no authority or interest.

"How does the prosecution feel about the request?" asked Judge Alderman.

"Due to the seriousness of the charges, the state requests Prince McGee be held over 'til the next court date," replied Marianne Boyce. Like the judge, she too kept her eyes down during the verbal exchange.

"Sorry, Mr. Priestley, but your client will be held until the next court date. I suggest that you and the state get together and discuss a plea. The court's calendar is full and both dependents may be guests of the state of Ohio for some time."

With that being said, the judge slammed his gavel, and Shy watched her son be led out of the courtroom. Cherise rose from her seat, expecting Shy to follow her lead. Shy's legs felt so weak she was sure to fall if she tried to stand. She tried to wrap her mind around what just happened, but fear would not allow it.

"Shy, honey, come on, let's get out of here," Cherise said. She rubbed her friend's back in an attempt to snap her out of her daze. Cherise's eye caught sight of a handful of other women who looked to be in need of a best friend. *This must be their first time in court behind one of their children,* thought Cherise. Though she understood their current positions, the only woman she gave a damn about was Shy. "Everything is going to be okay. Just grab my arm and lean on me. I won't let you fall. Prince is safe as long as Raequan is with him and, anyway, his lawyer is probably in the hall waiting for you."

Shy had no idea how long she was zoned out but she snapped back of it at the mention of Raequan being behind bars with her baby.

"Yeah, Raequan will watch out for Prince, right?" asked Shy in a childlike voice.

"Yes, Raequan will watch out for Prince. Hold my hand and follow me outside, so we can find out what happened to the lawyer you hired."

Early the next morning, Shy sat in a small white room at the detention center with Edward Teague, Prince's lawyer, waiting for the guard to return with Prince. Unfortunately for Prince, his lawyer was involved in a bad car accident yesterday morning, causing him to miss the arraignment. Edward was carried away from the accident with a fractured leg and was released from the hospital after receiving a cast. By that time it was late afternoon. He felt bad for not being able to represent his young client.

"You look worried and tense," said Edward. "Don't worry, we are going to get your family through this."

"I pray that we do. I didn't sleep at all last night for worrying about my baby," said Shy as tears escaped her eyes. She swept them away as fast as she could when the door suddenly opened. The faint glimmer Prince held on to inside of him immediately lit up when he saw his mother. Since witnessing the death of his father, Prince had caused problems and given his mother heartache, but she never gave up on him. Prince loved his family more than anything but his mother was special to him. Their mother-son relationship was strong and unbreakable.

Shy rose to meet Prince halfway and embraced him with open arms.

"Are you okay, baby?" asked Shy.

"Yes, Mommy, I'm fine. Don't worry about me, 'cause you know I can take care of myself," Prince replied with closed eyes and a heavy heart. He hated the fact that his lifestyle sometimes brought pain to his mother's heart, but he saw no way out of the street hustle. It was in his blood.

Edward watched the touching scene between mother and son and his heart went out to them both. He too was caught up in the streets as a teenager, but being locked up when his father passed away from a stroke was enough to make him turn his life around. Understanding what was being shared between his clients, Edward sat quietly until Shy and Prince broke their embrace.

"Hello, Prince. My name is Edward Teague and your mother has retained me as your lawyer."

"What's up, man?"

Prince eyed his lawyer up and down, trying to size him up. Despite being draped in a tailored suit, Prince could tell the man had some street in him.

"Let's sit down and get to business," Edward said while pulling a chair out for Shy. "I need to hear everything about that day. And Prince?"

"Yeah?"

"Don't leave anything out. I want to know exactly what you did the day of your arrest, from the time you woke up to the exact minute you arrived here at the juvenile facility," instructed Edward. "Everything you say will be kept in the strictest confidence." Edward pulled a legal pad and ink pen from his mahogany-colored briefcase. "Before we begin, tell me if you're comfortable talking with your mother in the room with us."

"Yeah, it's cool. My mom already knows the story," replied Prince.

Prince went over every single minute with his lawyer and painted a very clear picture for Edward. It was evident to Shy and Edward that Prince was his own worst enemy. He had no involvement with the crime but he knew who did.

"You have to tell the judge the truth so we can get you out of here," said Shy.

"No, I ain't a snitch, Ma," replied Prince.

"So you just willing do to someone else's time for a crime you didn't commit?" Shy asked in disbelief.

"Your mother is right," interjected Edward. "If you are charged as an adult, this crime will follow you for the rest of your life. You are going on eighteen and facing felony status."

"At least I will still have a life. Do you know what will happen to me in here and when I touch down on the street if I'm labeled as a snitch?"

"Prince, you have to think about your future. All this no snitching bullshit makes no sense," cried Shy. His rationale angered Shy. Prince would have rather remained behind bars than tell the truth and be set free. "His father used to pound that 'snitches get stitched' bullshit all the time like it was some kind of gospel."

"It is the gospel of the streets. I know because I used to be out there myself," explained Edward. "I was in a similar situation when I was your age, so I understand where you're coming from. Before you decided your fate, listen to what the prosecutor proposes. He will reduce the felony car theft charge to a simple joy ride if you agree to give them the other person involved and testify against him."

"Hell no! Are you crazy, man? That's a fucking death wish," fumed Prince.

"Watch your mouth, boy," snapped Shy. "Let the man finish."

"Or you will have to serve six months behind bars and another six months on probation upon your release," finished Edward.

Shy was scared for Prince. He wanted so much to be like his father that Prince made bad choices without intent. Their father/son mindsets were why Shy knew Prince was going to make the wrong decision, and she would not be able to get him out of the mess he was in.

"I'm good, man. Just let them crackers charge me as a juvie and I'll do the six months. Shit, time in here is better than life six feet in the ground." Prince tried to justify his decision but Shy knew it was a front.

"You sure that's what you want to do? You can think on it for a while," explained Edward.

"Prince, please think about this before you make a rash decision," said Shy with tears staining her face.

"I'm sorry to put you through this, Ma, but I got to do my time," responded Prince. "Please don't cry."

"But it's not your time, baby; you will be doing somebody else's," reasoned Shy.

"I love you, Ma, and I'll be home in six months." Prince hung his head low for putting tears in his mother's eyes. He did not know how to get her to understand the code of the streets. Being behind bars for six months for something he didn't do was the last thing Prince wanted to do, but he was stuck and nothing his mother said could change that.

Shy reached out for her son and held him as tight as she could as he cried on her shoulder.

"I'm sorry, Mommy. I'm so sorry. I love you," declared Prince through tears.

"Shhh, I love you too, baby. You know Mommy got your back, no matter what."

Chapter 13

You Know I Still Love You Girl

A month crept by slowly with Prince's and Raequan's absences being felt in the streets. Cherise was exhausted from trying to stay on top of her catering business and supplying her son's hustlers with their street candy. Each day that passed was one less to count, but there was at least one more to get through. Cherise was the first to admit her many faults but eager to declare her greatest attributes; she was a natural-born hustler. It was bred inside of her to make a way out of no way. No matter what it took, Cherise got it done. Without her son to do some of the heavy lifting, all Cherise could do was hope that the next seven months would soar by at lightning speed. Raequan's criminal record had netted him two month's longer in jail than Prince.

The beginning of the month meant it was time for Cherise to make the two-hour drive south to visit B-Boy. With Raequan behind bars, Cherise would have to take the trip alone. The ride would give her plenty of time to work out a plan to stay on top of her game while Raequan was away. Before she could head down the highway, Cherise made a list of things to be done around the business while she was away. Cherise was happy she could depend on her assistant, Brianna to take care of things for her.

Brianna was a trustworthy employee. She helped Cherise out on a part-time basis during the school year and full time during the summer. Cherise paid Brianna well and often treated her to goodies from her lavish shopping sprees. Brianna was the only girl at her high school that carried authentic Coach and Dooney & Burke bags. Apple Bottom, Baby Phat, True Religion, and 7 were designer names that hung in Brianna's closet. Brianna appreciated every paycheck and all of the gifts Cherise showered on her. Shopping relaxed Cherise, and being able to buy for a girl was fun for her. Raequan was her only child and picking out clothes for a boy offered little.

"Brianna, baby, it's that time again. Are you going to be okay?" asked Cherise.

"Yes, ma'am. You know I got this," Brianna smiled.

"I'm writing a list of things to be done while I'm gone. Everything is listed in order of importance but you'll still have plenty of time to study for the SATs. Here are the keys, you know the code to the alarm, and you have my cell phone number. Make sure you have Jayden help you close up and tell him I'll pay him when I get back," Cherise said mindlessly. She paced the tile floor jotting down things for Brianna to do as she spoke.

"I'll be fine, Miss Cherise, and I already spoke to Jayden about helping me close up. He can be a little overprotective sometimes so I didn't have to ask him to come by, he volunteered. You have a safe trip and keep watch for the highway patrol. The last thing your lead foot needs is another speeding ticket. If you keep it up, you're going to need a driver."

Brianna and Cherise laughed together and joked about the police having Cherise's license plate memorized. After going over things together, Cherise said good-bye to Brianna.

Until Bossy's retirement from the game, Cherise paid her to prepare and warehouse her drug inventory. Cherise did not trust anyone else so she was forced to take care of her own business. There was plenty of room in the kitchen for Cherise to cook the drugs, and the secret trapdoor to the basement was a perfect place to house the work.

Cherise's routine consisted of loud music, three various-sized aluminum pots, boxes of baking powder, and bricks of powder cocaine. She also dealt in heroin for her more financially stable clientele. The heroin was only one-fourth of her shipment and didn't require the time and attention that cocaine did. Cherise only cooked the drugs after hours. She didn't need anyone to discover what was really going on behind the doors of A Piece of Soul Catering.

Cherise sat in the visiting area, waiting to see B-Boy. He would want to know how and why she let his son get hemmed up on a car theft charge, like she could have done anything about it. The wait offered Cherise time to mentally prepare for that pointless argument. She watched a small child race toward a prisoner and thought back to when Raequan reacted the same way when his father appeared from behind the steel doors. B-Boy had spent all of his son's life behind bars. With the exception of B-Boy being in the hole, Cherise made sure her son got to see his father at least once a month. At one point Cherise had packed up her life and moved to Mansfield for a number of years so father and son could spend quality time together. It was important to Cherise that Raequan got to know his dad. She was a product of an absent father and wanted to protect her son from that pain having known her own.

Four years into his sentence, B-Boy's behavior earned him a tour of Ohio's various prisons. During his time behind bars, B-Boy had been housed at six different correctional facilities before finally ending up back where he started, in Mansfield. Cherise had long moved her son back to Youngstown. It was a decision she always regretted. She wondered if making a life in a better city would have produced a son of greater character.

Following B-Boy was a task. Cherise looked forward to Raequan's eighteenth birthday. He would be able to visit his father without her accompanying him.

"What's up, Reese?" B-Boy offered dryly. His voice snapped Cherise from her daydream.

"Hi, it's about time those slow-ass CO's told you I was here," Cherise complained about her forty-five-minute wait. She smiled up at her husband and stood to embrace him. After a quick hug, the two sat at a table in the corner for some measure of privacy.

"How's my boy holding up behind big walls?"

"He's his father's son. You know he's all right," Cherise replied.

"Yeah, well, if his momma was on her job, he wouldn't be locked down," B-Boy snapped smartly.

"Don't start that shit, nigga. You always running off about shit you know nothing about. I can't teach him how to be a man, that's his daddy's job. You have no idea how hard it is for a woman to raise a boy, especially when his so-called father is locked up and never coming home," Cherise said, irate.

"I know my son ain't supposed to be sitting behind no damn bars," B-Boy countered.

"Blame that on you, mutha fucka. Had you been on the street instead of providing free labor on this modern-day plantation, all our lives would be different." Cherise felt steam blowing out of her ears.

"Yeah, I'd be beatin' ya fuckin' ass right now. You better watch how you talk to me," B-Boy warned.

"Shit, nigga, you need me. You keep forgetting that little detail," Cherise said matter-of-factly.

"Man, whatever." B-Boy blew off Cherise's painful reminder of his dependence on her.

They spent the next few minutes in silence. B-Boy knew Cherise had grown tired of their arrangement. He never expected it to last as long as it had. It was true Cherise had always been ride or die, but a wheel should have fallen off after riding on it for so long.

Cherise was amazed at how quick her mood had changed. Dealing with B-Boy was not usually such a chore when they sat face to face. It was the norm for him to press her buttons during their phone conversations but Cherise felt B-Boy was downright tripping. She had to wonder why.

"So, what up? We cool?" B-Boy attempted to break the tension.

"That depends. Are you done tripping on me?" Cherise asked.

"We good." B-Boy smirked. "How's the catering going for you lately? Have you had to hire new help?"

B-Boy couldn't have cared less about the café or the catering services. All he wanted to know was if she was keeping up with drug sells and if she was continuing to supply the corner boys during Raequan's absence.

"Business is good all the way around. With the economy the way it is, I'm not looking to hire anyone anytime soon. Maybe by the summer I'll get somebody in there." In other words, Cherise could hold everything down until Raequan's release. "How are you holding up? Did you get the new underwear, books, and snacks I sent last week?"

"It came just in time. My stock of beaters was running low. Do you know how hard it is keeping whites white?" B-Boy and Cherise shared their first laugh since the visit began.

"Sorry I forgot the socks. I left two packs for you to-day." Cherise smiled.

"If you don't mind, I need new music to listen to and my phone card refilled," B-Boy voiced.

Cherise got the message loud and clear. B-Boy was low on drugs, mostly cocaine. What Cherise brought for him would hold him off until her next visit. B-Boy would call her if the situation changed.

"Time is flying by. Let's get in line for pictures before our times up," B-Boy suggested.

"Good idea. How did you like Tysha's book, *Cheating in the next room*? Wasn't it good as hell." Cherise wanted to change the subject.

"It was a beast. Dem joints ya girl be putting down be tight. When was the last time you hollered at her?" B-Boy asked, genuinely interested.

"Two weeks ago. She's promoting her book and traveling right now. She just treated her sons to a vacation in Miami. You know they kicked it." Cherise laughed.

"Tell her I said good lookin' out and to keep 'em coming."

"She said to look for a visit next month. She'll be in Mansfield, meeting with author Brandi Johnson about some project," Cherise said as she looked around at the other visitors.

"Dat's what's up. Your cuz is cool as hell." B-Boy gave a nod of the head.

The two found any mundane topic to discuss while others were in earshot. Though B-Boy did enjoy reading some of his time away, he did not care to talk openly about it. He nodded to let Cherise know it was time to do her thing.

"I don't feel well." Cherise gagged and covered her mouth with one hand and placed the other over her stomach. "I think I'm going to be sick."

"You cool?" B-Boy rubbed her back.

"I'll be right back," Cherise said, running off to the bathroom.

After finding an empty stall, Cherise pulled on the string of dental floss stuck between her back teeth. She slowly pulled on the string and began to gag. The longer she pulled, the more her natural reflexes worked against her. Finally, it was over and Cherise held a balloon filled with cocaine out of her mouth. After rinsing the small package off, she wrapped a thin layer of toilet paper around the package and tucked it inside of her front jeans pocket. Cherise had gotten the idea from a movie. Sneaking drugs into the prison by way of her vagina was too predictable. She had to be more innovative with her risk taking.

Cherise emerged from the bathroom with a blank look on her face. The way she was acting made B-Boy nervous.

"You straight?" B-Boy inquired and hugged Cherise.

"Yeah, I'm good. I must've eaten something that didn't agree with me. I feel much better now." Cherise's answer told B-Boy the package was in place for him to retrieve. He was able to do just that while they posed for pictures.

An hour later, Cherise was rounding the Lodi exit, headed toward the small outlet mall. Her anxiety level was sky high. Doing some serious shopping was therapeutic for her. Buying retail was more effective than popping a Xanax.

Chapter 14

What Family Love?

Jayden knew he needed a high SAT score if he wanted admittance in to a top HBCU. As a little boy Jayden dreamed of going off to college and never returning to his hometown. He'd mapped out his life a long time ago. First stop college. Nothing was going to keep him from his studies or block his five-point plan.

He found it hard to concentrate. Jayden was hurting on the inside. It seemed his entire world was falling apart. Prince was locked up and it was tearing Jayden up. The twins bond was undeniable. Right or wrong, the brothers always looked out for each other. Jayden missed his brother so much his heart ached. To make matter worse, one of the most important people in his life had been forbidden to associate with him. Quincy was more than just his first cousin, he was his best friend. Jayden felt he was being punished for crimes he did not commit.

"Jay, did you hear me?" Brianna asked.

"I'm sorry, what did you say?"

The sound of Brianna's voice snapped Jayden from his thoughts. They were in his living room, studying for SATs and babysitting Princess.

"What's going on with you? Are you not feeling well?" Brianna was becoming concerned about her boyfriend's state of mind.

"No, it's nothing like that. I just can't concentrate. There's too much going on right now," Jayden replied somberly.

"Are you still worried about Prince?"

"Yeah, a little I guess. But he was cool yesterday when we talked. You know Prince, he's keeping it together. It's so unfair that I can't visit my own brother."

"That is a stupid rule. You can't change it so don't waste time worrying about it." Brianna smiled. She reached over and gave Jayden a kiss.

"You know firsthand how twins are. You and Monica might be fraternal but you're twins nonetheless," Jayden said through a small smile.

"Our relationship doesn't compare to you and Prince." Brianna shrugged her shoulders and twisted her lips. She and Monica were sisters but Brianna would not label their relationship as being close.

In an attempt to relax his body, Jayden inhaled deeply. He had to figure out how to change his aunt's mind about Quincy without getting his mother involved. Jayden knew the situation was volatile. Shy would explode if she heard the things her sister had said about her children.

"My Aunt Tara won't let Quincy have anything to do with me or my family anymore. She says my mom has done a horrible job raising us and that Prince is a bad influence for Quincy," Jayden explained. He fought back the tears welling in his eyes. Jayden had to tell someone and he trusted Brianna.

"Jay-Jay, I'm hungry." Princess interrupted her brother's conversation with his girlfriend.

"What do you want to eat, little girl?" Jayden inquired while getting up from the floor.

"Cookies and ice cream," Princess said excitedly.

"Nope, try again." Jayden laughed.

"You so mean," Princess pouted. "I never get my way." Princess plopped herself down on the couch next to Brianna. She crossed her arms and poked her lips out. It was her version of a tantrum.

"Mom will be home soon and she's bringing dinner. Do you want a bowl of cereal to hold you over?" Jayden asked.

The mention of being treated to her favorite cereal put a smile on the six-year-old girl's face. She raced into the kitchen with her big brother following her. Jayden never minded babysitting his little sister. No matter what was going on in his life, Princess always made him smile. Hanging out with two of his three favorite girls was nice, but it didn't alleviate the pain of being banned from both his cousin and brother.

Jayden returned to the living room to find Brianna thumbing through their collection of DVDs.

"Don't tell me study time is over already," Jayden said, joining Brianna on the couch.

"I just thought we could take a break and watch a movie. Maybe it will help you relax and clear your head. How long are you going to keep from talking to your mother about Tara?" Brianna kept her eyes on the movie titles when she spoke.

"I don't think you've met my mom," Jayden joked. "You know how my mom is when it comes to her kids. I was hoping the situation would work itself out before my mom found out about it. My Aunt Tara is a trip at times but I never imagined she would tell Quincy he's not allowed over here anymore. Apparently, I'm not welcomed at their house, either. Did I tell you that she said it wouldn't be long before Prince's ghetto ways took over my mind and that we're both natural-born thugs like our dad was?" Jayden's soul ached.

"She said *what?*" Shy yelled, surprising Jayden and Brianna.

Shy walked in just in time to hear of her sister's latest antics. She was livid. Of all the things Tara had pulled over the years, she had gone too far.

"Jayden, please tell me I heard you wrong. Your Aunt Tara didn't really tell Quincy he's not allowed at my house, did she?"

"Oh, hey Ma." It was impossible to hear the front door open from the family room. He hadn't heard his mother come into the house and was startled by her presence "I was going to tell you about it tonight. Aunt Tara said Prince is a bad influence and you are not raising us right because my brother wouldn't have so many character flaws. Quincy's not allowed to be around us unless she's with him," Jayden further explained.

She heard the pain in her son's voice. She knew how close Jayden and Quincy were. Jayden's eyes watered when he told her what was going on. Sadness had washed over his face. Shy walked over to Jayden and gave him the tightest motherly hug she could muster. All she wanted at that moment was to take all of his pain away. Jayden's emotional state was unnecessary. She was happy that Brianna was there with him.

"Hi, Mommy!" Princess squealed. "I want a hug too." She skipped over to her mother's open arms.

Shy bent down and gave her daughter a hug. She was furious. It took great pains not to show it. There were more pressing things that needed her attention before she dealt with her childish older sister.

"I'm hungry and Jay-Jay wouldn't fix me anything to eat," Princess fibbed.

"Ooh, Princess, you know that's not true." Brianna pretended to be shocked by the little girl's false statement.

"Hey, Brianna. It was rude of me not to speak. I'm sorry," Shy said.

"It's okay, I understand." Brianna smiled.

"Come on, Mommy," Princess whined. She took her mother by the hand and pulled her into the kitchen.

Jayden felt horrible. The last thing he wanted was for his mother to overhear his conversation with Brianna. Jayden knew his mother would have gone off had it not been for Princess.

"It'll all work out. You can't get distracted from your ultimate goal, though," Brianna said while rubbing Jayden's back.

"You're right but it's hard to watch my family fall apart. Things have deteriorated overnight. There's no telling how bad it'll be after my mom talks to Aunt Tara. I don't know what I'll do if Quincy is snatched away from me forever," Jayden said in a gloomy tone.

"He won't be," Brianna promised, not knowing what else to say.

"All I know is my mom does not play when it comes to her kids. My aunt would stand a better chance facing Laila Ali in the ring than going up against my mother. This isn't going to end well."

"They're sisters, how bad could it get?" Brianna asked naïvely.

"Unfortunately, we'll soon find out," Jayden replied, and shook his head in distress.

Chapter 15

Is This Family Love?

Tara was loading the dishwasher when screeching tires echoed throughout her small cul-de-sac. It sounded like the car had stopped in front of her house if not in the driveway. She looked out the kitchen window to find headlights beaming down the length of her driveway. Seconds later, someone began banging on her front door, shaking the frame.

It had to be an emergency, and worry washed over Tara because Quincy was not home. She swung the door open to find her sister with a scowl on her face. Shy was obviously upset about something. Tara had a good idea about what.

"What in the hell is your problem?" Tara asked sarcastically.

"Funny, that's the same question I was going to ask you," Shy spat.

Shy brushed past her sister in an uproar. She was full of venom and Tara was about to get bit. The sisters had their share of differences over the years but things had never dropped to the point of no return. There would be no coming back, no right turns, and no apologies to be made or accepted. Shy was incensed. She wanted to slap Tara on sight but also wanted to give her a fighting chance to defend herself.

"When did your heart get so cold? How can you live with yourself?" Shy demanded.

"What are you talking about?" Tara pretended not to know.

"Naw, bitch, we are so far past that point. You told Quincy to stay away from my boys and me? You've made that declaration before but I've never taken it seriously. Despite whatever is going on between us, you've always left the boys out of it, at least after you calmed down." Shy stood with her fists balled against her hips.

"Look, Shy, I know you love him but Quincy is my son. He has a great future and I don't want anyone or anything distracting him." Tara tried to sound reasonable. "Besides, he needs to stay away from bad elements, family or not."

"Since when is Quincy and Jayden's relationship a distraction?" Shy snarled.

"Since it became apparent that my baby sister's household is breaking down," Tara snapped.

Tara felt strong about her decision to separate Quincy from the bad air surrounding the McGee family. Relatives or not, Tara had to do what was best for her own family. She had asked Shy to let her raise Jayden shortly after Melvin's death. Tara could see back then that Jayden was special and would be able to write his own ticket in life. She thought that by taking Jayden, Shy would have an easier time dealing with the traumatic state Prince was in. Shy had refused to separate her boys or to allow Tara to have any say in their rearing. Tara felt Shy's strength was her greatest attribute and her biggest weakness.

"I never claimed to be a perfect mother. We all make mistakes, including you. You try to present yourself as flawless. My children are as loved as anybody else's. Prince, Jayden, and Princess are my world. I would die for them all. I've sacrificed my life for them so don't you dare stand there and judge me." Shy was infuriated by her sister's snobby attitude.

" Why is Prince locked up if he's so loved? You know this is your fault, don't you?" Tara said snidely.

"Tara, I'd be careful if I were you. Be real careful," Shy warned. "We may be sisters but I will beat the shit out of you in your own house, trust that. Prince is no different from any other teenage boy struggling to survive, especially where we live. He's made some bad choices but so did you," Shy said cunningly.

Shy and Tara faced each other with mixed emotions. Love versus hate. Looking into her sister's eyes, Shy knew they would never be close again. Tara had cut her too deep far too many times. Betrayed a number of hurtful times because Tara chose friends over sisterhood, Shy felt it was time to let go of their one-sided relationship. She was no longer going to be the only one putting forth effort to have a friendship. Shy was done.

Sisters knew things about each other that no one else would ever know. That's the way it was supposed to be. Shy and Tara were no different. Tara just had more secrets to hide.

"I'm all Prince has. Not you, our half-brother, your fake-ass husband, or anybody else who claimed to love my sons embraced him when he needed it. You and that judgmental asshole you're married to stood on the sideline watching and waiting for Prince to fall. If anything, you and his uncles failed him. The people in his life who mattered talked about him instead of talking to him. Prince watched his father be shot down and your resolve was to turn your back on him." Shy wagged an accusatory finger at Tara.

"This is the problem, Shy. You get defensive when it comes to Prince," Tara said matter-of-factly, as if she wouldn't do the same if Quincy were being degraded and insulted.

"No one else is protecting him. Prince is just as much your nephew as Jayden is. You need to remember that," Shy exclaimed.

"I never said he wasn't. I love that boy. He's just not on the right road," Tara replied with attitude.

"So instead of helping me you're going to leave him out there lost?"

"Face it, Shy, your son is a thug," Tara barked.

"Fuck you, Tara!"

Tara got scared. She knew her words had gone too far. Shy was a mother lioness and Tara had no doubt that her sister would hurt her without a second thought.

"Shy, it's just that we feel—" Tara began.

"We feel? We feel? I knew Bruce's holier-than-thou stick in the ass was behind this," Shy said angrily.

"He's my husband, Shy," Tara said almost apologetically.

"He's a hypocrite, Tara."

Tara had to admit that Bruce was a dictator. She usually had no say in the decisions he made regarding their family. Tara ultimately went along with what he wanted to keep him from going upside her head. Bruce was a mean person, plain and simple. Tara liked her big house and luxury car so she dealt with her husband's shortcomings. There was no way Tara could maintain the lifestyle she was accustomed to on her own.

"But he's still my husband," Tara replied.

"And he's not Quincy's father," Shy countered with bitterness.

Tara felt as though the air had been knocked out of her. She was exasperated. Tara never thought Shy would ever play that trump card. Shy had Tara at a loss for words.

"If you want to keep that piece of information between the two of us, I'd rethink my position on keeping our boys apart," Shy threatened.

"How dare you?" Tara cried.

"How dare you treat my kids this way? Like they're throw away parts of your life. You want to act like an enemy, so be it. You fuck with mine, you had better be ready to stomp with the big dogs. I'll protect mine by any means necessary. That includes cutting my sister off at the knees." Shy was ready to go to war if it meant taking Jayden's pain away. "You can't fuck with me, dear sister. I'm not that bitch to be fucked with, remember that."

Shy stormed out of the house, leaving Tara standing in shock. Tara was speechless. She felt on the verge of having an anxiety attack. If her secret were to surface, her entire world would be destroyed. She had been dependent on someone her whole life. Tara was not like Shy; she didn't have the strength to be a single parent. As far as Bruce knew, Quincy was his son. Tara vowed to take her secret to the grave and that is what she had every intention of doing.

Tara feared the repercussions would be more than she could bear should Bruce ever discover the truth. The impact on Quincy's life would be irreversible. She had to figure out a way to change Bruce's stance on keeping their son away from his cousins. Tara sat down and stared out the window as tears streamed down her cheeks. Memories of that regretful time in her life washed over her. If only she could reverse the hands of time, she would have made better choices when she was younger. All Tara could think of was all the if only's and what ifs. She'd cheated on Bruce after he joined the Marines and left for basic training. She'd slept with at least five men in a six-week period. Based on probability, Bruce could not be her son's father. Truth be told, Tara wasn't sure who fathered her only child. For the sake of everyone involved, Tara selfishly went with a lie that best fit her own needs. Bruce was able to provide for her and the baby. He was a mediocre husband but a good father and wonderful provider. Tara's life was comfortable and she wanted to keep it that way.

Chapter 16

Recoil

Once he accepted his reality, Prince got in line with the program and abided by the rules as outlined. Shy had pointed out the wasted time he spent fighting an unbeatable opponent. The rules were set in stone way before his stay behind bars and they would remain in effect way after his release. Prince agreed with his mother's logic and canned his rebellious attitude. Life had become much easier since doing so. The appearance of surrender to the system got the staff off his back and the teachers on his team. The weeks had crawled by at a snail's pace. Prince was finally adjusting to having his civil liberties temporarily taken away and time was passing a little faster without incident.

"Mr. McGee, stay behind after class. I'd like a minute of your time," Mr. Karl requested. Karl Wilkins IV didn't look much older than his students. To bolster a rapport with the kids, the teacher allowed them to address him by his first name. It was Mr. Karl instead of Mr. Wilkins for the at-risk teens.

"Yes, sir," Prince replied.

An hour later, Prince sat in the empty classroom, waiting to hear the reason for keeping him behind.

"I've been seeing great improvement in both your work and attitude, Mr. McGee."

"I promised my mom I'd do better," Prince responded.

"It makes me wonder why you weren't regularly attending school before trouble found you," Mr. Karl pondered.

"Things are different on the streets." Prince lowered his eyes when he spoke. He was trying to make changes but had to adjust his thinking one step at a time.

"It's obvious to me that you are very intelligent. You have great potential, but for some reason, you're selling yourself short," Mr. Karl tried not to sound preacher-like.

Prince had no response to the compliment. He was so used to the negative things people had to say about him that flattering remarks made him uncomfortable. Prince gave the young black man a smile. He sat half paying attention to the encouragement his teacher was trying to offer him.

"I gather life hasn't been easy for you. I'd like you to keep in mind that only you control your future. There is a different world waiting for you somewhere outside of Youngstown. You have to believe in yourself," Mr. Karl said sincerely.

"Yeah, I hear you, man. I mean yes, sir," Prince corrected himself. He didn't want his teacher to feel disrespected. "My mom says the same thing. I'm working on changing my life. I want my mom and brother to be proud of me." Prince began gathering his things. "Good looking out, Mr. Karl."

With that being said, Karl watched as Prince walked out the classroom door. He was not done with his best student. Not by a long shot. Karl Wilkins IV had lost his only son to senseless violence eight years ago. Not long after, he and his wife divorced and Karl fell into a deep depression. Therapy and soul searching led Karl to his life's calling: saving at-risk boys within his community. Teaching had become his saving grace. Prince was the first student he encountered who reminded him of his deceased son. Mr. Wilkins felt a strong connection with Prince. He could see success in Prince's lost soul. Karl knew it was his responsibility to help Prince heal from what ailed his young heart.

Shy helped make her son's stay comfortable by making every visiting day, writing letters, and sending encouraging greeting cards. Parents and grandparents were the only people allowed to visit inmates so Shy allowed Prince to call home daily. The support Prince received made him a target on the inside. On more than one occasion, Prince had his personal items stolen. He'd even been jumped by fellow inmates during lunch. There was no other reason for others to hate on him. Prince could only reason that his fellow inmates were jealous of him. He spent most of his time alone. Prince knew the rules of the street carried over into the inside so he trusted no one. At times, he didn't even trust Raequan.

Prince was bothered by his best friend's inconsistent attitudes toward him. He understood Raequan being upset that the judge gave him a longer sentence but it wasn't Prince's fault. Raequan had a record, Prince had none. In spite of it all, Prince remained loyal to his partner in crime.

After lunch, Prince joined in on a pick-up game of basketball. He and Raequan were on opposite teams. Nothing was at stake but the boys played hard to be slated the winner.

"What's up with all the hacking?" Prince shouted.

"Man, shut the hell up and play the game," Raequan barked back.

Prince dribbled the ball down the court, stopping at the top of the key. He searched for an open man as Raequan tried to steal the ball. Unable to find a teammate,

Prince squared up and took the jump shot over Raequan's head. Prince hit the three-pointer with nothing but net.

"Hell no, dude stepped over the line, that ain't no three," Raequan said angrily.

"Whatever, man, don't hate the player, hate my game," Prince mocked. "Just play the game, nigga."

"Fuck you, trick," Raequan snarled.

Raequan was intent on winning the game. He was fed up with Prince and his superior attitude. He now had his hand on the ball. He saw a clear path for a layup and charged ahead. Raequan pushed forward with his left shoulder down when Prince stole the ball and took off in the opposite direction. The team's power forward chased after Prince. Prince made it to the hoop and went up for a dunk. His shot was hacked from behind and he was hit with a hard foul. Prince went down with a loud thud. He grabbed his right arm, curled up into a fetal position, and rocked from side to side in obvious pain.

"Bro, get'cha punk ass up." Raequan laughed deviously.

"Fuck you, man, you broke my arm," Prince said through clenched teeth.

"Get help! Call the CO over here," Rex, a cool, tall white boy, instructed.

"You wrong, Rae, this ain't shit but a game. Your slimy ass meant to do that shit," Tyrell voiced. He was a young thug with prison in his future.

"That's dat bullshit right there. Raequan, nigga, you ain't shit," Sam snarled. Sam was a natural-born criminal with hatred in his heart for people like Raequan. He knew his type. Raequan would sell his own momma up the river at the drop of a dime if he'd benefit from it.

"What are you trippin' about? You don't even like dude," Raequan countered.

"That doesn't have shit to do with it. Anyway, we like him more than your bitch ass," Tyrell declared. He too had distain for Raequan. The two had crossed paths on the streets and Tyrell knew what Raequan was capable of. Prince was supposed to be Raequan's boy and he had just broken his arm over a meaningless basketball game.

Prince made it to his feet with help from Rex and Sam. He was still gripping his arm and in excruciating pain. Prince and those around him heard the bone crack when he hit the floor. At the time, Prince was in too much pain to recall how the incident happened. He put it on pause until he could see the replay clearly, in slow motion.

After having his arm X-rayed, set, and placed in a cast, Prince was back inside his cell asleep. The doctors had given him a shot of morphine for the pain when he first arrived in the emergency room. When he returned to the facility, the detention center nurse gave Prince two Percocet pain pills. The medicine put him out like a light. It would be his first full night's sleep since being locked up.

"Hey, Jackson, my boss wants to see you," Baldwin announced. He was Raequan's least favorite corrections officer.

Raequan immediately followed Baldwin down the long corridor. It wasn't the first or second time a staff member woke him in the middle of the night. Raequan may have been a menace to society but there was a method to his madness. He had made a deal with the devil and was playing an award-winning performance.

"Come back in an hour, Baldwin. Jackson, have a seat," the night shift staff supervisor directed. His job

mostly confined him to a desk. The $9.85-an-hour po-
sition did not compare to his last job. Mr. Roberts was
once Roberts, the crooked undercover police officer
who killed Melvin McGee in front of his ten-year-old
son. Since the highly publicized scandal that rocked the
city, no one would hire him. He had to take whatever
he could get.

Holding the dead-end job was both humiliating
and emasculating for the man but he had to live. The
menial position was all he could find. Loss of his position of authority within the department dried up his
side cash flow as well. Even his drug connections quit
dealing with him. In the past, Roberts was a high-level
drug dealer, earning hundreds of thousands of dollars;
unfortunately he was a horrible money manager. What
came in immediately went right back out. Roberts had
very little saved when his career fell apart. His wife had
divorced him years before his life had fallen completely
apart. After public opinion pinned him as a common
criminal, his kids became ashamed of him and cut all
contact with their father. They moved across the country to escape the shame of sharing his name. The house
was foreclosed on, cars were repossessed, and family
and friends turned their backs on him.

In the years since being thrown off the force, Roberts lived off various women, and pulled robberies and
every single-minded hustle in between. Roberts was
able to wiggle his way into his current position seven
months ago. His life was slowly returning to a sense
of normalcy but memories of that fateful day haunted
him. He blamed all of his misfortunes on Melvin. Roberts often fantasized about exacting revenge on the
dead man. Payback was only a dream until the seed
of his nemesis was sentenced to juvenile hall. If he
couldn't make Melvin pay for every bad mistake, poor

decision, and immortal sin, he'd have to settle for the next best thing. Torturing and breaking the soul of Melvin's son had become Roberts's new life's mission. Making Prince's life a living hell was his obsession.

"You went over and above today, Raequan. You're even more ruthless than your father was in his glory days." Roberts laughed.

"Don't talk 'bout my pops. Just pay up, bro," Raequan griped.

"Here you are." Roberts handed over Raequan's reward. "You've earned this Bellaria pizza, my man."

"True dat," Raequan joked.

"Why'd you do your boy like that?"

"Shit, we all gotta get it in," Raequan replied, taking a bite of pizza. He had no conscience and no qualms about double-crossing his god brother/best friend. When Roberts stepped to him, Raequan instantly knew who he was. Prince kept newspaper clippings of Roberts. Prince, much like Roberts, had a mission one of retribution. Raequan kept that piece of information to himself. It might serve him well in the future.

"Give the little nigga a couple of days before getting at him again. Spread a rumor that he's snitching on everybody, including you. That's how he scored less time than you," Roberts suggested.

"Shit, I got that. It's probably true anyway. You know some of these dudes are gonna try to get at him," Raequan warned.

"Let them. I want him to get a beat down, a serious beat down," Roberts replied through an evil smirk. "I won't reveal myself to him until the time is right. If you play the game long enough, we might get more time added to his tab."

Raequan nodded his head as he bit into the pepperoni and mushroom pizza. *This fool's tripping. How long does he think he can hide out in this office before Prince spots him? Prince will beat his ass on sight,* Raequan thought, shaking his head. *That boy will do a life sentence just to watch this fool die. I should tell on him myself.*

Monica sat on her bed with the phone cradled between her ear and shoulder while she flipped through the cable channels. It was her favorite time of day, she was home alone and talking on the phone with Prince.

As his deep voice sang in her ear, Monica looked at the wall calendar. In three short weeks, Prince would be home and Monica's world would make sense again. Everything would be back on track.

"So, what's up, girl? What you into?" Prince asked with a grin.

"Nothing, boo. School was boring, as usual, and my mom's is still on my case about everything under the sun. Of course my perfect, prissy-ass sister still can't do any wrong," Monica whined.

"Baby girl, if you wanna start with the complaints, I can holler at you later," Prince warned his young girlfriend.

"Naw boo, you right. I'm good. You down to the last turn, boo. I can't wait to see you. It's some bullshit that your mom is the only visitor allowed to come see you. I want to see you so bad my body aches. I miss you so much." Monica sniffed.

"You don't miss me, girl, you just miss my backstroke," Prince joked.

He heard the sadness in Monica's voice. She was feeling like she didn't belong, like she was being punished just for being born. Prince understood her pain; it was the same anguish he was forced to live with, day in and day out. It was only one of many similarities Prince and Monica shared.

Both of the seventeen-year-olds were the oldest of a set of twins. They were born on the second day of a new year at the same hospital. Their parents had been high school sweethearts. Prince and Monica felt like their existence on the earth was a mistake. Their lives had been filled with heartache and disappointment. Prince and Monica shared a bond that could never be broken. They had an unspoken understanding that no one else could never understand.

"You have no idea how much I miss you. All I do is think about you, boo. I love you," Monica said with sadness.

"I miss you too, girl. Have you been doing what I asked? I want you to be prepared when I touch down." Prince smiled at the thoughts he was having.

"I'm watching one right now."

"Are you seeing anything you want to try?"

"Yes, there's one called the joystick joy ride. It's when I would straddle you and put my feet near your head and tilt my back slightly," Monica explained proudly.

Prince was much more experienced with sex. He'd been kicking it with older women since he was fourteen. Those older girls taught him things that he wanted Monica to learn. He was her first and she wasn't comfortable with her sexuality. Certain things embarrassed Monica and kept Prince from totally enjoying having sex with her. Prince asked Monica to watch movies, videos, read books, and study up on the *Kama Sutra*. He also suggested she learn how to masturbate. Prince explained that if she knew how to please herself, she could teach him how to please her. Monica was willing to do anything to keep Prince from cheating on her again. So, she did as he asked. Her letters to him were reflective of her good study habits.

"That sounds good, babe. What else?"

"We can try a tight squeeze where we're both hori-
zontal with you on top of me. I thought we could take a
shower together and attempt the frisky floor show position too," Monica said excitedly. She thought it would
be fun taking a shower with her man.

"You're starting to get me hard, girl. I'm not sure
what that is but it sounds real good." Prince took a deep
breath.

"I'd bend over, touching my palms on the floor, and
you'd enter me with one strong penetration. The book
says this position puts you in complete control."

Monica was proud of her findings and sharing them
with Prince. She hoped he was proud of her too.

"Yeah, keep doing those stretches and learning yoga.
We're going to put it in the day I get out of dis bitch. I'm
gonna be all up in that. I'll be able to tell if you've been
giving my shit away," Prince warned excitedly.

"You know this pussy cat is all yours." Monica blushed.

"A'ight, I have to go. I love you, baby girl," Prince
declared.

"I love you more."

After hanging up with Monica, Prince put in a call
to his cougar. She was stacked like a brick house and
straight hood. Vanilla Cream was her stage name and
Prince considered her his chick on the side. She had
no expectations of him and they had great sex. Prince
described her skills at performing oral sex as phenomenal. Vanilla Cream was a grown-ass woman who
hustled hard for hers. Prince had nothing but respect
for her drive.

Prince spoke with Vanilla Cream for five minutes
before heading back to his cell.

"Aye, aye, nigga, aye," Tyrell called out.

Prince turned to find Tyrell trying to catch up with
him. They greeted each other with a handshake and
one-arm hug.

"What it do, my man?"

"Some straight up shit," Tyrell announced.

"What up?"

"I know he's your boy and all but don't turn your back on him. Dude dirty and your broke arm is proof," Tyrell explained.

"For sho," Prince replied, appreciating the heads-up.

Prince had suspected that Raequan was tripping on him for some reason. It was hard to accept the idea that his lifelong friend would suddenly have a vendetta with him. As far as Prince knew, things were cool between them. Prince thought that Raequan was upset about the time he had to put in but quickly pushed the idea aside. Raequan should have known he could trust Prince. Tyrell wasn't the first person to tell Prince about Raequan. Prince never put anything past anybody so he'd keep a watchful eye on his best friend. Things done in the dark always surfaced in the light. If Raequan was dirty, Prince would be able to find out. Raequan was sloppy. His arrogance always gave him away.

Chapter 17

That's How I Do

Shy and Cherise were primped and primed for a girls' night out. After dinner at Ruby Tuesday, the best friends stopped in for a drink at Frieda's Bar. Shy wore her hair flat-ironed and parted down the middle. Her off-the-shoulder lavender blouse showed off the tattoo of her children's names and offered a hint of sexiness to complement her look. The torn-at-the-thigh jeans hugged her curves perfectly but it was the royal purple peep-toe, four-inch stilettos that screamed diva.

The olive green sleek material of Cherise's above-the-knee dress turned heads when she walked. Her hair was pulled back into a perfect ponytail, showing off the contours of her neck. Cherise stepped high in black sling-back heels and she carried a matching satchel.

It was a little before eleven when they walked through the door looking like hood stars. Only a handful of patrons surrounded the square-shaped bar situated in the middle of the establishment. The DJ played mellow sounds from the seventies. Shy and Cherise found two empty barstools and made themselves comfortable. They were able to see both the front and back entrances from their seats.

"Hi, babies, what are you drinking?" the barmaid asked after looking the women up and down.

"Gin and cranberry juice," Cherise replied.

"Long Island Iced Tea, all top-shelf dark liquor please," Shy said, adding her drink choice. She planned on having fun after being a couch potato queen for so long. Cherise had suggested they go to a bar known to serve their patrons stiff drinks of generous proportions, but Shy opted for a place where she could drink all night and keep hold of her whereabouts.

The best friends laughed, joked, and chatted. They were both enjoying their rare evening out, mostly in part to the funk and old school slow jams blasting through the speakers. The unmistakable sound of Roger Troutman's classic "More Bounce to the Ounce" filled the bar. The song never failed to fill the dance floor; that night was no different. Anyone who was lucky enough to secure a barstool remained seated. They swayed back and forth to the beat for fear of losing their seats. The large crowd in the bar forced some to lean against the wall. Sore feet did not keep them from moving their bodies to the music.

Shy was deep into the funk and failed to hear the husky voice speaking to her.

"Excuse me, Shayla," the stranger extended his hand and smiled.

"Oh hey, how are you?" Shy spoke.

"This might sound like a weak line but I'm doing fine but not as fine as you are." He took in Shy's undeniable beauty and the scent of her hair.

Shy laughed at the stranger's awkwardness. He reminded her of Derwin from the hit show *The Game*. From what she could tell, he passed her height requirement by an inch. It was close but he made it. He was well groomed and sexy.

"Do we know each other?"

"We've never formally met but I remember you from high school. My name is Dwayne."

"So, you went to South?"

"No, Chaney. We had English class together our freshman year," Dwayne explained.

"I was only at Chaney the one year before transferring to South. I'm sorry but I don't remember you. What did you say your name was again?" Shy quizzed.

"Dwayne Willis."

Cherise watched the meeting from the sideline. Dwayne looked all right but he wasn't her type. She gave Shy and Dwayne another glance before smacking her lips and standing to leave.

"Shy, I'm going to the restroom. Your friend can save my seat for me," Cherise flirted.

Cherise walked away, shaking her hips, hoping Shy's man of interest was watching. She was certain the sway of her hips would garner some male attention. Her body moved with precision. There was no way she would be outdone. *If Shy thinks she's the only one who can get a man, the bitch is crazy,* Cherise thought. The bar was elbow to elbow and everyone was having a good time. Cherise scanned the crowd for something to get next to but came up empty.

Shy sat laughing with Dwayne. It had been a long time since she was able to relax and she was going to enjoy her night. Dwayne was easy on the eye but not as handsome as Melvin. He measured up to be two inches shorter and didn't possess those deep, dark eyes of her late husband. Despite the negatives, Shy decided to give him a chance. She caught herself comparing every man to Melvin. It was a habit she was trying to break. No matter how much time passed, Shy knew there was no substitute for the only love of her life.

"I see your girl is making her way back over here. I know she wants her seat back," Dwayne recognized.

"Yeah, I enjoyed our conversation. It was nice meeting you," Shy replied.

"Do you mind if I hit you up sometime? I know you have a cell."

Shy hesitated before responding. Dwayne had just lost some points by the way he'd asked for her number. He sounded like Prince asking some hood rat for a casual date. There was too much going on in her life and Shy did not want another issue added to her to do list. She looked into Dwayne's eyes and saw sincerity. He had approached her respectfully and had made no sexual innuendoes during their conversation. Shy smiled and finally ran off her number.

"Okay, I'm going to be in touch soon," Dwayne promised with a wink and a smile.

Again, Shy's level of interest dropped two points. The wink, smile combination put her off. She liked a little thug in her man. It was completely different from being a hood.

Shy turned around in her seat and swallowed the last of her drink. She felt like it was a gamble getting to know Dwayne so she would keep it casual. Her hope was that she wasn't betting on a horse posing as a stallion.

Chapter 18

Mommy Taught Me How to Play the Game

Cherise found Raequan in a better mood than she expected. She was taken aback by his upbeat attitude and positive demeanor. His previous stays behind bars kept Raequan angry and defiant. Cherise knew her son and that whatever was behind his mindset, it was surely against the system.

"Have you been writing to your dad? I don't want a lecture on my poor parenting skills just because he hasn't heard from you," Cherise fussed.

"Yeah, I hit 'em up. Everything was cool," Raequan asked sarcastically. "I don't even know why you still be dealing with dude." Raequan turned up his nose. Since he was able to understand what was going on, Raequan wondered why his mother stayed loyal to his father. Raequan hated the way she allowed him to treat her. He was the one locked up, not her. As far as Raequan was concerned, B-Boy needed his mother, not the other way around.

"For now, but you know that door is forever revolving. I think that nigga keeps a list with 'ways to fuck with Cherise' scribbled at the top." Cherise laughed but was dead serious.

"Don't let him get away with dat shit, Ma. You need to let dat nigga go if he can't respect you, Ma." Raequan's good mood blew out the other side of Cherise's head along with his advice.

All of his life, it seemed his parents discussed their
dysfunctional relationship with him. The good, the
bad, and everything in between. Cherise spoke in one
ear and B-Boy in the other. Raequan had watched his
mother do things no son should ever see. Sharing the
intimacies of a broken-down union with a product of
that environment was a mistake of catastrophic proportions. Cherise and B-Boy set their son up to fail
from the day he was born. They were so wrapped up
in destroying each other's lives that Raequan's needs
were overlooked. As a result, Raequan evolved into a
straight-up menace. His mental and emotional defects
were instilled deep inside of him.

"I've tried to get away from that deviant so many
times that I don't have the energy to try anymore,"
Cherise said mindlessly. Raequan had heard it all before. He decided to change the subject.

"So anyway, are you good at the shop?" Raequan
asked, uninterested in the answer. He was ready to end
their visit before his mother totally ruined his day.

"No complaints. The books are good and business
is holding strong. I do want to find a building to buy.
I plan to rent out the place for parties, wedding recep-
tions, and shit like that," Cherise announced.

"Dat's what up. You do you and keep things moving,"
Raequan said. He was actually proud of his mother for
thinking ahead. He knew if she'd let go of the past, she
could be happy.

"You were in a good mood when I first got here.
What's up with that?" Cherise quizzed.

"I came up on a way to make my time slide by. All I
gotta do is fuck wit' dis dude's head and make his time
crawl like the snake he is," Raequan explained.

"How'd you come by that?"

"A night supervisor got me up on it. He has a major issue with dude so he reached out to me."

"How'd you get in good with the target?"

"We've been homies for life. It's data snitchin'-ass nigga, Prince," Raequan snarled.

"What did Prince do to piss the supervisor off?" Cherise was skeptical.

"You already know that dude hates Prince and his fam, especially his dad," Raequan answered with venom in his voice.

"What's the supervisor's name?"

"He's that dude that took Melvin out, Keith Roberts."

"Roberts?" Cherise shouted.

"Yeah, he works the midnight shift and stays in his office so Prince not even up on him working here."

"Raequan, get out of it," Cherise demanded. "You don't need to be dealing with him. He's crazy and dangerous. That combination is like dynamite."

"I'm already in, Ma. Prince's broke arm was no accident," Raequan confessed.

"What did you get for your trouble?" Cherise asked with attitude.

"A pizza from Bellaria and I watched *Scarface* on the flat screen in his office," Raequan replied.

"Are you serious?" Cherise was surprised by her son and his arrogant attitude.

"Look, the unhappier Prince is, the more I get in return and the happier I'll be," Raequan reasoned.

"I understand making your time comfortable but this won't end well. Roberts has something bigger on his mind. Prince watched that man kill his father. What could Roberts possibly gain from messing with that boy? Trust me, sooner or later, that nigga's going to claim you owe him," Cherise promised. She had a bad feeling about Raequan's mission.

"It ain't even that serious, Ma," Raequan said dismissively.

"Rae, that man killed Melvin; why is he fuckin' with Prince? If anything it should be the other way around," Cherise fumed.

"That ain't my problem. As long as Roberts got me, I'm in it to win it," Raequan said with a shrug of the shoulders.

Cherise grew up on the streets. She knew if a man went up against another, he was ready for war. Melvin's death had affected everyone who knew him. He'd done dirt when called for but Melvin was always fair. No man deserved to be shot dead in front of his child. Cherise took total offense to Roberts's tactics. Her son had made a deal with the devil and Cherise had to get him out of it. If not, Cherise knew they were in for another tragedy.

Chapter 19

Wrong Is Wrong

Tara was so engrossed in her phone conversation that she didn't hear Quincy walk into the kitchen. Quincy assumed his mother was gossiping with her best friend, Nyla. She was the only person he could think of who would participate in stomping on his aunt's name. He was insulted by the malicious lies his own mother was spewing about her own sister.

"No, no, if I were you, there's no way I'd allow my daughter to keep dating my nephew. I stand behind my statement. Shy failed one son and it's just a matter of time before the other son follows suit," Tara ranted.

Quincy's jaw nearly hit the floor. He could not understand why his mother was saying such things. How could she even believe what she was saying? The longer he listened, the worse it got. Quincy wondered why his mother had nothing better to do than put her own sister down.

"Listen to me. My sister has to be smoking, popping pills, or something. Her decision-making process is horrible. Shy has no one to blame but herself for the way Prince has turned out to be. He's just like his dead daddy used to be: a hoodlum. Shy should've given Jayden to me after Melvin got himself killed. She never should have had another baby, either. All of her time and energy should've gone into saving Prince." Tara went on and on with her slamming Shy.

Quincy could hear no more. He was devastated. That was enough.

"*Ma!*"

Tara jumped at the sound of her son's voice. She spun around to find a look in Quincy's eyes she had never seen before. Tara stood frozen. Her mouth tried to will itself to speak but she was speechless; unfortunately, it was five minutes too late. Tara never meant for Quincy to overhear her. It slipped her mind that he was home.

"Quincy, you scared me." Tara exhaled and held her hand to her chest. She felt lightheaded and guilty.

"How could you talk about Aunt Shy and the twins like that? To say Princess shouldn't even be here? Why, Ma? That was foul," Quincy said, near tears.

"It's complicated," Tara offered as a weak apology.

He loved his cousins and admired his aunt. Prince and Jayden were like brothers to him. Not a soul on the earth could change how important the twins and Shy were to Quincy. Growing up, Quincy spent more time with Shy than his own mother. All he wanted was to be with his cousins and enjoy their company. The three of them were so close they felt like triplets.

Quincy had never disrespected his parents, especially not his mother. As he stood looking deep into her eyes, Quincy was on the verge of losing it. He needed to put space between him and his mother before the situation got out of hand.

"Let Dad know the coach called a mandatory second practice and our golf game will have to wait," Quincy communicated to his mother. He was incensed by her behavior and ashamed to be her son.

Tara could hear the resentment in her child's voice. She felt a permanent shift in their relationship. It was obvious his opinion of her was forever changed. Fear washed over Tara's heart. The butterflies in her stomach caused her to be nauseated. Tara didn't realize she was still holding the phone to her ear until it almost fell from her shoulder. Nyla sat on the line, listening to everything.

"Nyla, I'm going to call you back," Tara said into the phone. Her eyes fixated on Quincy. He turned his back on her to leave.

"Wait, Quincy, don't leave yet," Tara begged. She tried to grab his shirt but Quincy stepped out of reach.

He picked up his pace and walked out the front door. Tara was left alone to ponder what had just transpired. She knew how much Quincy felt Shy and his cousins. At times, Tara thought Quincy viewed Shy as his mother and her as his aunt. Tara was jealous of Shy's relationship with Quincy. She took it as a threat.

Playing basketball was therapy for both Quincy and Jayden. Problems were left on the court after the rush of the game. That day was different for Quincy. Tara's berating words played in his head like a song with a catchy tune.

"Let's go hit up IHOP," Jayden suggested. "I'm starving."

"So am I. My treat," Quincy offered. "Grab Lawrence and Davis, too. Tell them we'll meet there." Quincy and Jayden sometimes hung out with the team's point guard and power forward. The four had played ball together since their seventh grade year. Quincy could use Lawrence's sense of humor. He was in desperate need of a sidesplitting laugh.

An hour and a half later, Quincy was at Jayden's house helping to clean up. Jayden was tired from basketball practice and sleepy from eating multiple stacks of pancakes, but he wanted to knock out his chores before his mother got home. He didn't want to deal with the repercussions if she came home to a dirty house. After scrubbing down the bathrooms, Jayden moved into Princess's bedroom. He had to move her existing bedroom furniture to the basement. Her new canopy bed and dressers were scheduled for delivery the next day.

"Set it down while I move these containers out our way," Jayden directed.

"I never realized how big it is down here. Aunt Shy should put a game room with a pool table down here," Quincy suggested.

"I know, right? She says she'll think about remodeling next summer. With college coming up for me, I don't see it happening."

Jayden moved the last crate from the space. He noticed a square piece of dry wall cut out of the wall. Jayden was astonished by the contents inside the wall.

"I don't believe Prince! Q, look at this," Jayden raged.

In all the time Prince had been gone, it never occurred to Jayden that his brother might have drugs and cash hidden in the house. Jayden was upset because Princess could have found them.

"Whoa! How much money do you think that is?" Quincy asked.

"It's too much for it all to belong to Prince. This is crazy."

"What are you going to do?"

"I don't know but I can't chance my mom finding it. Maybe Unc will come pick this stuff up and hold on to it for Prince."

If anyone would know what to do, it was their Uncle C-Lok. It wouldn't surprise Jayden if Prince had gotten the drugs from him anyway. C-Lok promised to pay for his nephews' college educations since he was hustling so hard in the streets. Jayden and Quincy didn't like how their uncle made his money but they were happy to know they could attend college without putting a strain on their parents' finances.

Quincy pulled out his phone and pressed the button assigned to speed dial C-Lok. He answered after three short rings.

"What it do, nephew?"

"Hey, Unc, Jayden and I need you to come by Aunt Shy's house."

"What's wrong with my sister?" C-Lok immediately became concerned. These types of calls from his nephew could only mean trouble. Though C-Lok was hard-pressed to imagine what type of trouble Quincy or Jayden could be in. Shy had calmed down immensely over the years but things happen.

"Here, I'm going to let Jayden explain."

Quincy handed the phone to his cousin.

"What's up, Unc?"

"You tell me, nephew. Is everything okay with ya momma?" C-Lok asked nervously.

"Yes, this isn't about her. I moved some stuff around in the basement and stumbled on some stuff that must be my brother's," Jayden explained.

"Like what?" C-Lok was slow on picking up Jayden's hints.

"A stack of money and—" Jayden began.

"Whoa, whoa, whoa. Please, say no more," C-Lok cut Jayden off. He had to stop Jayden before he said too much over the phone. There were certain things not meant for electronic ears. C-Lok knew where Jayden was going without him verbalizing it. "I'll be there within the hour. What time does Shy get home?"

"In about two hours," Jayden replied.

"I'm on the way, nephew. One," C-Lok said, ending the call.

"So, does he want us to bring it to him or is he coming to get it?" Quincy inquired.

"He's on his way. You know he's not going to let us ride with this stuff in our car." Jayden smirked.

Jayden and Quincy looked at each other and laughed. They knew their only uncle was always there for them.

"Unc to the rescue," they said simultaneously.

Chapter 20

Nothing Less, Nothing More

Shy was so excited she could hardly contain herself. The past six months were grueling but the difficult ordeal was finally over. Shy was so happy tears were streaming down her face.

Prince emerged into the freedom light feeling like a king. You can't keep a natural-born hustler tied down like an animal and take for granted that upon his release, he won't be rabid. Prince was a natural-born hustler and ready to hit the streets like a beast. In due time, the old heads would recognize him as the son of a legend known as Legend.

"Prince!" Shy screamed and ran into her son's open arms.

"Hi, Mommy!" Prince was just as excited to return his mother's affections.

"My baby's home." Shy began to cry. She was floating on air. Her arms were wrapped so tightly around Prince's neck he couldn't breathe.

"You're going to choke me to death, Ma. I missed you to but don't kill me before I get a hot shower and a home-cooked meal," Prince joked.

"Oh, I'm sorry, baby. Come on so I can get you home. I have all of your favorites cooking so it's fresh and hot. I'll put the mac and cheese in the oven while you take a shower," Shy rambled and fumbled with her car keys.

"Ma, you know I like my wings hot out the grease."
Prince gave a slight frown. He never liked leftovers. If
food sat for an hour or longer, Prince considered it left-
over and would have none of it.

"No, boy. I know what you like. Fried chicken wings,
mac and cheese, collard greens, sweet potatoes, corn
bread, and potato salad. Did I forget anything?" Shy
joked.

"Yeah, banana pudding," Prince blurted out.

Shy and Prince joked and laughed the rest of the
ride. Mother and son felt blessed to be together again.
Prince couldn't wait to see his brother, sister, and
cousin for the first time in months.

Prince walked into his home and finally received
proof he was not dreaming.

"What's up, bro?" Prince and Jayden said simultaneously. They embraced and exchanged loving pats on
the back. Their reunion had been a long time coming.
Prince missed his brother terribly. Jayden felt whole
again. Without his brother within arm's reach, life was
different, uncomfortable, and boring.

"Good to have you home, bro," Jayden admitted, finally breaking their hug.

"Prince is home, my Prince is home," Princess sang
while jumping up and down. She was ecstatic to have
her big brother back. Talking with him on the phone
didn't compete with having Prince to play with.

"Come give me a hug, little girl," Prince happily requested. Though it wasn't his favorite pastime, Prince
missed having tea time with his baby sister. She was his
pride and joy.

Prince looked around the house, trying to take it all
in. He never realized how good freedom would taste.
Prince went to get settled in while Shy finished preparing dinner. He enjoyed a long, hot shower and felt like

a new man by the time the family of four sat down to eat. Shy had outdone herself with the menu. Prince savored every bite.

"Hey, cuz!" Quincy greeted with enthusiasm.

"What's up, bro?" Prince returned his cousin's energy.

Prince rose from his chair and hugged Quincy. The two were genuinely happy to see one another.

"Look at you. I see you've finally cut those braids and shaved. You're all groomed, man. You almost looking as good as me," Quincy teased.

"I couldn't get my stuff twisted in there. It was either get a cut or look like a motherless child, as my mom would say."

"I feel you, man. You and Jay are hard to identify to the average person," Quincy replied.

"Well hi to you too, favorite nephew," Shy said with a sarcastic laugh.

Shy knew Quincy was happy to see Prince so she let his rudeness slide. Any other time, she would have gone upside his head.

"I'm sorry, Aunt Shy. How are you doing?" Quincy gave her a kiss on the cheek.

"I'm glad to have Prince home too. Are you hungry? I can fix you a plate," Shy offered.

"Yes, ma'am. Give me some of everything."

Prince, Jayden, and Quincy sat at the table eating, joking, and reminiscing. It touched Shy's heart to see them all together. Shy decided to start cleaning the kitchen to give the boys some privacy. She had Princess give her a hand.

"Mommy, who's that plate for?" Princess inquired.

"My friend Mr. Dwayne is coming by," Shy answered.

"Oh." Princess sounded disappointed.

"What's wrong, baby girl? I thought you liked Mommy's friend."

"No, ma'am, not really. He acts funny when you leave the room or not looking," Princess confessed.

"Funny how?" Shy stopped loading the dishwasher and gave Princess all of her attention.

"Mean," Princess replied simply.

Shy was very in tune with her kid's personalities and reactions to different things. She knew Princess was not telling a lie or exaggerating her words. Shy knew the judgment of babies and puppies was to always be trusted. Shy and Dwayne had been getting to know each other and she was starting to feel him, though not so much that she wouldn't heed her daughter's misgivings.

"He's not my friend, Mommy," Princess said in a sour voice.

"Baby, why didn't you tell Mommy that Mr. Dwayne was being mean to you? Don't you know it's my job to protect you?"

"'Cause he really don't be here to bother me, and Jay-Jay said you seem a little happier since you got a boyfriend. Maybe your heart was ready to like somebody other than Daddy." Princess explained her reasoning.

"Lilac Princess, if you're not happy, Mommy's not happy. Now go get ready for your shower. I'll be up to check on you soon."

Shy could hear the twins and Quincy laughing in the dining room. The sound was music to her ears. She had missed Prince and Jayden laughing and talking with each other. Talking to Jayden about her earlier conversation with Princess could wait. There was no way she would interrupt Prince's celebration. Shy knew Monica, Brianna, and Quincy's girlfriend, Caron, were coming to join the small gathering.

"I got it, Ma. It's probably the girls," Prince yelled out. He was eager to see Monica.

"No, Prince, it's most likely for me. You go on and relax." Shy smiled at Prince.

Shy reached the front door just steps ahead of Prince. He stood behind her as she opened the door. Shy found Dwayne standing under the porch light with a bottle of wine in hand. Her face was void of any expression. Shy felt nothing but indifference.

"Hi, Miss Lady, how are you?" Dwayne stepped inside the house.

Prince's blood pressure skyrocketed. He could not believe the gall of the man standing in his house and kissing on his mother's cheek.

"What the fuck is this nigga doing here?" Prince yelled.

Jayden and Quincy rushed from the dining room. Shy jumped at the vibration and hatred in her child's voice.

"Prince, what the hell is wrong?" Shy demanded.

"You don't recognize this nigga?"

Dwayne was stuck. He stood in fear of the ambush he felt coming but also held hate in his heart for the McGee family.

"This is my friend, Dwayne. Do you know him?" Shy asked.

"His brother was that punk-ass nigga Silk. The snitch that was working with Det. Roberts when he killed dad." Prince was in a rage. "Oh, nigga, you think you gon' play with my momma?" Prince had sought out, studied, and lived the entire situation surrounding his father's death. When he was old enough, Shy allowed him to read the transcripts of all of the witness interviews and Roberts's report. She had no idea Prince was also finding any information he could about every name mentioned. That traumatic event had never left Prince's mind or heart. His family only assumed it had because he never discussed that day with anyone, including Jayden.

Those were the last words Dwayne heard before his head was being beat in by the three athletically built teenage boys. They beat Dwayne for the sins he committed against their mother. Dwayne was stomped for disrespecting their father's memory. He was thrown out on the curb because he gambled and lost. The McGee family wasn't sure what Dwayne had planned out but after the hospital released him, they were positive he'd never step foot on their doorstep again.

Roberts was mad as hell. He was grabbing a nap to sleep off the alcohol he'd consumed. His shift started in less than three hours and he'd gulped the last of the Crown Royal Black twenty minutes before the disruption.

"Yeah," Roberts barked into the phone.

"Man, I fucked it up." Dwayne sounded wounded.

"What the fuck you mean?" Roberts demanded.

"Ya boy is home and he recognized me right off the bat. Man, those young thugs put me in the hospital. You're going to have to come up with another plan," Dwayne informed him.

"I knew I shouldn't have fucked with your stupid ass. You're just as weak as your soft-ass brother was."

Click!

"Look at this nigga. Bitch ass let some young boys lay him out. My bad for sending a boy to do a man's job," Roberts said aloud before passing out again.

Chapter 21

I Gotta Get Mine, You Gotta Get Out of My Way!

Prince and Monica found it impossible to keep their hands off one another. Monica had missed her boyfriend so much that at times, her body ached. She closed her eyes and devoured his tongue, afraid to open her eyes and discover it was all a dream. The reality of it was Prince was back in her arms. His touch alone made her feel protected and loved. Prince had a way of making Monica feel beautiful, sexy, and happy to be alive. He was the only person able to love her the way she needed. Whether he was taking care of it or breaking it in half, her heart belonged to Prince.

The hotel room was much nicer than Monica expected. She could tell Prince had put a lot of thought into making their first night together special. When Monica saw Prince she raced to him and jumped into his arms. The fact that his mother was witnessing their reunion didn't matter. They were each other's first loves and Shy understood how they felt.

Prince was in love with Monica. Her letters, cards, pictures, and voice over the phone helped him hold his head up while he served out his time. Their time apart gave Prince a lot of time to think about how much he truly loved Monica. He'd cheated on Monica multiple times and been busted a handful of times but she was always there for him. Prince regretted the disrespect-

ful way he'd treated Monica. She held him down while
he was locked up and for that, Prince owed her better.
Prince promised to make Monica feel the love he held
in his heart for her.

"This is so sweet. You really do love me, don't you?"
Monica spoke with tears in her eyes.

"You know I love you, girl," Prince replied, followed
by another wet kiss. He walked up behind her and
wrapped his arms around her small waist. The smell of
her hair always excited him.

"When did you get the room and how?"

"I ain't gon' lie, Unc helped me out. You know I'm
not with this romance bull but I wanted to make you
happy. You deserve it after holding me down," Prince
admitted.

"Boy, don't you know I'd do anything for you? We
ride or die, always."

"Go check out the bathroom," Prince ordered.

Monica was breathless. The tub was filled with floating candles, and a tray of white chocolate-covered
strawberries was strategically placed beside it. Two
white terrycloth bathrobes were laid out with slippers
to match. A mix of slow tunes played through speakers
in the wall. It was like something out of a movie.

"What do you want to do first?" Monica asked, already knowing the answer.

"Not what you think." Prince smirked. "I'm hungry
as hell. Let's order room service and chill out." Prince
kicked off his shoes and picked up the menu. After a
quick glance, his decision was made.

"Whatever you say, boo. Can I order a steak?"

"Order what you want, it's cool."

After dinner, the young couple settled into their relaxing tub. Prince took his time with Monica. They had
sex together before but that night would be different.

He was going to take Monica places her mind and body would dream about.

"Lie back, just relax," Prince directed.

Monica did as she was told. She let her body go and Prince quickly took it over. He gently and slowly washed her from head to toe. Her body was flawless, perfect in every place. Prince felt good to call her his own. Monica's head was spinning. Prince was making her feel like a woman. His touch sent tingles up her spine. After Prince finished taking care of her, Monica returned the favor. As their kisses intensified it was time to take it to the next level. Prince helped Monica out of the Jacuzzi by lifting her up and carrying her into the bedroom.

"I wanna do some freaky shit to you, girl," Prince whispered.

"I want you to do some freaky shit to me," Monica replied.

"Like what?"

"Make me feel good, the way a man is supposed to make a woman feel." Monica smiled and looked directly into Prince's eyes. "Then make me feel like a slutty bitch."

Prince didn't know where that request came from but he was going to make it happen. After years of sleeping with older women, Prince knew how to handle a woman's body. He was much more skilled than Monica could have imagined. She was about to become proficient in making love. Prince was intent on putting in work.

LOCAL ATHLETE STAR ON ALL-STATE H.S. BASKETBALL TEAM headlined the *Vindicator* newspaper.

The city of Youngstown is all abuzz about seventeen-year-old senior Jayden Prince McGee being named one of the starting five for this year's all-state basketball team . . . .

"This is huge, man," Quincy said, ecstatic.

"I almost fell out when Coach called me into his office to tell me. There were reporters everywhere. It was crazy. I barely had a chance to tell my mom before it ran on the news last night." Jayden was overwhelmed.

"I'm proud of my little bro. We gotta celebrate and I'm taking you shopping. My brother's gonna be styling during his news interviews. Jayden!" Prince shouted for his brother in excitement. "I just realized that you're going to be on *Sports Center*. Bro, I swear you're headed for the NBA."

"I don't know about all of that. I'm just trying to get a free ride to college. Be it by basketball or not, my future is not written here. One of us is going to give Ma a better life." Jayden smiled at the thought.

"Right, right," Prince agreed as the brothers bumped fists.

"I'm hyped for you, Jay. Everybody is talking about this accomplishment. Prince is right, we have to head over to PA and grab you some gear," Quincy stated.

"That's cool, let's head out now," Prince suggested, still hyped.

"What about Princess? Ma won't be home for a minute," Jayden informed.

"Bring her with us. I'll buy her a doll, or outfit or something. Or see if Monica or Brianna can keep an eye on her 'til Mommy gets here," Prince replied.

"Not to change the subject but are we the only seventeen-year-olds still referring to their mothers as Mommy?" Quincy laughed.

"Not in private," the twins answered in unison and joined Quincy in laughing.

"Let me go grab something and I'll be ready," Prince said.

Prince turned and headed toward the basement door. Jayden had completely forgotten about finding his brother's stash of drugs and money. He hadn't told Prince about their uncle getting it out of the house.

"Yo, bro, hold up," Jayden called after Prince.

"Wat up?"

"While you were gone, me and Q had to move Princess's old furniture in the basement. We found your stuff and called Unc. He's holding that for you."

"What?"

"I didn't know where you kept that stuff. We stumbled up on it and didn't know another safe place to put it. I didn't want Mommy to find it and couldn't chance Princess uncovering it," Jayden explained.

"Yeah, we called Unc and ask him what we should do with it," Quincy added.

"Man, I don't ever want y'all caught up or connected to any of my shit. I'm sorry you had to do it but good looking out for me."

Prince felt bad about Jayden and Quincy finding his inventory, but was happy his mother hadn't stumbled upon it.

"It's nothing. Just call Unc and hook up with him. You know he has your back. I just assumed you were working with him anyway," Jayden stated.

"I can't make a move until Unc gets with me so let's go to PA tomorrow and hit the outlet malls. We can head out in the morning."

"We can go after practice. Coach makes us practice early morning every Saturday," Quincy told Prince.

"I thought the season was over," Prince responded.

"It's not practice, its conditioning. Coach wants all of his players to stay in shape year round. I don't mind because we can use the school's equipment. No monthly membership fees," Quincy joked.

Prince sent C-Lok a text while he kept up simple chatter with Jayden and Quincy. The three picked up their joysticks and the twins began a game of *2K11* on Xbox. Quincy would play the winner. Two hours later, the tournament was rolling along and Princess had gotten restless. She was bored and demanding attention. The boys took turns playing with Princess until their turn on the game came back around. Prince and Jayden were heavy into their game when C-Lok returned his nephew's text message. He replied simply: Main spot in 2. Prince was to meet C-Lok at his house in two hours.

Shy walked through the door tired and happy to be home. Prince had been home for a week but due to her work schedule, mother and son hadn't spent much time together. Though Prince was home, Shy still worried about him. She knew it would only be a matter of time before he was back with his old friends and running the streets. Over the years, Shy spent many sleepless nights trying to figure out where she went wrong. She repeatedly asked herself what she could have done different, what it was she had done to push Prince to answer the call of the streets. Shy blamed herself for his unhappiness, poor decision making, and dangerous lifestyle.

Every time the phone rang Shy held her breath. She couldn't sleep until both of her boys were home each night. Like most mothers, Shy worried about her teenagers even when she knew where they were. For some reason, Prince thought very little of himself. He failed to dream and set goals for the future. Prince and Jayden were equally intelligent. Jayden was focused on his future whereas Prince focused on the right now.

Shy joined the kids in the family room and plopped down on the couch between Princess and Quincy. She was thanking God it was Friday because she had the weekend off. Shy was hoping to spend it with her kids. Some mommy love would do her a world of good.

"You looked great in that picture the newspaper printed, Jay. All of my coworkers were acting so excited and happy for you. Half of them have never said a word to me before. Now they fronting like we're the best of friends," Shy complained.

"Thanks, Ma. Did you have a long day?" Jayden responded to his mother's words.

"Yes, working with the public is difficult. I had to draw blood from more than just a few today. I'm glad all of you are here because I need to talk about something," Shy announced.

The twins, Quincy, and Princess all looked a little worried. It was rare for Shy to need to speak with them at the same time.

"What's wrong, Aunt Shy?"

"Everything cool, Mommy?" Prince asked, concerned.

"Yes, everybody calm down. I've been thinking about going back to school. I found out today that I was accepted into the hospital's nursing school," Shy began.

"Go for it, Mommy, if that's what you want to do," Prince encouraged.

"There's also another two-year program that interests me. It will allow me to become an X-ray and sonogram technician. So what do y'all think I should do?" Shy asked nervously. She'd been thinking about her career in the medical field and decided she could be doing much more than just drawing blood. It was hard deciding what field to go into so she decided to ask her family for their opinions.

"Aunt Shy, if you become a registered nurse, you can work in any state across the country. Plus, the pay is great." Quincy offered his vote.

"I'm leaning toward you being a nurse too. They make good money and we wouldn't have to worry about you and Princess so much," Jayden voiced.

"I say do whatever makes you happy, Mommy. We want you to live the way Dad wanted," Prince added.

Shy smiled at her boys. She loved the relationship they shared. They'd always been comfortable talking to her, no matter what. No subject matter was off-limits.

"I'm going to take a little more time and think it over. Money is always a deciding factor but there are other things to take into consideration. This is going to be my career and I have to love what I do in order for me to be good at it. My heart is in the healthcare field, I'm just not sure where my passion lies," Shy explained.

"Man, all I care about is the money part," Prince blurted out.

"Not everything's always about money, Prince. There are other things in life than just money," Jayden countered, perturbed at his brother's limited thinking.

"Money makes the world go round. Money made my daddy's world go round and it's gonna keep my world spinning," Prince announced.

"You sound stupid," Jayden said, irritated.

"Here we go, Mr. College-bound with all the answers to shit he don't know nothing about."

"Hey!" Shy snapped at Prince for his language. "I can see this is about to get out of hand so this little powwow is over."

"Naw, I'm sick of him always judging me." Prince was heated. Jayden had an air of arrogance and Prince had grown tired of it. His brother didn't live in his world and had no idea about hustling for a dollar or surviving outside of their mother's presence. Prince was fed up with Jayden putting him down.

"I'm not judging you, Prince. You have the same potential as Q and me but you refuse to see that. The only one between you and a way out is you. It always has been."

"Jay, you don't know shit 'bout them streets. You know even less about what I carry on my shoulders so shut the hell up," Prince barked and rose to his feet.

"Prince, calm down, man. It ain't even that serious." Quincy attempted to defuse the situation.

"It is that serious. All my life people been pointing fingers and judging me. Everybody always got shit to say about me. Fuck that! Why my brother gotta be one of 'em? He should be with me, not against me." Prince dropped down on the couch and started to cry. He couldn't take it anymore. There was no more room for pain on his back or in his heart. For the past seven years he'd had to live with people looking down on him. No matter what he did or said, Prince always felt like he didn't measure up. He was the bad twin, the one whose fate was set when his father died in his arms. Prince was fragile and weak from carrying that pain around.

Shy was heartbroken. All the hurt inside Prince was pouring out. She knew there was much more to it than the argument with his brother. They had gone at each other much worse but Prince had never reacted so emotionally.

Jayden's heart sank. He never wanted his brother to believe he didn't love him. Prince was half of Jayden; good, bad, or indifferent, they were brothers unconditionally. Jayden understood Prince but sometimes lost sight of being a good sibling. He'd die for his brother without hesitation. Prince had to see that.

"Man, I'm sorry. You're my heart, bro. I love you." Jayden cried with Prince. Seeing the pain his brother was in was overwhelming.

"Prince, I always got your back. You're my big bro, man. Nothing can change that," Jayden explained with a despondent heart.

Prince felt like he'd been hit in the chest with a mallet. The emotional pain had taken over his soul. He felt alone and lost. His head fell down to his chest. Unable to gain control of his emotions, Prince continued to cry. Soon, everyone in the room was crying with him.

Shy knew this day would come. A person can hold on to emotional pain, disappointment, and anger for only so long. Prince had been in pain for seven long years. She knew he had tried to be strong for her. Shy always suspected that Melvin told Prince to take care of her before he died. That request was beyond a child's ability. The request from his father mixed with the traumatic events of the day were haunting Prince. It was time to release those demons.

"I just want to make Daddy proud. It's my fault he's dead." Prince rocked back and forth, trying to ease the pain.

"Don't say that," said Jayden.

"No, it isn't," Quincy added.

Shy wrapped her arms around her son. She felt his pain. It was clear that Prince was traumatized by that horrific day. Shy knew Prince never stopped mourning his father but she wasn't aware he felt responsible for Melvin's death.

"Jayden and Quincy, let me talk to Prince alone. He'll be okay," Shy promised.

They reluctantly did as they were told and left the room. Jayden didn't want to go far so he and Quincy sat in the dining room. He had to be sure his brother was fine.

"Prince, you listen to me," Shy demanded. She pulled Prince up in order to see his face. "You are not responsible for what happened to your father. It's a parent's job to protect their child, by any means necessary. If a situation ever came up where your life was in danger, I'd die for you without hesitation."

"But if I'd just done what that cop said, Daddy would still be here and everything would be different. You shouldn't have to work so hard or be worrying about going to nobody school."

"Prince, I don't work because we need the money. I work because I want to," Shy admitted.

"What you mean it's not for the money?" Prince was confused.

"We've never wanted for anything. All of our needs have always been met. You kids have everything you ever asked for and more. Trust me, it's not because of that change I make at the hospital." Shy chuckled.

"Where do you be getting your money from, Ma? Uncle C?"

"No, not Uncle C. My brother has offered to pay for college for you boys and Princess but that's something he wants to do. We are financially stable. Your father made sure of that."

"How then?" Prince couldn't figure out how they could still be living off some insurance money after seven years. It just didn't make sense. "I know you ain't got some dude taking care of us," Prince said angrily.

"We'll get to that in a minute. First, we need to talk about all this guilt and pain inside of you. Prince, stress will havoc your body. If you don't let this go, I can see you having a nervous breakdown."

"I don't know how, Mommy. Don't anything ever go right for me. I just spent time locked up for somebody else's crimes. Then, while I'm doing the time, I see that Raequan is on some foul shit. He's supposed to be my boy. Jayden don't respect me because I'm not doing what he thinks I should. I hear people talking about 'he crazy' or 'he's a time bomb waiting to explode' because my father died in my arms. Why is that anybody's business? You're the only person in my life who never betrayed me. Even Aunt Tara thinks I'm headed for prison," Prince said.

"No one on this earth has a right to judge you. They don't have a heaven or a hell to put you in so fuck all the hypocrites. People always point attention away from themselves so their faults and mistakes won't shine through. The only opinion about you that matters is your own. Prince, let go of this guilt. That cop had it in his mind to kill your daddy before they kicked our door in. Your father died because he loved you. That's the only reason he jumped to protect you, believe that. I'm sorry you've been in so much anguish but it's time to move on, baby. Just because you live your life doesn't mean you've forgotten about your dad. He's always with us in our hearts, he watches over us every day. Live to honor him instead of living to avenge his death. Your father's dream was for his family to be happy and to know he loved us."

Shy hugged Prince and kissed the side of his face. Prince returned the gesture. His mother's words made sense. He finally had permission to release the pain and move on. Prince physically felt the weight lift from his shoulders. He could breathe.

"Thank you, Mommy. I feel a lot better. I love you." Prince smiled. "Now, back to this money thing."

Shy laughed at her son. She knew he wasn't going to forget about that. Jayden and Quincy returned to the family room as Shy instructed. They could tell Prince was feeling better by the look of relief on his face. "I'm sorry, bro," Jayden said sincerely.

"We good, man. I'm sorry too." Prince smiled and embraced his brother.

"You good, man?" Quincy asked Prince.

"Fo' sho," replied Prince as he extended his hand to Quincy. They bumped shoulders, hugged, and let go of the situation.

"Jay, Mommy said she works because she wants to, not because we need the money. I asked her how that's even possible but she hasn't said yet." Prince laid out his conversation with their mother.

"Here's the thing. Your daddy had life insurance that paid me enough to pay off this house, bury him the way he deserved, and to keep us secure for a couple of years," Shy explained.

"How are you paying bills and buying food? I can go get a job to help out," Jayden offered.

"No, your job is to finish high school and go to college. You won't have to work while you're away at school, either. That goes for you too, Quincy. Prince, if you one day choose to finish your education, the same goes for you. We set up college funds a week after I had you, plus your uncle is going to take care of housing and buy the three of y'all cars."

"Okay, Ma, how are we surviving now?" asked Prince.

"Your daddy had his own insurance policy. He left behind a very large sum of money for us. We've been living off it since the insurance money ran out. I only take what we need each month to pay bills and eat. When you kids need clothes, shoes, or pocket money, I go into it. Unlike a lot of women, I didn't blow that money by buying cars, rings, expensive clothes, and flossing around town. I had three kids to take care of and I'm always mindful of that."

"Dang, Aunt Shy. It's been seven years and you still using money Uncle Mel left? How much did he leave?" Quincy inquired.

"That's my business." Shy laughed. "Just know that financially, we never have to worry about going without."

Shy left the room before the boys could ask another question. She'd kept that information to herself for a reason. She did not want Prince and Jayden thinking they were rich and becoming spoiled brats. Shy did splurge on her kids on holidays and birthdays but that was it. That money had to last. To avoid drawing attention from the IRS, Shy left the money exactly where Melvin had it stored. When Shy discovered the amount of money Melvin had put away, she was amazed. She knew he was high on the food chain but had no idea he was standing at the top.

Melvin also left some product behind. C-Lok was continually flipping the drugs and adding all the profits to his sister's savings. It's what Melvin intended when he stocked his wife's inheritance. Shy was, indeed, a hustler in her own right.

Chapter 22

I've Always Looked Up to You

Prince looked around C-Lok's house, admiring the way he lived. The four-bedroom house was big but not too flashy. Genuine African American artwork hung on the walls, plush cream-colored wall-to-wall carpet lay throughout the living, den, and family rooms. Deep cedar wood stretched the long entry way, half bath, and dining room floors. The gourmet kitchen was equipped with all stainless steel appliances, topped off with a vaulted ceiling and skylight. C-Lok limited the number of people he allowed inside of his home. His number one rule was never let them know where you rest your head.

C-Lok and Prince were in the den playing a game of pool. Prince had to pick up the stash of drugs and money his uncle was holding for him. Unbeknownst to him, C-Lok had a proposition that would change his life forever.

"You held up well while knocking out that stretch you took on for ya boy," C-Lok said proudly.

"It's all part of the game." Prince shrugged.

"See, that's what I like: a young hustler who under-stands the rules of the game." C-Lok nodded.

"This is all I know, Unc. I'm a born hustler just like my pops. It's in my blood," Prince voiced.

"I agree, nephew. I didn't know you were handling the amount of weight that you are. Is Cherise holding

you up?" C-Lok needed confirmation that Prince was
working for Cherise, which ultimately meant he was
putting money in B-Boy's camp.

"Yeah, Unc. She got her prices at a doable rate, feel
me?"

"Look, ya old man and B-Boy weren't all that tight
when he died. I don't trust him or his bitch," C-Lok
explained.

"It's crazy you said that, Unc. Since we did that stretch
of time together, I don't know if Rae is being straight up
with me. I've been hearing some foul shit, feel me?"

It felt good for Prince to finally share his suspicions
with someone about Raequan betraying him. He wanted
more proof than just the word of random street dudes
and his gut before he dealt with Raequan. After a lifetime of friendship, Prince felt he owed Raequan that
much.

"That's fucked up, nephew, but it brings us to why I
brought you here." C-Lok paused for a sip of beer before continuing. "It's time to jump ship. You're ready to
run with the big dogs and join the FAM."

"Is this for real, Unc?" Prince asked, completely taken
off guard.

"That means family prices, discounts, and protection. You'll be working for yourself. I want you to build
your own team." C-Lok could tell by the look in Prince's
eyes that he was all in. He looked like a kid on Christmas who'd just received exactly what he wanted from
Santa Claus. "Melvin the father didn't want this life for
his boys. I ain't too happy about it either but I'm always
going to look out. He wanted you to go the college route
alongside your brother and Q. Since it's obvious that's
not where your head is at, I know Melvin the hustler,
the Legend, would keep you close to him. He'd teach

you how to do this shit right." C-Lok rationalized his decision to bring Prince over to his side.

"Are you sure 'bout that, Unc? I want him to be proud of me. I feel like maybe I'm letting him down," Prince confessed.

"He set certain things in motion before he was killed. You may not know this but he's still taking care of his family, even in death," C-Lok began.

"My mom just told us about the money," Prince told C-Lok, who was surprised by the news.

Since Prince only mentioned the money, C-Lok figured that was all Shy told them about. He was going to follow her lead and keep his mouth shut. Prince and Jayden never needed to discover all of their mother's secrets. What boy wants to find out his mother has a past?

Every once in a while, Melvin would allow Shy to keep him company while he weighed and packaged drugs to prepare them for the streets. Shy would ask questions like, "How do you know how much to charge? What are you weighing and how do you know how much money you should be making off this stuff?" Melvin would smile at how inquisitive Shy was despite the fact that she claimed not to want to know the details of his hustle. He always took the time to school her and break down the information she was seeking. Shy wondered how Melvin could be so gifted in mathematics and chemistry but hated school to the point of barely graduating.

Once Melvin began doing business with C-Lok, the partners quickly became a force to be reckoned with. It wasn't long before they had every city within reach on lockdown. Pillow talk between Melvin and Shy went unimaginable places. Throughout their years together, Shy grew well versed in how her husband did things.

Shy knew the drug money was addictive, dangerous, and plentiful.

"I'm gonna need you to give Cherise her shit back and settle your account with her. Just tell that bitch you're out. Our business ain't hers, feel me? It's no secret but she doesn't need to know what's up. "

"Done," Prince agreed.

"Let's get shit poppin', nephew. We've got an empire to build."

Chapter 23

Nigga, Please

Another three months passed and Prince was doing big things. Material possessions became his second priority; the first was making money. He was spending $500 a day to outfit himself from head to toe in name-brand gear. The charcoal-gray Chevy Impala he pushed sat on twenty-four-inch chrome rims. Custom eight-inch screen monitors had been installed in the back of each headrest, both visors, and one in the dash. Prince was turning heads everywhere he went. The newness of his car was wearing off. He decided it would be best for him to purchase a good running used car for work. The last thing he wanted was for a hater to pump holes into his Impala. That was always a possibility in his world.

Prince bobbed his head to the sounds of his friend Je'Vohn. He was an up-and-coming rapper out of Columbus, Ohio who went by the stage name Jesse Mr. Hello. Je'Vohn had sent Prince a copy of his latest mix tape. He and Je'Vohn lived in different cities but had the same life experiences. Life on the streets was hard and like them, only the strong survived. With his younger brother, Lil Reese, producing his sounds, Prince was positive that his friend would become an industry success story.

A few of the boys standing in front of a corner store caught Prince's eye as he rode down the street. Even from a distance, Prince recognized Raequan. Prince had heard Raequan was back on the streets but had yet to see him. The two had not spoken since Prince was released from juvie. Prince pulled over and immediately got love from his boys NuNu and Mike Frank. A few of the other street hustlers also gave him respect. Raequan fell back, taking in the love Prince received from the streets. His hesitation didn't go unnoticed by Prince.

"Hey, what up, bro?" Prince got out the car. "When'd you touch down?"

Raequan paused before he responded to Prince. Jealousy had taken over his heart after receiving word that Prince had jumped ship on his mom. The desertion only confirmed for Raequan that Prince was a traitor. As far as Raequan was concerned, Prince was just another nigga on the streets. They were nothing more than competitors.

"Ah, man, I've been pounding the pavement for a minute. You know how it is," Raequan said dryly.

"That's cool, man. Happy to see you breathing fresh air again. Rae, why don't you let me holler at you real quick? Come sit in the ride with me," Prince requested.

Raequan nodded his head and walked around to the passenger side door. He sat with his right leg outside of the car door. Raequan had no intention of talking to Prince for too long. After hearing what Prince had to say, he was going back to the street corner to hustle.

"I know you might be a little salty about me doing business elsewhere but it was an offer I couldn't pass up. Feel me?" Prince spoke candidly.

"Shit, it ain't no thang, nigga. We all gotta get it the best way we can, I feel you," Raequan lied. He was annoyed with Prince turning his back on Cherise. Prince knew what it was and he still left his mother for dead. Raequan couldn't let his betrayal go unpunished.

"We've been friends for life, man. I had to make sure we were straight," Prince explained, suspicious of Raequan's reaction.

"We good," Raequan lied. "This ride is sweet as hell. How long you been pushin' this?"

Raequan reached behind his back and pulled out his gun. He set it down between his legs and continued admiring the interior of the Impala. Prince leaned on his door and gave Raequan a look that said, "don't play."

"What up, Rae, we got problems like that?" Prince stared at the gun.

"Nigga, chill, it was pushing into my back. I just copped it this morning from some geek. He let it go for a fifty dollar rock." Raequan laughed at the addict's bad business deal. The .38 was new, probably stolen, but Raequan didn't care. He was never one to pass on a good deal. He picked up the gun and showed it to Prince.

"Check it out; this look fresh, ain't no bodies on this one," Raequan bragged.

Prince saw Raequan position his index finger on the trigger. He saw it happening before he could react.

Boom!

Prince couldn't believe what had just happened. So much so that Prince took pause before he reacted. Raequan had sat in the passenger seat and shot out the car's engine. That was no accident and Prince knew it. Raequan had gone too far this time and would have to answer for his actions.

"Man, what da fuck!" Prince was livid.

"Damn, my bad, nigga. It just went off, my bad." Raequan smirked. He jumped out of the car.

"Just went off my ass, nigga. What da fuck? You meant to shoot my shit. How da fuck it just go off with ya finger on the trigger?"

"You know I wouldn't do no shit like that to my man. It was an accident." Raequan walked around the front of the car to face Prince. Treachery was in control and Raequan knew Prince wasn't going to let it ride.

Prince popped the hood as smoke seeped into the air and fluids pooled underneath the car. The bullet had gone through the engine and continued its path past the grill. Just that quick, Prince' pride and joy was disabled. It would cost thousands to get repaired. Prince was infuriated and quickly becoming homicidal. Raequan had shown himself to be a bitch. Despite what everyone else said about him, Prince always had Raequan's back. It became obvious that the rumors of Raequan setting him up to be jumped and robbed were true. Prince was certain that his arm getting broken was no accident.

"Man, you's a simple-ass bitch. You must be out ya monkey-ass mind," Prince barked before punching Raequan in the jaw. Raequan stumbled and Prince caught him with haymakers before he could get his balance. Prince threw all his strength behind each blow. Raequan eventually grabbed Prince around the waist, attempting to slam him to the ground. Prince was stronger and more skilled than his victim and refused to go down.

NuNu, Mike Frank, and the other hustlers watched as Raequan got what he had coming. They were all fed up with Raequan's slimy business practices. He had played them all at one time or another. When it became apparent that Prince was going to kill Raequan, they broke up the fight.

"Get dat away from me. I'm gon' kill that bitch," Prince insisted.

Raequan was led off leaving a trail of blood behind him. He was embarrassed by taking a loss out on the streets for all to see but that didn't matter as much as getting his wounds mended. Prince would be dealt with later. All Raequan wanted was his momma.

Prince calmed down after a few minutes. He called a tow truck to take his car to the dealership for repairs. After his car was secured on the flatbed, Prince called C-Lok to let him know what went down. C-Lok ensured his nephew that he would have Raequan dealt with. He couldn't let Prince catch a charge behind something so petty. Quincy arrived on the scene fifteen minutes after getting Prince's call. He and Jayden rushed to Prince. They were relieved to find him in one piece.

"Get me to the crib, bro. I got this nigga's blood all over me." Prince chuckled.

"What happened?" Jayden inquired.

"Raequan's a bitch and I beat his ass, that's what happened. He shot my fuckin' engine out then gon' claim it was an accident. That pussy-ass nigga fucked up. Every time I see him, I'm fuckin' him up on sight!" Prince continued to go off.

"Yeah, Aunt Shy is going to go off. I'm glad I'll be there to see it," Quincy said while shaking his head.

"Is Mommy home?" Prince asked.

"Yeah, bro," replied Jayden.

"Good, wait 'til I tell her about this shit."

Chapter 24

Girlfriends

Cherise was exhausted. She'd just returned from another visit with B-Boy. Despite the fact that Cherise held everything down for their family, B-Boy was always very critical of her parenting skills and business sense. B-Boy was never satisfied. She took Raequan to the wrong barbershop, purchased Reeboks instead of Nikes, and dressed him in Southpole not True Religion. Cherise picked up shipments too slow, counted money too fast, and her weight calculations were always off even though she used a scale. Let B-Boy tell it, everything she touched crumbled beneath her feet.

Thanks to her, B-Boy had so much money on his books, Cherise wouldn't be surprised if the warden was embezzling from him. If that were the case, Cherise knew B-Boy would find a way to blame her for it. Cherise had taken care of him since the day they met. B-Boy showed his love for her by being mentally and emotionally abusive but still she stayed. It had gone on for so long, Cherise felt worthless.

She filled her soaking tub with hot water and poured in her favorite lavender-scented bath beads. The warm water slowly melted the tension from her tired muscles. Twenty-five minutes later, Cherise spread out on her bed with only cocoa butter lotion covering her body. The hot bath wasn't relaxing enough. Cherise needed some type of sexual release to completely erase the negative thoughts from her mind. She put new batteries in her favorite B.O.B. and touched herself. It took five minutes before the vibrating against her clit moistened her love box. Just as she was about to reach her first climax, someone began beating on the front door.

Cherise cursed under her breath and grabbed her bathrobe. She peeked out of her bedroom window to see who was on her doorstep trying to knock the door of its hinges. It was Shy. Cherise rushed down the stairs thinking there was an emergency. She feared it was about Raequan. He hadn't checked in with her all day.

"What's wrong? What happened?" Cherise asked with a racing heart as she swung open the door.

Cherise was taken aback when Shy pushed her way into the house. Shy was fuming. She'd tried to lower her blood pressure the entire ride over to confront Cherise but her attempts were futile.

"Shy, what's going on?"

"I am so sick of you and your jealous ass. Now your immature, entitled son is pulling the same bullshit," Shy said angrily.

"What are you talking about?" Cherise asked defensively.

"Oh, Raequan hasn't come running home yet? He shot a gun off inside of Prince's car today. What the fuck was he thinking?"

"First off, you need to calm down. I don't know what Prince told you but that don't even sound right. Raequan wouldn't do anything like that," Cherise responded. She immediately jumped into protective mode. Raequan was her son, and right or wrong, she would defend him no matter what.

"Why wouldn't he? Because you taught him better?" Shy sarcastically asked with hands on her hips.

Cherise was beyond insulted. Shy had picked the wrong day to attack her parenting skills. She'd already taken enough disrespect from her baby daddy earlier in the day; she refused to take it from her best friend.

"What makes you think the twins are any better than Raequan? You ain't special, Shy. Women are raising boys into men every day," Cherise snapped.

"Too bad you ain't one of 'em. You've been so busy holding on to the inside of B-Boy's ass that you barely raised Raequan. The streets raised that boy. The only message he got from his parents was that money trumps everything. You should be the spokeswoman for all of the weak-ass women of the world."

Shy stared in Cherise's eyes, waiting for her to say one foul word about Melvin. Melvin had been more of a father in death to his children than B-Boy was in life. He was behind bars but in Shy's opinion, B-Boy could've and should've made more of a difference in his son's life.

"Who are you to talk? You've been holding on to a ghost for seven years. You're holding on to Melvin's memory so tight it's sad. That nigga still got you stuck on stupid."

Smack!

Cherise never saw it coming. She covered the side of her face and looked at Shy as if she'd grown a second head.

Smack!

Shy gave it to Cherise again on the other side of her face before she recovered from the first slap. If Cherise crossed the line again, Shy was prepared to beat the breaks off her ass.

"Bitch, you just made that shit up. For over thirty years I've been a good friend to you. I've always been there for you and ain't ever asked your ass for shit.

You've gotten my ass in street fights, bar fights, got my car windows busted out all because of a sick obsession with a nigga that ain't shit!" She was so angry tears fell from her eyes. "You want to talk about Melvin? How many times did he save your ass when B-Boy was beating the shit out of you? Should I add up the money he dealt out to keep a roof over your head? If B-Boy was about his business, you wouldn't have had to ask my man for help."

Cherise was stunned by Shy's words. The slaps, the insults, the verbal attack, it all came out of nowhere. She was caught completely off guard. Though Shy's words hurt, Cherise knew that everything being thrown at her was the truth. Shy had always been her rock. Until she gave birth to Raequan, their relationship was the only positive constant in her life. Truth be told, Cherise had betrayed Shy on more than one occasion. If the ultimate disloyalty Cherise committed ever came to light, she was sure Shy would kill her. Shy stood before Cherise with disgust in her eyes.

"You know I've been a friend to you. I've always been there for you," Cherise lied. She had been selfish when it came to her best friend. Their relationship wasn't based on mutual give and take. It was more like Shy gave and Cherise took, always. "Don't act like Melvin ain't never hurt you. You know that nigga cheated on you so don't act all high and mighty. Your life ain't perfect."

"I've heard rumors that you fucked Melvin, more than once, but I never paid them any attention because I trusted you. Melvin wasn't perfect, he made his mistakes, and I forgave him for that shit with Theresa. If I remember correctly, we broke up behind that bullshit for over a year. During that time you were chilling with that bitch. You remained friends with her knowing she'd stabbed me in the back. I should've beat ya ass for that but I just let it ride." Shy's heart ached at the memory of that difficult time. Having to deal with the fact that her best friend could remain close to someone who'd hurt her while trying to get over Melvin was overwhelming. "Cherise, you've never been a true friend to me, ever. You don't know how to be and neither does your son. Prince would never do something so foul to him. He thinks of Raequan as a brother, you know that."

Shy was angry with herself. She'd allowed Cherise to pull her down to her level. The ghetto girl had awakened in her. Shy hated giving someone the power to dictate her emotions and behavior. This side of her rarely came out but she was as dangerous as a mother bear protecting her cubs. She would rip her prey apart to protect her children.

"Why we gotta go through all of this just because of an accident? You know Raequan would never hurt Prince on purpose; if anything, you need to be worried about what Roberts gonna do," Cherise snidely said.

"What does he have to do with anything?" Shy asked, totally confused. There was no conceivable reason for Roberts to pop back up in her life. Instinct told Shy that something was not right. Shy repeated her question when Cherise was slow to respond. "What does Roberts have to do with my son?"

"He recruited Raequan to fuck with Prince while they were in juvenile hall. If anybody's trying to do Prince harm, it's him. Why don't you go find his ass and harass him?" Cherise said in a loathing tone.

Cherise had not meant to blurt out Roberts's name but it was too late to turn back now. It was out there and Shy would just have to deal. Raequan wasn't a saint but he also couldn't always play the role of Satan.

Cherise would never be a contender for mother of the year but she was going to protect her son as best she could.

"I want to know everything about Raequan and Roberts," fumed Shy. "Now!"

Shy took slow, calculated steps toward Cherise, who was now cowered in the corner of her foyer. Cherise knew she was no match for Shy in the ring. The last thing Cherise wanted was to be beat on again. B-Boy had done that enough.

"All I know is that he's the supervisor of the night shift at juvie hall. He was careful not to let Prince see him."

"Keep going," ordered Shy.

"He recruited Raequan to fuck with Prince and make his time miserable. He has nothing but hate for everything McGee," Cherise explained.

"Did Raequan take the bait?"

"Yes, Roberts paid him with privileges."

"What did Raequan have to do with my son's stuff getting stolen and those boys jumping him?"

"He set it up," admitted Cherise.

"And his broke arm?"

"It wasn't an accident," Cherise cried, fearful of Shy's response to the news. "I told Raequan to get out of the deal with Roberts but he wouldn't listen. He did what he had to do to make his time easy."

"Do not try to justify that bitch-ass move with me. What is wrong with you? It's all right to stand by your child but admit when he fucks up. Raequan is turning out to be just like his daddy and you condoning that shit ain't right," Shy uttered in disbelief.

"How long have you known about Raequan dealing with Roberts?" Shy asked suspiciously.

Cherise refused to answer that question. She knew that telling Shy a lie would be as bad as the truth. The hurt in Shy's heart was evident in her eyes. Cherise was well aware there was no coming back from what transpired. The line between love and hate was miniscule and Cherise had leapt to the other side. She'd lost a lifelong friend. Cherise prayed that Shy would forgive her one day.

"I'm sorry, Shy. I never wanted this to happen. Raequan is all I have and I'm all he has, you know that. I couldn't stop it. Roberts lured him in before I knew anything about him even working there."

"If that were true, Cherise, you would've told me. That man killed my husband and you didn't think enough of me or my kids to tell me his killer was overseeing my son's wellbeing. Prince took a charge for Raequan. He refused to give the prosecutor any names or details about Raequan. Prince sacrificed his freedom and all along Raequan had plans to leave him for dead?"

Shy was outdone. How could someone who claimed to love her commit such treachery? What had Prince ever done to deserve Raequan's disloyalty? The answer was simple: there was no love in the game. Melvin had drilled the number one rule in her head but it never occurred to Shy that the rule applied to her friend of over thirty years. Shy had to get out of that house before she caught a murder case. Cherise underestimated Shy. That was a huge mistake.

"You know you fucked up, right?"

"I'm sorry," Cherise said sincerely.

"Not as sorry as you're going to be," warned Shy as she walked out the front door of her best friend's house for the last time.

Chapter 25

One Plus One Equals Two

In spite of the three boys being together, the McGee household was quiet. As expected, Shy was livid after hearing what had gone down between Prince and Raequan. Prince had barely finished telling her the story when she stormed out of the house. There was no question where Shy was headed. Over two hours had passed and Shy still wasn't home. Prince, Jayden, and Quincy knew without a doubt she could take care of herself but they were still worried.

"Bro, you don't think she got arrested do you?" Quincy hesitantly asked.

"No, you think so?" Jayden replied after a brief pause.

"She would've called us by now. Maybe they were able to talk without Mommy havin' to give it to her ass," Prince speculated.

The boys burst into laughter at the thought of Shy being rational. She was defending her kids; logic and anger are like water and oil. They just don't mix.

Silence filled the room once again. The boys sat staring at each other as if the others had the answers they searched for. There was a knock at the door.

Jayden went to open the door. He found an average-built, light-complexioned man with long, neat dreads standing on the porch.

"Hi, may I help you?" Jayden asked the stranger cautiously.

"Hey, man, how've you been?" The stranger extended his hand for a proper greeting.

"I'm sorry, do I know you?"

The man looked confused and a little offended.

"Hey, Prince, it's me, Mr. Karl. Remember, your teacher from juvie?"

"Oh, I'm not Prince, sir. Hold on a minute," Jayden instructed.

Jayden disappeared behind the door. Mr. Karl stood on the porch wondering why Prince wouldn't remember him. Prince hadn't been too interested in his education but Mr. Karl thought they had mutual respect for each other. He'd been thinking about Prince and wanted to check on him. Karl hoped Prince would be receptive to his friendship. It seemed he was wrong.

Prince came to the door and smiled at Karl. He extended his hand and gave a shoulder bump.

"Hey, Mr. Karl, how you doing, man? It's good to see you."

"What's going on? Am I being punk'd? Just a second ago you didn't know me."

"That was my brother you saw." Prince laughed. "You know I'm a twin, right?"

Now it all made sense. Karl had no idea that Prince had an identical twin brother. It was a little eerie how much they looked alike. They were identical without question.

"No, I didn't know that. You guys are mirror images of each other. That's crazy. I thought you were trying to play me," Karl joked.

"Never that. Come on in, Mr. Karl," invited Prince. He stepped aside for his visitor.

Prince let Karl into the family room where Jayden and Quincy were playing Xbox. After introducing everyone, Prince offered Karl a seat and something to drink. It was kind of strange to have a teacher relaxing in his house. Prince handed a bottle of water off to Karl and sat across from him, right next to Jayden.

"What brings you by?" Prince asked.

"I've been trying to call but could never get an answer so I thought I'd come check on you. My bad for just popping by like this." Karl made an apology.

"You must be calling the house number. My mom keeps the phone off the hook all the time. I don't know why she even has a house phone."

"The last time we talked, you said you'd think about finishing school. What's up, man?"

"I ain't trippin' 'bout that. I'm out here making moves. School has to wait," Prince answered honestly.

Jayden glanced at Prince and rolled his eyes. That was the lamest excuse Prince had ever come up with. Karl saw the disapproving look Jayden had to Prince's explanation and assumed that he wanted his brother in school as well. Karl looked around the room, impressed with its organization and décor.

"So what's your plan for life?" Karl inquired.

"To make as much money as possible and become hood rich. I'm my daddy's son." Prince smiled.

"Oh, you never mentioned your father. Is he around? I'd like to meet both of your parents," Karl said.

Prince, Jayden, and Quincy suddenly looked ill. Their eyes became glassy and the carefree smiles they held were now sad, subdued expressions. Karl didn't know why the mood in the room changed but he knew he'd said something wrong.

"Our father was killed seven years ago," Jayden announced.

"I didn't know. I am so sorry. That's my bad for sure," Karl said, surprised.

"It's cool. I thought you knew about it," Prince stated.

"No, why would you think that? The only information I had was school records. I don't need all the in-depth reports on my students."

"It was big news around here for months after it happened," Quincy added. "My uncle was killed by a police detective. Prince witnessed it." Quincy hated the story of how his Uncle Mel died. They were close and Melvin always took Quincy along when he and the boys went fishing and played ball and stuff. Quincy thought of Melvin as his second father. His own was always working. When he wasn't working, he claimed to be too tired to do anything. As a child, Quincy couldn't understand. It hurt him not to have a tight relationship with his dad but he had Melvin. After Melvin was gone, so was Quincy's father figure.

Karl remembered the story. He had no idea Prince was the young boy whose father had died in his arms. That explained why Prince didn't think very much of himself. Karl took notice of Prince's lack of desire to learn. Prince had to be holding on to guilt and pain. From past experiences with kids, Karl knew that in order for Prince to really live his life, he'd have to let go of the past. That information would help Prince change his way of thinking. He only hoped Prince would be receptive to his helping hand.

"Please forgive me, I had no idea. I didn't connect that tragic story to you, Prince. If any bad memories surfaced because of me, I am sorry," Karl said sincerely.

"It's cool, man, don't sweat it. I ain't trippin'. Hey, Mr. Karl, what you know about this latest *Madden?*" Prince asked, trying to change the subject.

"Boy, you don't want any of this. I'm fierce on the sticks," Karl bragged.

The three boys laughed, doubting the older man knew anything about their electronic toys. Prince grabbed a stick and handed his teacher the other. They played three games back to back. The third game was the tie-breaker and the winner would have bragging rights. Being with the McGee family felt comfortable to Karl. They discussed and sometime argued about professional sports. Everyone had their opinion about LeBron James leaving Cleveland, Shaq retiring from the game, Dwayne Wade's personal life, and Michael Jordan's stats. Prince, Jayden, and Quincy liked Karl. He was easygoing and didn't take himself too seriously. All of the other teachers they had known only cared about grades and behavior. Karl seemed to care about them.

"Where is everybody?" Shy yelled as she stepped in the door.

The boys could hear anger in her voice. They immediately knew Shy was still furious and her visit with Cherise only made it worse.

"We're in the family room," Jayden replied.

"I almost had to beat the breaks off that bitch," Shy vented. "I have to tell y'all something explosive." Shy continued her walk toward the family not knowing the boys had company. She had to let the boys know what Cherise confessed to.

"That bitch told me Raequan has been . . ." Shy stopped. Her eyes locked with the stranger as she stepped down into the family room. She was embarrassed by her language.

Karl was sitting on the couch with Prince playing a game. He heard the woman walking through the house clearly upset about something. Karl had assumed it was a girlfriend of one of the boys. He never imagined the voice belonged to the twins' mother.

"Ma, we have company," Jayden announced with a nod of his head.

"Ma this is my teacher from when I was in juvie. This is Mr. Karl. Mr. Karl, this is my mom, Shayla McGee," Prince happily introduced.

Karl shifted his attention from the game to the woman standing near him. She was beautiful. Shy's pretty face was like a magnet pulling him to her. Karl scanned her hourglass shape, causing him to fight off the erection growing in his pants. This woman was stealing his heart without even knowing. Karl wanted to speak but was tongue tied. He looked into her eyes and his heart skipped a beat. At that moment, Karl knew they would be together one day.

Shy saw something in Karl's eyes that she hadn't seen since Melvin died. He was a pretty boy but didn't seem arrogant. Shy found his dreads and eyes sexy. Her stomach had butterflies. Their eyes locked along with an undeniable connection. She forgot all about her anger.

Quincy noticed something going on between Karl and Shy. He wondered why they hadn't said hello to each other. At a closer glance, Karl's mouth was open. It looked like he had something to say but his mouth wouldn't let him. Quincy laughed. He had had that look when he met his girlfriend Caron. After a few seconds of awkwardness, Shy blinked and shook her head.

"Hi, Karl, everybody calls me Shy. It's nice to meet you." Shy blushed.

"It's nice meeting you too. I, umm, I just stopped by to check up on Prince. You raised a very respectable young man," Quincy complimented as he stood to shake her hand.

"Thank you. I'm sorry about my language when I first got home. We have some complicated issues going on right now. That's not a daily thing, please forgive me." Shy giggled, a little embarrassed.

"Don't worry about it. We all get to that point from time to time."

Karl had a knot in his throat. He cleared his voice and glanced over Shy's body. She looked well put together. Karl wanted to kiss her to see if her lips were as soft as they appeared. His eyes fell down to her hips and long, smooth legs. He felt his manhood move and put a hand in his pocket. It was his turn to feel embarrassed.

"Have a seat. Do you make home visits to all your students' homes?" Shy fished for information on his marital status.

"No. Prince is very intelligent and I tried talking him into returning to high school. It would be tragic for him to waste his intelligence. I know with some focus he would hone in on his skills and perfect them. Something about Prince reminds me of myself," Karl admitted.

"You see it too? Prince is his own person and he's going to be who he is though I want better for him. I want all my children to get college degrees and move away from this city."

"I don't appreciate being talked about like I ain't here," Prince interjected.

Shy and Karl laughed. They apologized to Prince through laughs.

"I should be going. I have a few errands to run," Karl said.

Shy was disappointed to hear he had to leave. She enjoyed their brief conversation. His voice gave Shy goose bumps. Karl stood up and Shy smiled. It was good to see he was taller than her and his physique was exactly as she'd hoped. His body was a beast. *This brother is sexy as hell.*

"I'll walk you to the door."

Karl said his good-byes to the boys and promised to keep in touch. He followed Shy to the front door, his attention focused on her wide hips and firm behind. It took great willpower for Karl not to grab Shy and run his hands over her body. From talking to her, he knew Shy was a lady and deserved to be treated as such. There was something about Shy that made him want to know her better. Karl was thirsty.

"It was nice meeting you," Shy said.

"You too, I appreciate the hospitality. The boys were very welcoming."

"That's good to hear. Well, don't be a stranger." Shy smiled with a racing heart.

"I don't want to be forward but do you mind if I call you sometime? Maybe we could have dinner or something," Karl stammered.

"I insist," Shy flirted. She ran off her cell number and stood in the doorway until Karl was in his car.

Shy was smitten and totally taken aback by the instant attraction between her and Karl. She didn't know what it was but Karl felt familiar. They'd never met or run into each other before but the connection was undeniable. Something was awakened in her the moment she laid eyes on this complete stranger. With everything that went on earlier in the day, meeting Karl was a welcomed distraction. It almost made Shy forget about her fight with Cherise, almost. She still had to tell Prince just how deep Raequan's betrayal lay.

The boys pounced with a million questions as soon as Shy returned to the family room.

"Did you get his number?" Jayden joked.

"Where does he live?" Quincy inquired.

"He was the coolest staff people in lock-up but I don't know that nigga all like that. Who are his people?" Prince voiced suspiciously.

"Yeah, we don't want another Dwayne coming through here," Quincy added.

Shy stood quietly while her sons and nephew talked among themselves. They spoke as if she weren't even in the room. If she weren't dealing with her best friend and godson's disloyalty, the scene would have been comical.

"I didn't even think about that. I'm just happy dude had a job. Mommy don't need a thug," Prince stated.

"Hey, there's nothing wrong with a thug. Ya daddy was a thug. Remember, every thug ain't a gangster and every gangster does not deal in street pharmaceuticals," Shy educated them all.

"Any man you bring around has to be good enough for you, Aunt Shy. He needs stability," Quincy said matter-of-factly.

"You're right, Q, but it takes a certain type of man to handle a woman like me. I prefer a man to be taller than me and he has to have some thug in him," Shy stated with a neck roll and huge smile. She also liked a man with his own money and a pole at least eight inches long and as thick and fatty as a cut of prime steak. Shy didn't think they needed to know that.

"He gon' have to see me if he hurts you," Prince threatened.

"Stop jumping ahead. I'm going to enjoy a meal with the man, not walk down the aisle."

Shy's heart was touched. It felt good to know she was so loved. Melvin had treated her like a queen. With him, she never wanted for anything. Melvin took care of her every need. Shy missed that feeling of a strong body next to her at night. Her battery-operated boyfriend couldn't take care of all her needs. At times the loneliness felt overwhelming but, somehow, she always worked through it. She had resolved herself to being alone if the alternative meant settling for a man who wasn't right. All of that didn't matter because she had just met the man. He had asked her out for dinner. Dinner was just that: dinner.

The boys knew Shy was right. They were overprotective but only because she was such an important part of their lives. Quincy felt like more than just a nephew; he felt like a son to Shy. Her love for him was invaluable to Quincy. Prince and Jayden saw the sacrifices their mother made for them and their baby sister. They wanted her to be happy and supported her desire to find it. The twins could tell by the look on their mother's face that she had more on her mind than going out on a date. Something was wrong.

"Prince, turn that game off for a minute. We need to talk," Shy instructed. She sat on the ottoman next to Quincy. Prince and Jayden sat across from them on the couch. Shy could only imagine Prince's reaction; she knew it was going to be explosive.

"What happened when you went to talk to Cherise?" Jayden asked cautiously. He thought back to how Cherise came home and assumed she was going to drop a bomb. Jayden never expected the news his mother was about to deliver.

"Cherise and Raequan are no longer a part of our family. They have both betrayed us in the worst way. I never want to hear of any contact with them again. This situation is so foul that I almost pulled my .22 from my purse and shot that bitch in her own house," Shy declared angrily.

"What's going on, Ma?" Jayden asked worriedly.

"Prince, your broken arm and all the other bullshit you dealt with in juvie were calculated," Shy began.

"I'd been hearing that Raequan was behind all that bullshit. I ain't trip on it 'til that nigga shot out my engine," Prince responded nonchalantly.

"Why didn't you ever mention it, bro?" Jayden worried.

"It wasn't nothing I couldn't handle."

"Wrong. Raequan wasn't working alone. He didn't just turn on you overnight. That boy had somebody pulling the strings," Shy explained.

"What you mean?" Prince immediately grew heated.

"The night supervisor paid Raequan to make you unhappy. Basically Raequan got special treatment to fuck with you." Shy was infuriated. She hated the thought of not being able to protect her child from the evilness of the world.

"Ma, that don't make no sense. I ain't trip with no staff all like that." Prince tried to make sense of it all.

"I know, baby, none of this has anything to do with you. It's about your daddy." Shy tried not to show the anger in her voice.

"What?" the three boys asked in unison.

"Roberts works there. He put all of this in motion. He's probably who dropped Dwayne into my life." Shy was furious.

"I ain't ever seen that bitch nigga. How you know all this?" Prince grew more and more livid.

"That was probably by design. He worked at night and stayed out of sight. Cherise knew all about it and never said a thing to me. She supported that spiteful shit. I understand having your child's back but as a parent, you let them know when they're wrong. It does not mean I wouldn't have your back but I damn sure won't rally you on. There's no rationalizing what they did. Raequan is just like his daddy: an immature, jealous, think the world owes him everything, asshole."

Prince felt as if a knife had been jammed into his back. He had been a loyal, lifetime friend to Raequan. Prince was probably the only true friend Raequan ever

had. Jayden and Quincy never trusted or cared for Raequan. As kids, he always got jealous when all of Prince's
attention wasn't focused on him. Raequan would break
their toys, steal money, and lie to get them into trouble.
Prince treated Raequan like a brother because he was
their god brother. Even though Raequan was older,
Prince felt responsible for him. After a lifetime of dealing with all his bipolar ways, Prince felt used and de-
ceived.

Jayden was outraged. He knew Prince was hurting
and Jayden resented Raequan's treatment of his brother. The twins felt each other's happiness and hurt.
When Prince broke his arm, Jayden felt the physical
pain. He told their mother that Prince had gotten hurt
before the juvenile facility called to notify her. It had
been that way their entire lives. Jayden also knew that
Prince was homicidal. If Prince were to leave the house
and find Raequan, he would kill him for sure. Jayden
could not let that happen.

Prince paced the length of the family room, punching his fist into his hand and breathing hard. He was so
angry and hurt that tears stained his face. Shy, Jayden,
and Quincy were nervous. They had no idea what
Prince was going to do but Shy's hypothesis was correct: things were about to explode.

"Ma, fo' real? This nigga played me like that? He
stepped on my neck, bro. How am I supposed to let
that shit slide?" Prince cried angrily.

Before Shy could find the right words to calm her
son, Prince punched a hole in the wall. Quincy rushed
to grab Prince before he could do any more damage.
Prince threw a vase against the wall before his cousin
could stop him.

"Bro, calm down, bro. We got you," Quincy demanded.

"Bro, he ain't worth all this. You need to bring that down, bro. Mommy right here and she's upset, man. Come on, Prince, calm down." Jayden pleaded with his brother repeatedly.

Everyone in the room felt the pain inside of his heart but Prince was giving Raequan too much power. Until Prince understood that, anger and hatred would rule his life. Shy was determined not to let that happen. Somehow she would make this right for her son. By any means necessary, Shy was going to take his pain away.

Jayden swept up glass and Quincy picked up drywall while Prince sat staring off into space with Shy by his side. She would not leave his side for anything in the world. Princess was at a friend's sleepover and wouldn't be home until morning so Shy could take care of her oldest baby. Her soul ached for him. She refused to let him see how angry she truly was. Cherise and Raequan had hell to pay for what they'd done to Prince. There was no way Shy could let things go. Cherise knew better than anyone what lengths Shy would go to in order to protect her family. Roberts was also in Shy's sight of revenge. No one needed to know what Shy was about to put into action, it was best that way, but when the dust settled, there would be three fewer people walking the earth.

Chapter 26

Didn't See It Coming

It was obvious by his black eyes that Raequan had taken a loss. Cherise knew without asking who had beat her child. Shy was right about one thing: Raequan was just like his father. He had no conscience. B-Boy never cared who he double-crossed and neither did his son. They would lie, rob, and steal out of pure greed. Raequan possessed the same character flaws as his father. Cherise justified her son's actions by believing there was a genetic link to the habitual lying and their shared emotional abuse of her. She believed Raequan was entitled to be angry with the world for having a loser for a father. It wasn't his fault B-Boy was sent to prison before his birth or that the streets had raised him. Cherise always made excuses for her only child's behavior but shied away from acknowledging her failures as a mother.

Cherise refused to take ownership of any bad choice she had ever made. To her, life had been unfair because of her upbringing or it was all B-Boy's fault. She was full of excuses but never searched out the reason behind her disastrous decision making. Shy had called Cherise out on her being a user of people. Cherise had taken advantage of Shy countless times throughout the years. Something inside Cherise was programmed to get the things she wanted by simply taking them. It was in her to take the quickest and easiest routes in life. Much like Raequan and B-Boy, Cherise saw nothing wrong with how she lived her life.

"I've been trying to get in touch with you for hours. Where have you been, boy?" Cherise demanded to know.

"Making moves," Raequan arrogantly replied on his way to the kitchen.

"Looks more like you were taking an ass whooping or two," Cherise snapped.

Raequan looked at his mother with contempt. He couldn't stand her at times. She was always judging him and expecting the worst. Raequan never felt loved by his mother. He held a lot of resentment in his heart for both of his parents.

"What did you want?" Raequan asked dryly while dropping ice into a Baggie for his eye.

"Shy told me what happened between you and Prince today. I was trying to warn you that they know everything."

"What da hell you talkin' 'bout? What everything?" Raequan frowned and turned to face his mother.

"Prince has no love left for you. There's a way to go about doing shit so the person you're fuckin' over won't know about it. Come on, I mean damn! That's probably why Prince started to cop from somebody else. You've always been sloppy about ya shit," Cherise ranted.

"I ain't tryin'a hear dat right now. You don't see my face? Fuck Prince and his new connect," Raequan hollered as he pushed past his mother.

"Shy cut me down today behind ya shit. Our friendship is probably over for good this time. We almost came to blows thanks to your little deal with Roberts's punk ass," Cherise said with much attitude.

Raequan stopped in his tracks. At first he wasn't sure he'd heard his mother right but the look in her eyes confirmed it for him.

"How did Shy find out 'bout me fuckin' with Roberts?"

"I told her," Cherise responded matter-of-factly.

"What da fuck, Ma! You always doin' grimy shit like that to me. You ain't right, man." Raequan swung his arm and knocked a vase off the sofa table.

"And what about you? What did you think was going to happen? Did you really believe you could get away with some petty-ass deal all for some pizza and watching a movie you've seen a hundred times over?" Cherise didn't care how mad Raequan was, she was just as angry. "The only time you snake on somebody is for your enrichment, nigga. You can't do shit just for the sake of doing it and think it ain't coming back full circle. How many times do I gotta tell you that a young-minded hustler won't get far in the game?"

"And how far you gonna get, Ma? Your circle is from here to Mansfield and back," Raequan said with venom. He stabbed the knife deep.

For the second time in one day, Cherise's feelings had been trampled on and she could take no more. She decided to throw in the towel. The fight had been drained from her body and she was tired. Cherise turned her back on Raequan and started up the stairs. Raequan thought he had all the answers so nothing she said would penetrate his thick skull. She refused to waste any more energy on him.

"Go figure it out, Raequan. I can't do shit for you."

"You never have." Raequan gave another turn of the knife.

Raequan was outraged. No wonder Prince had gone off on him the way he had. Yeah, he had shot the gun off inside of the car on purpose but Prince didn't know that for sure. It never crossed Raequan's mind that he'd left a trail of hints and evidence in his wake. Just like his parents, Raequan had a one-way mind. He was smarter than everyone and nothing was ever his fault.

He didn't know if it was the safe thing to do but Raequan had to pay his partner in crime a visit. Prince would be gunning for him and Raequan knew his skills didn't match his opponent's. He'd never be able to withstand his god brother's wrath, especially with his mother and uncle protecting his back. Raequan only had his mother and he didn't trust that she would have his back.

Raequan went up to his room, showered, and changed clothes. After he double-checked the clip of his 9 mm, Raequan grabbed a pair of dark sunglasses to cover his eyes and headed out the door. There was no way around it; he and Roberts had to talk.

Roberts was a semi-functioning alcoholic and drug addict. He'd become a disgrace to everyone around him, including himself. Guilt ate away at him from the inside out while hatred fueled his determination to see another day. He lived his life trapped in a closet with shame, humiliation, and self-hatred. His mind was stuck in a state of misery; the only thing he missed was company. Dwayne and Raequan had visited his dark world but hadn't set up residency yet. It would be just a matter of time before they signed a lease. Roberts was also determined to lure every person with the last name McGee to his prison of desolation.

Roberts lay on the floor of his studio apartment in a daze. The event that changed his life constantly played in his head. Being a cop had been a goal of his since middle school. Back then, he thought he could make a difference in the world by arresting anyone who thumbed their finger at the law. He worked hard to make detective quickly. His aim was to become a lieutenant and supervise his own squad one day. Melvin McGee changed all of that.

Roberts had identified Melvin McGee as the drug kingpin who would make his career. The streets knew him as Legend. Roberts believed busting the largest and most powerful drug enterprise in the city would make his career. All he had to do was bust someone on Legend's team to get his foot in the door. He'd planned on making multiple buys from Legend before making his arrest. Roberts was still oblivious to the identity of Legend's partner. It was imperative that he implemented his plan slowly. He needed a snitch on his team. Arresting a low-level drug dealer would get things in motion.

Albert Silk Willis was a student of the game. Unlike the true hustlers living the life, Silk lacked natural ability to survive the life. Silk cried before Roberts had even started the interview. He didn't have a hustling bone in his body, so flipping him after his arrest was like taking candy from a baby. The ambitious officer used Silk in order to get into Melvin's circle.

He posed as a new player in the area from Pennsylvania by the name of Skrill. His cover story was that the hustler he usually dealt with had been popped and in federal custody. Silk vouched for Skrill and told Melvin that they had history. That got Roberts a deal for ten kilos of pure cocaine. Melvin trusted no one except for his elusive partner. He never touched a drug; he had people for that. All shipments Roberts received were from one of Melvin's loyal workers. Melvin was so vigilant, he never verbally communicated with customers, only those under his employ. It took Roberts over a year to get close to Melvin.

Melvin's guarded business practices made it difficult to take his empire down. After nine months of dealing with the family, Roberts was no closer to getting a warrant. He had no interest in making multiple arrests of lower-level workers; he wanted the two men in charge. Roberts wouldn't rest until Melvin and his partner were serving life behind federal walls. The worst part about the failing undercover sting was that the identity of Melvin's cohort remained a mystery. Because he was too low on the pyramid, Silk had no idea who co-chaired the family. Had that information been available to Roberts, he could've brought down their entire organization. Melvin McGee was only one half of the drug enterprise in Roberts's sights. Roberts reasoned that knowing the identity of Melvin's partner would've allowed him to bring down their entire organization. Instead, killing Melvin became the springboard of his demise as a man.

In Roberts's mind, Melvin was the reason for his failures. He chose to overlook the fact that he had been a horrible husband, a mediocre father, and a subpar police detective long before his nemesis entered his life. After twelve years of trying to change him, Roberts's devoted wife packed up their children and disappeared. It had taken her over three years of skimming money from their joint bank accounts before she could leave. Through infidelity, a child outside of their marriage, and mental and emotional abuse, Brenda stuck in there with her man for as long as she could. Even a strong-minded woman like Brenda could only take so much. Brenda was pushed past her breaking point when she discovered her husband had fallen in deep with drugs, money, and loose women.

Roberts had slipped off into a deep sleep with dreams of better days when banging at his door jarred him awake. The drugs had his mind in a daze. He had trouble lifting himself off the floor.

"Man, what in the hell are you doing here?" Roberts slurred angrily.

"You told me to come by today." Dwayne was confused. They'd run into one another the night before at a bar. Roberts wanted to put together another plan to get close to Shy. Dwayne was all in if it meant he got to get close to Shy again. In the few weeks they'd spent together, Dwayne started to care about Shy. He missed her. "We're supposed to put a plan in motion to hurt the McGee family." Dwayne walked past Roberts into the messy apartment.

Roberts had an all-day-type hangover. He made a pot of coffee as he tried to remember what he'd done the night before. The lingering high blocked his memory.

"You need to clean up and open a window; it's stuffy in here." Dwayne took it upon himself to open the only two windows in the apartment. Fresh air was only a fraction of what the apartment needed. Dwayne was tempted to grab a bucket and cleaning solution but decided against it. He did little cleaning at his own home.

"I don't remember shit. We gon' do this later," Roberts said, taking a sip of coffee. "My head is spinning right now." Roberts sat on the tattered couch when another knock echoed through the cramped living space. "Now who is this? Y'all niggas kill me not calling before just coming over."

Raequan stood on the other side of the door, feeling as nervous as a virgin sharing the most valuable part of her for the first time. He had no other choice. Roberts had to know what had happened. It was possible that Prince and his family would be out for payback. Raequan found it difficult to get past the fact that his mother had ratted him out. Her betrayal had to take a back seat. Raequan had bigger trouble ahead of him and he refused to get caught slipping.

Roberts flung the door open in a huff. All he wanted was to be alone with a glass of Alka-Seltzer. "What da fuck you doin' here?" His head was thumping hard at that moment. Raequan had no business being on his doorstep. Roberts was furious.

"It's all out, man. We gotta come up with a plan before these niggas come gunnin' for me," Raequan said frantically. Raequan stepped past Roberts and began pacing the dirty floor. He was so preoccupied with his thoughts that Dwayne went unnoticed. He hadn't noticed Dwayne until he opened his mouth.

"What is so important that you feel comfortable walking up in here?" Roberts demanded to know. He poured a second cup of coffee while he waited for Raequan's explanation. Had he looked up, Roberts would've seen the aftereffects of the ass beating Raequan took earlier in the day.

"Prince and his mother know everything. They up on you being behind that bullshit I pulled on him. He came at me today and we had it out in the middle of the fuckin' street. That punk-ass nigga lucky the homies broke it up 'cause he'd be in a body bag right now," Raequan exaggerated.

Roberts and Dwayne looked at Raequan and knew he was lying. It was obvious he'd been knocked on his ass since he was sporting two black eyes, a crooked nose, and busted lip. They were more interested in how Prince and Shy found out he'd been working with Roberts.

"Did Prince beat the information out of you?" Dwayne laughed in Raequan's face.

"Man, go to hell. While you all giggly over there and ya ribs just healed from the twins and Q puttin' it in on that soft ass," Raequan retorted smugly. Raequan wasn't worried about Dwayne. He was one person he knew he could knock out for sure.

"Hey, I told y'all niggas my head is pounding so bring that shit down. Raequan, tell me what went down," Roberts directed.

Raequan was hesitant to tell Roberts the truth. No one had to know it was his mother who started the impending war with the McGee's. All Roberts needed to know was that his enemies had found his hiding spot and his plan of attack failed.

"All I know is Prince was all rah-rah about knowing you put me up to fuckin' with him while we were down. Then, when I get to da crib my mom's is all up in my face 'bout that same shit. She said her and Shy fell out about it and that you better have a plan of survival 'cause ya days are numbered," Raequan said as dramatically as possible. He was really overplaying his lie. "I don't know what the fuck happened. Ya boy over dere probably ran to Shy 'cause he ain't get to hit it before they put his ass in the hospital."

"Ah, fuck you, man. Ain't nobody on that shit. If anybody fucked up it was your bitch ass. It wouldn't be the first time you bitched out about some shit," Dwayne defended himself. He had no idea Prince knew who he was or he'd have stayed clear of Shy when her son was around.

Roberts looked at Raequan and waited for the real story. The tale he'd just told had far too many holes in it to be believable. "Calm down. Both of y'all fucked up the mission so stop spewing bullshit. Raequan, you got a lot of nerve coming up in my home and lying to my face. Clearly you can't think fast on your feet 'cause you just made that shit up." Roberts gave Raequan the look of death. "If the McGee clan wants to play, tell them to come with it. I put Legend's ass six feet under and will do the same to his bitch and all of those bastards he left behind."

Dwayne and Raequan didn't have the confidence like their leader. Melvin had killed Dwayne's brother and he hated the man's memory too. He knew harming Shy and her kids wouldn't bring his brother Silk back so he failed to see the point of it all. So far, Prince had proved himself to be his father's child. Dwayne was scared of the boy. He was reckless.

Raequan knew Prince was crazy. He didn't give a fuck who got in his way but when it came to protecting his mother, Prince was like a pit bull: evil and fearless. Going to war against Prince was a mistake. Not only was he dangerous, his uncle had his back. The two of them together would eat Roberts up, slowly. Raequan had grown tired of being in Prince's shadow. It was time to become a man with an identity of his own. Raequan reasoned that if all else failed, he'd switch teams, again.

Roberts already had a plan to finally get his revenge on the McGee family. It was time for them to be as miserable as he'd been for seven years.

"Shy better have life insurance on all of her kids," Roberts said mindlessly. "She's gonna be putting in a claim real soon."

Chapter 27

I Can't Do This Thing Called Life Without You

It was early Saturday morning and Step It Up Cuts was crowded. Darrin and Jarell Houston were two of the top barbers in the city. Prince, Jayden, and Quincy were loyal customers of the brothers. The once neighborhood barbers opened their first barbershop a year ago. They were already turning a profit. Prince and Jayden grew up together with Darrin and Jarell. The twins introduced Quincy to their friends and he also became a loyal customer. The McGee twins and their cousin held an eight o'clock outstanding appointment every Saturday morning for haircuts and shaves. Once they're groomed and looking their best, Prince, Jayden, and Quincy headed to the YMCA to play basketball.

"So what's the plan for today? Are we trying to play together or not?" Jayden asked while they searched for a parking spot. From the looks of the parking lot, the Y was busting with activity.

"I don't care as long as we don't have to wait forever to get on the court," Prince replied from the back seat. He'd been texting with Monica since they left the barbershop.

Quincy circled the parking lot for the third time and finally found an empty parking spot. He pulled in between a new mint-green Lexus and a white on white old school Impala. Old school cars were one of Quincy's interests. He never saw one that didn't grab his attention. Owning a fleet of late-model Chevys, Lincolns, and Cadillac's was one of Quincy's goals in life.

"That ride is clean as hell. Man, look at the rims on it." Quincy beamed with interest. He walked around the car as if he were a customer at a car dealership. It took great restraint for him not to run his hand alongside the classic automobile as he admired its detail.

"That joint is a beast." Prince smiled. "I can see myself pushing this ride."

"Hey, bro, speaking of rides, what did the shop say about yours?" Jayden looked his brother in the eyes and felt as if he were standing in front of a mirror. They both rocked Caesar haircuts. Their six o'clock shadow beards were outlined and trimmed to perfection. Even those who'd known them their entire lives would have had trouble telling them apart. Their mother, baby sister, and Quincy always knew which twin they were addressing. Even their girlfriends mistook them for one another from time to time.

"I don't even want to talk about it. That bitch nigga is costing me a lot of money. The engine is shot and basically totaled out. I got my man checkin' for me something like this joint right here. This Impala is clean as hell." Prince followed Quincy, admiring the inside of the car. From their vantage point, it was obvious that the white leather was as soft as butter. They both wished the owner would appear and offer them a tour of his weekend toy.

"Have you seen him since that day?" Quincy assumed Raequan was in hiding since Prince hadn't been arrested for murder.

"Hell no. That bitch is lucky I ain't seen his ass. I'm a fuck that boy up when I catch up with his ass," Prince fussed angrily.

Quincy regretted asking the question. When Prince started using bad grammar, he was mad and ready to pop off. Quincy had noticed that his Aunt Shy did the same thing.

"It's almost ten; let's get in here or we'll never get on the court." Jayden abruptly changed the subject. He heard the anger in his brother's voice too.

"Cool, I'm ready," Prince agreed in a calm voice.

They grabbed their gym bags and headed for the front entrance. Prince walked ahead of Jayden and Quincy when the walk sign signaled it was safe to cross the street. His attention was drawn to his phone when a text message came through. Prince assumed it was Monica again and opted to read it later. Quincy lagged behind a few steps Jayden. He had difficulty tearing himself away from the car. Like Prince, his cell alerted him to a new text. The message was cryptic and anonymous. It read: dis my perfect dream cum tru, who gon run to da rescue now? No signature was on the message and the number was blocked. Quincy figured someone sent it to him by accident and paid it no mind. That was a mistake. Even if he had made something of the text message, there was no way he could have prevented what happened next.

Prince reached the sidewalk with Jayden on his heels when the sound of screeching tires came out of nowhere. An old, beat-up dark-colored car flew around the street corner practically on two wheels. The car sped past them, barely missing Quincy. The driver never slowed down and quickly disappeared around the bend.

"What the fuck was that?" Quincy's heart raced a mile a minute. There's no doubt he would've been killed had the car hit him.

"Who the hell was that?"

Before Jayden could respond to Prince's question, the same car came back at them from the opposite direction. The passenger's arm was extended with gun in hand. Both he and the driver wore black masks over their faces. Gunshots rang out, scaring everyone within earshot.

"Get down!" Prince yelled.

Jayden and Quincy hit the ground together. Prince dove on top of them in an attempt to shield their bodies with his own. People were screaming and running for cover. It felt like forever before the shooter emptied his clip in their direction. Once it was over, Prince heard someone scream out in fear and agony.

"Are y'all straight?" Prince asked, out of breath. He stood up and noticed blood on his clothes, sending him into panic mode. "Jay! Q! Are you hit?" Prince's question was met with silence at first. His heart was about to beat out of his chest.

"I'm straight, man. That was some shit." Quincy got up from the ground.

Jayden lay at his brother's feet in a pool of his own blood. He was unconscious and hit bad. Prince stood over his Jayden in shock. His mind told him to move but his body wouldn't follow orders. Quincy fell to his knees in tears. He checked Jayden for a pulse.

"He's still breathing. Prince, call 911," Quincy ordered as he removed his shirt to help stop the blood. "Prince!" Quincy punched Prince in the leg. His attempt to snap Prince out of his daze worked. Prince pulled his cell out and dialed 911. After giving their location, the operator told Prince to apply pressure to the wounds and to cover his brother with a jacket or blanket to prevent him from going into shock. Once it hit him that Jayden had just been shot, Prince kneeled over him and begged God not to take his brother from him.

Quincy's shirt soaked up the blood of the person he was closest to on earth. He was terrified for Jayden. Just the thought of losing his best friend terrified Quincy. The force behind his eyes pushed a rapid stream of tears down Quincy's face. He'd never been so terrified in his entire life.

"Come on, cuz, fight, man, fight," Quincy cried over Jayden.

"Hold on, li'l bro, they coming. We got you, Jay, don't you let go," Prince begged through sorrow and fear in his heart. He had been there before. Prince was reliving the entire scene with their father all over again. He was that ten-year-old boy holding his dying hero in his arms. Fear caused his body to seize up on him. "Jayden, I got you, man. I got you." Prince heard the sirens in the distance minutes after the emergency call was placed. The police station was only three blocks up the street and the hospital was five minutes away. Help reached them quickly.

"Sir, let me get to him please." The voice came from a female emergency response worker. She gently placed her hand on Quincy's shoulder when she spoke. "I'll take care of him, I promise." Quincy rose to his feet and helped Prince do the same. They held on to each other for dear life, both frightened beyond belief. Prince and Quincy watched as Jayden was loaded into the back of an ambulance with a portable heart monitor, oxygen machine, and IVs attached to his fragile body.

"Excuse me, sir, are you hurt?" An officer directed his question to Quincy. Blood was running down his left arm. Quincy was so focused on Jayden that he hadn't realized he'd been hit. One of the bullets had gone straight into his bicep. Quincy was in shock, oblivious to the pain. "It looks like you were wounded as well. Why don't you let them stop the bleeding before we get you to the hospital, okay?"

Prince's heart dropped when he saw that Quincy
had also been shot. How did a morning of haircuts and
basketball turn into gunshots and hospitals? Nothing made any sense to Prince. At that moment, all he
knew was his cousin needed help and his identical twin
brother might die. He felt so alone. Prince knew he had
a duty to take care of both his brother and cousin. Being the oldest of the three, it had been his responsibility
to look out for them since they were little boys. It was
an obligation he took seriously.

"No, I'm fine," Quincy barked at the officer.

"Q, just let them stop you from bleeding and then
we'll go straight to the hospital. I gotta know that
you're okay, man, please," Prince said, near tears. He
took a deep breath trying to contain himself. If he was
strong, Quincy would be too. Prince prayed he had it in
him to be strong enough for Quincy. What he felt inside
didn't matter.

"Can I ask you some questions while they get him
patched up?" the young police officer requested of
Prince.

Prince snarled at the man. He had nothing to say to
him or any other cop. Experience had taught him they
were not to be trusted. They all carried a license to kill
without any accountability. The streets would spit up
the shooter's name soon enough. When it did, Prince
would serve his own brand of justice.

"All that's gonna have to wait. My brother needs me
as soon as possible, I can feel him," Prince said defiantly.
"If they're done with my cousin, we need to go up the
hill. I'm sure you'll follow us anyway." Prince walked
around the officer toward Quincy. It was taking longer
than it should have to stop a flesh wound from bleeding.
Another bad feeling washed over Prince. Quincy's situation was more serious than the emergency workers first

thought. There was a bullet still in his arm. He would probably require surgery. Prince took the news in stride. His demeanor seemed robotic, void of any emotion. "Can I drive my cousin to the hospital?"

The EMT started to protest but she could see that Prince was on the verge of losing it. Being an identical twin herself, she understood the bond the brothers shared. She knew the young man before her was doing his best to be resilient in the face of a traumatic event. Her heart went out to both Prince and Quincy.

"That will be fine. My partner and I will meet you at the emergency entrance."

"Quincy, let's go see about Jay and get you right," Prince said gently as he led his little cousin away.

Shy stood in the middle of the walk-in closet agonizing over which pair of jeans to wear with what top. She had under an hour to make her decision and get dressed. Her date was expected at noon and Shy didn't want to make a bad impression by not being ready when he arrived. Shy owned at least fifty pairs of jeans, some still had price tags, but not one pair seemed right for a simple lunch date.

"Miss Shy, you aren't dressed yet?" Brianna giggled. She took a seat on the bench in front of the bed.

"I don't have anything to wear." Shy sighed.

"What?" Brianna was in disbelief. The closet looked as if it would explode if another piece of clothing was stuffed into it. Shy owned so many shoes that she could've opened a shoe store. "Miss Shy, I can't believe you. Most of this stuff hasn't been worn, the price tags are still on them." Brianna looked around and decided to take matters into her own hands. "You have a seat, let me find something cute."

Shy left the closet feeling flustered. She usually wasn't so indecisive. Her nervousness was a surprise to her. Shy was always a confident woman and seldom made to feel uncomfortable or insecure. For some reason, it was important that she made a good impression on Karl. She looked forward to spending time with him and wanted to look her best.

"Here you go, Miss Shy. This pair of dark denim 7 jeans will go perfect with this Baby Phat powder-pink tube top and these Jessica Simpson pink heels. I know the shoes are a bolder shade of pink, but trust me, it works," Brianna explained with confidence in her choice. She held up the clothes for Shy to visualize herself in it. "Or, if you don't want to show off your curves, you can go with this white linen maxi dress and your royal purple flats from Bakers with the matching hobo bag. What do you think?"

"I think you should've been up here dressing me an hour ago." Shy laughed. Shy picked the maxi dress for comfort. It was hot outside and a lady does not like to perspire, especially in the presence of a man.

"Good pick, now get moving. You got about twenty minutes to get dressed and do your makeup. Good thing your hair is braided up for the summer. Just pull your micros up into a ponytail and you'll be good to go," Brianna instructed as she headed for the door. She wanted to give Shy privacy, plus she needed to check on Princess. Brianna was babysitting while Shy went to lunch. Princess was very talkative but never gave Brianna, or Monica, any grief when they sat for her. The twins were like big sisters to Princess.

Brianna found Princess stretched out across her bed watching the Nick Jr. channel. Her brothers and their girlfriends had treated her to Cedar Point Amusement Park the day before and Princess was still tired. She had the time of her life riding rides, eating junk, and running around. It was the five hours they spent at the waterpark that had Princess relaxing the day away.

"Hey, baby girl, you all right?" Brianna asked.

"Yeah, I'm fine, Bri," Princess answered slowly. Her attention remained on the television show.

"Okay, I'm downstairs if you need me." Brianna laughed.

Shy was finally dressed and ready for her date. The doorbell chimed as she descended the stairs. "I'll get it, Bri." Shy opened the door and was surprised by a bouquet of white lilies. She was impressed. Karl had just proven himself to be a gentleman. "Come on in," Shy said, welcoming him with a smile. She smelled his Unforgiveable cologne by Sean John when he passed by her. He looked sexy in his crisp white Sean John T-shirt and blue jeans. Shy admired how groomed and put together Karl was.

"These are for you, Miss Lady. What a coincidence, they match that dress you're wearing so well," Karl flirted.

"Thank you, Mr. Sexy Chocolate," Shy flirted back with a wink of the eye and a sweet smile. "Karl, go in and make yourself comfortable while I put these in water. Jayden's girlfriend Brianna is in there already," Shy yelled over her shoulder as she went in search of a vase.

Karl watched Shy walk away and enjoyed the site. The way she swayed her hips turned him on. He found Brianna in the family room reading a book.

"Hi, I'm Karl and you must be Brianna." Karl extended his hand as he walked toward Brianna.

"Yes, nice meeting you, Mr. Karl. Have a seat," Brianna offered with a smile.

"Thank you. What are you reading?" Karl made small talk.

Before Brianna could answer the question, her cell phone rang. The caller ID read: My Heart.

"Excuse me, please, I have to answer this."

Karl focused his attention on the television while Brianna took her call. It quickly became obvious that the caller was delivering some bad news. Tears exploded from Brianna's eyes and her breath became short.

"Oh my God no," Brianna cried. "I can't tell her that."

Karl hoped Brianna would be okay. Whatever it was appeared to be devastating. He called out for Shy. She would know how to help the young woman.

Shy walked into the room full of energy and anticipation. She was amped about spending the afternoon with Karl. Her upbeat demeanor immediately disappeared when she saw the look on Brianna's face.

"What happened?" Shy asked, concerned. Brianna's failure to answer gave Shy a bad feeling. "Is it the twins?" Shy held her breath and waited for Brianna to confirm the fear that took over her heart.

Brianna shook her head and continued to cry. Shy quickly grew impatient.

"What is it, Brianna?" Shy demanded.

"Miss Shy that was Prince. They're at St. Elizabeth's emergency room," Brianna cried. She took in a deep breath before continuing. "Both Jayden and Quincy were shot. You have to get to the hospital. Jayden's being rushed into emergency surgery. Quincy wasn't hurt as bad."

Shy couldn't believe her ears. Brianna had to be joking. Why would anyone play such a horrible game with her? Her body wouldn't follow her commands to move. Shy didn't know what to do.

Karl saw Shy was in shock. He didn't want to startle her and moved slowly toward her. With caution, Karl wrapped his arm around Shy's waist and guided her to the couch. He sat between Shy and Brianna, holding both their hands for support.

"Shy, Shy, can you hear me?" Karl spoke just above a whisper. "Is your daughter in the house?" The mention of Princess jarred Shy out of her daze.

"Princess is upstairs. I don't want her at the hospital worried about her brother and cousin. I'm sure Brianna wants to come with us to see about Jayden. Oh, my baby needs me." Shy sobbed.

"Is there anybody I can call to come pick her up or to sit with her?" Karl suggested.

"Yeah, call Bossy from my phone. Tell her what's happened and ask her to come get Princess for me. She'll come right over." The reality of the situation quickly set in on Shy. She went from shock to borderline panic mode in under a second. Shy jumped to her feet. There was no doubt Bossy would come right over but Shy couldn't wait. She had to get to her son.

"Bri, baby, listen to me." Shy kneeled in front of Brianna and wiped her tears away. "I know you love my son and that you're scared. Please, try to calm down. Jayden needs us both to be strong right now."

Brianna fought to stop her tears from falling. Her heart felt like it was in her stomach. She loved Jayden with all of her heart and didn't think she could go on without him in her life. Jayden was her anchor. There was nothing she wouldn't do for him. Brianna knew Shy was right; she had to be strong. She said a quick prayer and tried to slow her breathing. Her attention was now focused on Shy.

"I'm going to leave for the hospital. You wait here for Bossy. When she gets here, have her drop you off at the hospital. I don't want you driving like this. So you understand me?"

"Yes, ma'am, I do." Brianna sniffed. "What about you? You can't drive, Miss Shy."

"Don't worry, I'm not going to leave her alone. I'll stay at the hospital with her. Everything will be okay," Karl promised without reservation.

"Okay, I'm going to run up and kiss Baby Girl before I leave. Whatever you do, Brianna, do not tell her about what happened. I'll do that myself after I know exactly what's going on."

Shy found Princess asleep. She gave her a gentle kiss on the cheek before going back downstairs.

"Karl, I'm ready to go. Take me to my baby."

Chapter 28

Do unto Others Before They Do It to You

The shot to Quincy's arm wasn't as bad as initially thought. The bullet missed hitting any bone and was expected to heal quickly. Quincy was already in the recovery room and would be released into his parents care that night. He'd been stitched up, given antibiotics, and prescribed pain medication to take home. Prince wasn't physically hurt but emotionally, he was shaken. He sat in the family waiting room, feeling anxious and afraid for Jayden and Quincy. All he knew was that Jayden required an operation that would take hours.

Shy and Karl arrived at the hospital to find Jayden had already been taken to surgery. A small amount of relief washed over Shy when she saw Prince and found out Quincy was going to be fine. That good news was hampered by Jayden's absence, only confirming Shy's fear of how bad the situation really was.

"Prince," Shy called out.

Like a small child being picked up from daycare, Prince rushed into his mother's arms. Prince couldn't shake the vision of his brother being shot and lying in a puddle of his own blood. Having to relive that horrible scene from seven years earlier was overwhelming. Being in that same place twice in a seventeen-year lifetime was too heavy of a burden to bear. Prince was on an emotional rollercoaster ride headed for a tragic collision.

"Why again? Why is this happening again, Mommy?" Prince cried in his mother's arms.

Shy's heart broke into a million little pieces. She could not help but to cry. Life had been unfair to Prince. His entire world seemed imbalanced. There was far too much pain and not enough happiness surrounding Prince.

"I don't know, baby, but we'll get through this, you hear me? We'll get through this together," Shy promised with love.

Shy felt helpless. Seeing the familiar pain in Prince was tearing her soul apart. Mothers are supposed to protect their children. Standing there in a hospital waiting room, Shy was powerless to protect or help her boys. There was no worse feeling in the world for a mother.

Quincy sat on the couch, stiff as a board after receiving his aftercare instructions and release papers. Tara had yet to arrive at the hospital. Given the situation, Quincy received permission from the doctor to sit with his family while he waited for his parents. He was as relieved as Prince to see his aunt. Just having her near him gave him a sense of security. Shy looked at Quincy and didn't know what to say. He looked so fragile sitting in the corner of the room like a lost puppy. For as much time as Quincy spent with the twin, most would assume his street savvy was as honed as Jayden's or came natural the way it did for Prince but they'd be wrong. Quincy was built different. He may have spent most of his time in the hood but Quincy was a child of the suburbs. Drugs, guns, and violence weren't part of the world in which he lived.

"Come here." Shy invited her nephew into her open arms. Quincy melted when Shy wrapped her protective arms around him. It was at that moment Quincy knew he was safe. He knew his aunt would shield him and his cousins from any further harm. "Everything's going to be okay. We're going to band together and help Jayden heal. He's going to be fine." Shy tried to comfort Quincy and convince herself that she would not have to bury a son. "Are you all right?" A nurse interrupted them before Quincy could answer.

"Excuse me, ma'am," said the nurse as she stepped into the room. "Are you Mrs. McGee?" the brown-eyed, attractive nurse said in a soft voice.

"Yes, I am. What's going on with my son?" Shy asked in agony.

"He's in surgery right now. Jayden was hit twice in the lower back. One bullet pierced his kidney, the other hit the spleen. Our best doctors are in with him now. The head surgeon, Dr. Fitzgerald, will be out to give you an update as soon as possible but it may be a couple of hours before that happens," Nurse Gordon explained slowly and clearly. "In the meantime, there are some forms we need you to fill out and sign. If you would come with me, please." Her compassion came through with every patient and their families. She was a recent graduate of Kent State University and had returned home to be near family and give back to her community. That level of commitment made LaTonya Gordon great at her job. Her heart especially went out to victims of crime. When she was a child, her father lost his life when an assailant decided another man's life was his to take. She was dedicated to helping other victims of crime work through their pain and anger.

Prince's nerves were wrecked. He grabbed Shy's hand and held on to his mother for dear life. Prince didn't want to let his mother out of his sight. She tried to follow LaTonya out of the waiting room but Prince held her back.

"It's okay, baby. Mommy has to go take care of this so the doctors can do everything possible to save your brother. I'll be right back," Shy attempted to assure Prince. He maintained his grip on her hand. Shy noticed Prince was physically shaking. She decided to take another approach.

"Karl, will you sit here with Quincy while I take care of this paperwork?"

"Of course, anything you need," Karl replied.

"Come with me, Prince." Shy and Prince walked hand in hand behind LaTonya.

As hour after hour passed without word from the operating room, Shy was sick to her stomach waiting to hear if her son would live or die. She refused to break down in front of Prince and Quincy. They had been through enough. Shy would not force them to be her rock. She was determined to be theirs. Karl remained with Shy and her family for hours, only leaving her side to get food for everyone. He'd been where they were before and understood how they felt. Karl prayed for a different outcome from the one he experienced.

The waiting room was quiet. Brianna and Monica had arrived along with Quincy's girlfriend Caron. Aisha stayed back at the house with Princess. C-Lok and Bossy were in the hallway keeping tabs on their troops. While everyone else focused on Jayden, they were coordinating the hunt for the shooter. The city was in for an escalating rise in its murder rate. They wanted to know who was behind the attack before the clock stroked midnight.

Shy heard a female voice in the hallway talking loud and stupid. "I wonder what that's about," she said aloud. It quickly became evident who was behind the ruckus. Shy stood up and firmly planted her feet shoulder-width apart. It was time to rumble.

"Where's my son? No, no, C-Lok, I'm not trying to hear all of that. Where is my son?" Tara yelled and pushed past her brother. Nyla walked in right behind her best friend.

"This is all your fault! I knew something like this was going to happen," Tara screamed at Shy.

"I know you're upset but you need to calm down," Shy responded to her sister's rant.

"I don't need to do shit. I should have kept my son away from you like I started to. If you'd have done what you should've back then, we wouldn't be standing here now," Tara growled at Shy.

"Calm down, Tara. My son is back there fighting for his life. I'm not in the mood for one of your bourgeois temper tantrums right now. This ain't the time," Shy warned. She stood with her hands on her hips, ready to pounce. She understood her sister being upset about Quincy getting shot but that didn't give her a right to come at Shy the way she was. Shy knew this was about more than Tara being upset about Quincy since she hadn't acknowledged his presence in the room. Tara was so focused on fighting with her sister that she hadn't hugged Quincy or asked him if he was okay.

"You think everybody's supposed to be scared of you but I ain't," Tara lied. "Quincy got shot, Jayden's in surgery, and the reason behind it all got away without a scratch."

"Watch it, Tara. That's your last warning. If you were so worried about your son, why'd it take you three hours to get here? What was more important than you coming to see about him?" Shy demanded. She was steadily losing control of her temper. Tara was taking things to a dangerous level. Shy had an immeasurable amount of pain and aggression stored up inside of her and Tara could get it if she wanted.

Monica sat holding Prince's hand. She knew how his aunt liked to put him down but placing blame on him for what happened was so unfair. Her mother standing behind Tara only angered Monica more. Monica thought her mother was just as ignorant and selfish as Tara. Nyla hadn't consoled Brianna or even looked in their direction. Brianna was still in a daze. She didn't care about anything but Jayden. Monica simultaneously wrapped her right arm around her sister and rubbed Prince's knee with her left hand. That was all she could do to let them both know that she had their backs.

Quincy felt so embarrassed and ashamed. He could never figure out what was behind all the animosity between his mother and aunt but he hated it. She liked to put on airs and turn her nose up at people. Everything with his mother was about money and status. If it had a big name attached to it, Tara wanted one for herself. She had spent nearly his entire college fund on unnecessary status symbols for herself. Tara had name-brand clothes, cars, purses, and furniture, but her son had no way to pay for college. Quincy was able to attend college because of his Uncle C-Lok. His mother had lost all of his respect the day he overheard her disrespecting Shy. If he had his choice, Quincy would have moved in with Shy years ago.

"C, come get your sister," Shy called out to their brother.

"Jayden does not deserve to be suffering and fighting for life. Whoever did this was probably aiming for Prince. That's who should be on the operating table." Tara spit out her vile words.

"Ma! That's enough. You need to leave. What's wrong with you?" Quincy cried out as he jumped up from his seat. He was fuming.

Shy's next move was slow and deliberate. She paused and said to her nephew, "Quincy, baby, please forgive me for what I'm about to do." Like a mother lion protecting her cubs, Shy faced her prey and went on the attack. She punched Tara square in the face so hard it sent her falling backward into the wall. Her head made a hole in the drywall. Tara landed on her behind in an upright position. Shy stood over her sister, throwing haymakers faster than Laila Ali. "Bitch! I will fucking kill ya ignorant ass." Shy beat on Tara like she'd stolen her man. Nyla tried to grab Shy from behind. Bossy pulled Nyla back just as Shy turned around and knocked Nyla to the floor. Shy tried to stomp Nyla out but C-Lok pulled her off the helpless woman.

Enough was enough. Shy had no time to think before she pounced on Tara and Nyla. Tara had been trying to provoke Shy into mutual combat for years. Shy tried to steady her breathing as nurses, security, and other hospital personnel rushed the family waiting room.

"Somebody grabs a gurney," someone yelled.

"Better make it two," another instructed.

"What happened here?"

Shy went back to where she was sitting before Tara singlehandedly broke hell loose. If Tara and Nyla needed medical attention, they'd brought it on themselves. Shy had no time for regrets. Besides the condition of her child, Shy had no interest in anything going on around the room. Stoic was the only word to describe her demeanor. Shy's heart went out to Quincy, Brianna, and Monica. They had to bear witness to their mommas getting their asses whipped, but those apologies had to wait. Jayden was her immediate focus.

Karl was left in the dark. He had no idea what had just happened. Shy had spoken of her brother but never mentioned she had a sister. Karl assumed Quincy was her brother's child. Nothing he could think of to say seemed appropriate so Karl decided it was best for him to remain silent. When the time was right, he knew Shy would open up to him about the obvious feud with her sister. Until then, Karl would stay by Shy's side for as long as she needed.

When police detectives walked in, Shy didn't move or blink an eye. They would have to arrest her later. If they insisted on going against her wishes, Shy had no problem giving it to them too because she was not leaving without a fight. The police were not above getting the same beat down Tara and Nyla had just received.

Chapter 29

Letting Go

The detectives had interviewed the eyewitnesses who remained at the scene. Hours had passed and they still needed to talk to the victims. They knew Prince and Quincy had experienced a traumatic event but they had to do their jobs. Speaking with the family was always difficult, especially when critical injuries or death was involved. Emotions always controlled people's reactions to life's difficulties.

Detective Iverson scanned the roomful of sad and worried faces. His heart went out to them all.

"Excuse me, Ms. McGee, I'm Detective Iverson. I'm investigating the case with my partner here, Detective Selma."

Shy looked both detectives up and down, pausing before extending her arm to meet Detective Iverson's open hand to shake.

"How's Jayden doing?" Detective Iverson genuinely wanted to know. The worst part of his job was the number of young black boys losing their lives on the streets.

"We don't know yet. He's still in surgery."

Shy's right leg began shaking. An indication that her nerves were frazzled and on edge.

"Ms. McGee, we've spent the last couple of hours interviewing witnesses. I want to personally promise you that we won't stop investigating until we find those responsible." Detective Iverson offered assurance of his resolve to give Jayden justice.

Shy felt both detectives' sincerity but nothing would make her trust them. She was as leery of the police as her son Prince. Detective Roberts made certain of that the split second Melvin took his last breath.

Karl knew Shy didn't have the mindset to speak with the police. Though their relationship was in the beginning stage, Karl felt protective of Shy. Her body language screamed out how uncomfortable the police presence made her. Karl knew Detective Selma. She was the detective assigned to the shooting death of his son. Detective Selma was professional and empathetic. Karl was grateful for her role in bringing justice to his fallen son, Tubb.

"Mr. Wilkins, how've you been?" Detective Selma asked once she recognized the man standing next to Shy.

"I'm blessed," Karl replied with a weak smile.

"No parent should have to bury a child, especially as a result of violence. You seem to have come through that dreadful time much better than some. I admire that level of strength," Detective Selma said.

"I hope you're able to bring this case to a close with a better ending. We won't lose another child to the streets," Karl responded with sadness.

From what he'd learned about Shy and Prince, Karl knew another loss could crumble the McGee family.

"I'll do all that I can to find those involved. Right now, we really need to get a statement from Prince and Quincy," Detective Iverson interjected.

Karl was well aware of Prince's attitude. He lived by the code of the street. That meant no snitching. Prince's frame of mind and experience with the civil servants behind the gold shields would hinder the investigation. He'd solve it on his own.

Before Detective Iverson could open his mouth to ask his next question, he was interrupted by the surgeon. Dr. Fitzgerald had a presence that attracted attention. He stood just over six feet and sported salt-and-pepper hair with a thick mustache. His poor upbringing kept him humble and grateful. Education and a strong mother helped in his success.

Shy's stomach turned when she saw the doctor. It had been eight long hours since Jayden was first wheeled into the operating room. She was sick with worry.

"Doctor, how is my son?" Shy held her breath and waited for the answer.

"Ms. McGee, you have a strong young man. I'm Dr. Fitzgerald and please accept my apologies for the lack of updates on Jayden. The bullets to his stomach did massive damage. His condition is critical." Dr. Fitzgerald paused and took a look around the room. There were many concerned faces but he had to be sure he had permission to speak in front of them all. "Ms. McGee, would you like to talk alone or should I continue?"

"You're fine, what's going on with my baby?"

"Jayden has extensive damage to a few major organs. We had to remove his spleen and perform a colectomy. In layman's terms, we had to take a portion of his large intestine," Dr. Fitzgerald explained slowly.

"Oh my God!" Shy cried out. Karl and Prince embraced her tightly. "He will die if he can't play basketball. It's such a huge part of his identity."

"Most people recover fully. He will most likely be able to do most of the activities he did before surgery. Jayden is in very good physical condition. His body is that of a well-disciplined athlete," Dr. Fitzgerald reassured.

"Thank God." Shy exhaled.

"Jayden is far from being out of the woods. His kidneys are not functioning. The damage is far too extensive for modern medicine. If he doesn't receive a kidney transplant, Jayden will require dialysis for the remainder of his life," Dr. Fitzgerald said somberly.

Dr. Fitzgerald gave Shy a minute to let the news set in. He'd given her some difficult news and did not want to overwhelm her. The doctor looked on as Shy broke down. Her knees were weak and she needed help staying on her feet. Dr. Fitzgerald watched as the young man who mirrored his patient comforted his mother. Realizing that Jayden had an identical twin brother gave Dr. Fitzgerald hope that his patient could make a full recovery.

"Young man, what's your name?" Dr. Fitzgerald asked.

"I'm Jayden's twin brother, Prince. My little brother can have both of my kidneys if he needs 'em. Just tell me what to do," Prince said with urgency.

"He can have one of mine. I'd rather it be me donating a kidney. Prince doesn't need to go through this," Shy insisted.

"In all honesty, identical twins are perfect matches for one another. As his mother, there's a good chance that you would qualify as a possible donor. What we'll do is test you both but as I said, your son here will be more compatible. I want to test you both as soon as possible," Dr. Fitzgerald said before making notes in Jayden's chart.

"I'm down with givin' dat nigga a kidney."

Prince was livid. Who did Raequan think he was? Raequan had tripped over the line of friend; he was forever a mortal enemy. He stood in the doorway with a stupid smirk on his face and his mother standing by his side. They both sported obvious signs of having lost a physical battle. Shy and Prince were three seconds from going for their necks when Karl and Monica jumped in between the four of them.

"Not here, not now," Karl said. "Remember where you are and that Jayden needs you right now. What good would you do him behind bars?"

Shy took a step back and reached for Prince. Karl was right. Their focus had to be on Jayden. Cherise and Raequan would be dealt with another time.

"Testing multiple people is likely unnecessary, but considering my patient's condition, I'll have everyone who volunteers tested. It may take up to forty-eight hours to get the test results back and time is of the essence. Ms. McGee, let's take care of Jayden. You and Prince will be the first tested. We have to move as fast as possible. Nurse Gordon will be in with paperwork." Dr. Fitzgerald spoke with Shy a minute longer before he left the waiting room. There was thick fog of hate floating in the air. He wasn't sure what was going on with the family but Dr. Fitzgerald knew all hell was going to break loose soon.

Prince sat on the side of his brother's bed with a variety of emotions flooding both his mind and soul. Suddenly, Prince was overtaken by a tidal wave of sentiment inside his chest. Tears burst from the wells of his eyes. Prince leaned forward in his chair and rested his head on the side of his brother's hospital bed. He hadn't left Jayden's side since the nurses wheeled him in from ICU. Prince's head lightly brushed the side of Jayden's hand. Not since the loss of their father had Prince experienced such fear. For years Prince had been able to hold back his tears. Instead he expressed his disappointment, sadness, and fears through anger and aggression. Those repressed feelings looked like irresponsibility and lack of motivation. When children become depressed, they have no idea how to explain it. Many times the adults labeled Prince's sorrow as ADD, hardheaded, or just plain bad.

Prince gripped Jayden's hand and spoke from the heart.

"I can't lose you too, bro. I ain't built fo' dis right here. It just hurts too bad," Prince cried. He paused long enough to catch his breath as he used his T-shirt to wipe his face. Prince fell back in the chair. Tears continued to fall as he stared at all of the machines and tubes running in and out of his brother.

Beep, beep, beep . . .

Sounds of artificial life assisting his brother to breathe tore into Prince's heart relentlessly. The sight sent a paralyzing bolt of fear through his body. He felt lost in the world. At that moment, Prince questioned his own existence. No one person should be condemned to a life of agony. Prince couldn't help but think God must be angry with him about something. All he had done was be born. He would be the first to admit all of the wrong he'd committed over the years but Prince didn't know why so much sorrow haunted him. The emptiness he felt inside made him feel like God had turned His back on their family.

"What did I do to make my brother have to fight for his life? It should be me in that bed," Prince sniveled.

Prince reached for his brother's hand again. He'd give anything to trade places with Jayden. "I'm sorry, bro, it's my fault Daddy ain't here. I'm sorry." It seemed like forever that Prince had housed that guilt inside his heart. "If I hadn't jerked Dad would be here. Why did I move that day?" Like a spirit leaving its earthly being, guilt washed from Prince when he confessed his sins. Prince had never let go of his brother's hand. He thought their energy might recharge Jayden and bring him back to life. "Please forgive me, Daddy . . . I'm sorry for moving," Prince whimpered.

Shy stood inside the doorway, listening to her son sob his pain away. Hearing Prince's cries broke Shy's heart. Helpless didn't begin to describe the way she felt. As much as she wanted to rush over to Prince and hold him in her arms, Shy knew Prince needed to cleanse his soul.

Shy let her tears stream down her face. She too had to forgive herself for the mistakes she'd made as a single mother raising boys. Shy had done her best but she had no idea what it meant to be a man in this world, especially a black man. Through trial and error, Shy did the best she could. Witnessing the emotional scene between her twins made Shy proud. Somewhere along the way, she'd done a good job.

Prince's cries slowly changed to weeping as he sat with his head hung low. Prince jerked upright and gasped. He felt Jayden move. Jayden had clasped his brother's hand by moving his fingers. Prince was certain of it.

"Jayden, can you hear me, bro? Squeeze my hand again," Prince begged.

Shy rushed into the room. She stood on the opposite side of the bed and took Jayden's left hand into hers.

"Baby, Mommy's here. Give us a sign if you can hear us," Shy asked excitedly.

Shy and Prince waited patiently for Jayden to respond to their voices. He looked so weak and fragile. They stood over him with tears dropping down on the blankets covering Jayden. Shy thought that maybe Prince wanted his brother back so bad that he'd imagined Jayden moving.

"Jay, come on, man, holla at me." Prince encouraged Jayden to move.

"Do it for Mommy, baby. Can you hear us?"

Shy and Prince didn't have to wait long for proof that Jayden could hear them. Jayden moved his hands with just enough pressure for his family to feel it. His wiggling fingers brushed on both hands simultaneously.

Prince's tears turned into joy. His brother was going to be okay. He sat back down in the chair. "I'm right here, bro." Prince took a deep breath and silently thanked God for His forgiveness. "I'm not leaving you by ya 'self."

Shy broke down into tears. She bent over and held her son. Knowing Jayden could hear her meant he was fighting to stay alive. Shy knew without a doubt that Jayden could win the fight. He was a McGee.

Chapter 30

Look at This Bitch . . .

Shy used a washcloth to wipe down Jayden's legs while Brianna scrubbed his chest and arms. The nurse was happy to hear she had one less patient to give a sponge bath. The patient's mother and girlfriend would work things out.

"Like I was saying, Baby Girl has been begging to visit you. I told her you were still tired and taking a nap, so you have to wake up before that girl has a tantrum," Shy half joked. She felt Jayden could hear her and Shy decided to have a one-way conversation with him. After they got him cleaned up, Brianna planned to read him a book.

"Well, good morning, Ms. McGee," Dr. Fitzgerald gave a slight nod in Shy's direction. "How did I know I would find you in here?" Dr. Fitzgerald checked the machines helping to keep Jayden alive.

"Good morning," Brianna and Shy said simultaneously.

"Ms. McGee, I need to speak with you. Will you please follow me?" Dr. Fitzgerald stepped toward the door but waited for Shy to join him.

"Brianna, be sure to rub the cocoa butter lotion on his legs. You finish up and I'll be back in a minute," Shy promised.

Shy followed the doctor down the hall to the family room where Prince was cowered in a corner taking a nap. She was unhappy to find Tara there along with Cherise and Raequan. It upset Shy to find enemies that close to her son when he was oblivious to their presence. Just when Shy opened her mouth to cuss everybody out, Dr. Fitzgerald explained their presence.

"I requested those tested yesterday to be here. It will save a lot of time this way," Dr. Fitzgerald explained.

Quincy, Karl, and C-Lok sat quietly while the doctor took charge of the room. They knew Shy was a ticking time bomb. She could explode at any minute. For the sake of everyone involved, the men sat at attention.

"I didn't realize you actually tested everyone. I thought Prince and I would be the safest donors," Shy said, irritated.

"We want to help Jayden so we were tested. You never know what might happen," Cherise interrupted with a nervous smile.

Shy looked at Cherise like she'd just blown morning breath in her face. She was not impressed. Cherise and Raequan showing love meant nothing to Shy. It was just another way for the mother and son team to keep tabs on Jayden's condition. Shy stared Cherise down as she stood with her arms crossed and lip twisted. Prince woke up but remained seated where he lay. He paid close attention to the room. This was his second time seeing Raequan since their fight. Prince tightened his jaw and breathed deeply as he looked at Raequan. Anger and hate raced through Prince at lightning speed. For as much as he hated Raequan, Prince loved his brother more. *I've got plenty of time to drop his ass. All that matters to me now is taking care of my fam,* Prince told himself.

Dr. Fitzgerald cleared his throat and gave one last read of the chart in hand.

"There's no surprise that Jayden's identical twin brother is a perfect match. That is wonderful news." Dr. Fitzgerald scanned over the papers again. "Ms. McGee, if anything goes wrong, you and the half-brother are good matches."

Cherise and Tara gave slight gasps at the doctor's announcement. Cherise's heart raced and sweat beads formed on her forehead. She was having trouble breathing.

"What half-brother? He doesn't have any half-brother. You must mean my nephew Quincy is a match. He'd have some of my traits since his mother is my sister," Shy clarified for the record. A mistake had been made somewhere in the testing process.

Dr. Fitzgerald flipped two papers over and confirmed the test results. He'd gone over them so many times that morning he practically had everything memorized.

"Yes, here it is. According to the blood test, which includes DNA, the young man shares the same male, or fathers, markers as the twins." Dr. Fitzgerald was oblivious to the implications.

"Who? Quincy?" Shy demanded angrily. Her eyes were the size of half dollars and agitation took over thoughts. Was that the reason for Tara's jealousy? Had she and Melvin slept together? Shy had her fist ready to go on her sister again.

Tara delighted in the thought that Shy might find out that Melvin was not a perfect husband.

"No, not Quincy. Raequan Jackson, no relation, is the twins' half-brother." Dr. Fitzgerald unknowingly revealed the truth Cherise had planned to take to her grave.

Prince jumped to his feet. C-Lok, Karl, and Quincy followed suit. Shy was in shock. She was unable to move a muscle. *When was Melvin fuckin' with Cher-*

ise? There's no way they could have been gettin' it in without me knowing. He would never cross that line, especially with my best friend, thought Shy.

There it was for the world to see. Cherise's secret was out. The night of their high school graduation was just the beginning of many three-way trysts with her, B-Boy, and Melvin. It happened two or three times a year. Cherise's jealous heart gave her cause to betray her best friend. B-Boy always got the three of them together. He liked watching another man bang out his woman but it couldn't be just any nigga. B-Boy always lured Melvin in after a long night of drinking moonshine and smoking weed. Cherise kept their secret close to her chest.

There was nothing Cherise could say to explain her position so she said nothing. Cherise knew how Shy operated. She was afraid Shy was going to come for her. Raequan stood by his mother with a stupid look on his face. He stared at Prince as if to say, "I got street cred now, nigga." Raequan was being arrogant about the situation. Being a McGee mattered on the streets and he wanted the status Prince always had. Raequan was anxious to spread the word.

Prince was stunned by the news. He didn't care what the test said, there's no way Raequan shared his bloodline. Karl walked over to comfort and restrain Shy. C-Lok pulled Prince down next to him on the couch. Melvin's sins had been unearthed and that meant turmoil, but there was a bigger issue at hand. Jayden needed a kidney. Prince suspected that Raequan was the reason behind it all.

"Remember, we're here about Jayden. Nothing else matters right now," Karl said to Shy.

Shy felt homicidal and wasn't trying to hear Karl. She had temporarily found the strength to contain herself. Shy knew she could forgive him of his sins if it weren't for the fact that her best friend was Melvin's bitch on the side. The weight of her husband's betrayal was overwhelming. Knowing that Cherise and Melvin played with her heart in the most disrespectful manner hurt so bad Shy felt as if she wanted to die.

"Treachery comes with a high price, you scandalous bitch." Shy lunged at Cherise. No one was able to stop her. Shy wrapped her hands around Cherise's neck and put all of her strength into choking her out.

"Get her," Karl yelled as he and C-Lok tried to pry Shy and Cherise apart.

"I'm trying but Shy ain't letting go," C-Lok replied. He couldn't believe how strong she was.

Despite the devastating news, Prince remained focused on his brother. He had his mother by the arms as he begged her not to kill Cherise. "Ma! Don't do this here. Mommy, let her go," Prince urged.

The three men continued to scuffle with Shy. She had a vice-like grip around Cherise's neck and would not let go. Cherise was seconds away from passing out.

"Mommy, let her go. Jayden needs you," Prince implored his mother.

Hearing her son's name snapped Shy back to reality. She held Cherise's life in her hands. At that moment, Shy decided that being choked to death was too kind. Shy was going to torment Cherise but Jayden trumped her need for immediate retribution. Shy released her grasp, causing Cherise to fall to the tiled floor.

Prince hugged his mother for dear life. He was giving her time to catch her breath and refocus on saving Jayden's life. After Prince promised Shy that their plot for revenge would be relentless, she took a deep breath and apologized to the doctor. It was time to move on.

"Am I right to assume the twin will be donating a kidney to his brother?" Dr. Fitzgerald was uncomfortable. He had no idea that the test results would open Pandora's Box. The only thing that concerned him was saving his patient. They needed to get Prince and Jayden into the operating room. Time was of the essence.

"Yes, Prince is giving Jayden a kidney. When will the surgeries take place?" Shy asked with a tight throat.

"Right now. Prince, let's get you prepped for the operation. Jayden's waiting on your gift." Dr. Fitzgerald smiled.

"I'm ready," Prince responded without hesitation. "I want my brother back. I'm with you, doc." Prince gave Shy a long, tight hug and kiss on the cheek.

"I love you, Prince, and I'm so proud of you," Shy cried.

"Love you too, Ma. That bullshit will be dealt with later. We need to tell Jayden what's up with the operation." Prince held his mother's hand.

Shy and Prince headed for Jayden's room hand in hand. The three of them needed some time together before Prince was wheeled away. Everyone else in the room was left in mayhem. Cherise may very well have been taking her last breaths on earth. C-Lok would hold off on the retribution until Shy was ready to make a move.

"You shoulda been told me this shit," Raequan said, almost jovial. He was so focused on how his life was going to improve that the thought of a deadly war never crossed his mind. A street battle with Shy was all Cherise could think about. There was no doubt Shy would get C-Lok and Bossy involved. She was ill-equipped to face her enemy in combat.

Chapter 31

Strong as Steel

After multiple hours on operating tables and days spent in ICU, the twins were resting comfortably side by side in a regular room. Dr. Fitzgerald had been sympathetic with their family issues. He arranged for them to share a semi-private room. It was the first time Prince and Jayden had shared a room in seven years. Shy couldn't have been happier. Princess was even allowed to visit her brothers. Brianna and Monica helped her make the twins some macaroni artwork and colorful get well cards. Princess was looking forward to their return home, in part because Shy promised she could help take care of them.

Dr. Fitzgerald and Nurse Gordon were impressed with the twins' recovery. Jayden's turnaround was nothing short of a miracle. Shy's dedication to them was evident. She stayed by their side every day. Dr. Fitzgerald was pleased to deliver some good news.

"Good morning, sons, how'd you rest last night?"

"As good as we could with nurses waking us up every two hours," Jayden joked.

"That's the best part about being in here. Dr. Fitzgerald, you got some fine broads walking around here." Prince unconsciously adjusted his manhood when he spoke. Everyone laughed at Prince.

"Good morning, Ms. McGee," Dr. Fitzgerald greeted.

"Good morning, Dr. Fitzgerald. How are my boys doing and when can I take them home?" Shy inquired.

"Prince can go home today. Jayden will follow in a couple of days, perhaps a week at most. We want to keep close attention to how his body is reacting to the new kidney."

Dr. Fitzgerald examined Jayden and was pleased with how strong Jayden had become. He completed his assessment of both boys before excusing himself to get started on getting Prince's release papers in order.

He hated leaving his brother behind but Prince was ecstatic to be home. Taking a hot shower and tasting his mother's cooking were his immediate goals. Prince was exhausted after the hot shower. Dr. Fitzgerald warned him to take things slow because his body was still healing. The level of fatigue took Prince by surprise. He had to take a nap.

Shy and Princess went in search of Prince shortly after hearing the shower water turn off. He wasn't in his room when Shy and Princess went to check on him. Shy automatically knew he had gotten into her bed. The sight brought back a flood of memories that made Shy's heart smile. Shy thought back to all of the times Prince had crawled into his parents' bed. Prince had always found comfort being in his mother's presence. He'd lie and watch movies or just talk to his mother.

"Shhh, he's sleeping," Princess whispered.

"Do me a favor and stay here with him while I go cook. Can you watch your brother for me?"

"Yeah, I can watch him. I'm going to lie on this pillow in case he needs something. Will you put on a movie for me so I won't be bored?" Princess said excitedly.

It wasn't long before she fell asleep next to her big brother. Shy couldn't help but snap a few pictures of her babies. She left them to rest, feeling blessed.

Prince being comfortable was Shy's main focus at hand. Shy finished with the small details in the family room. The goal was to put the PS3, TV remotes, blankets, pillows, and anything Prince might need within reach. Shy had Monica purchase a dorm room-sized refrigerator and an oversized La-Z-Boy that Prince could sleep on comfortably.

Shy was in the kitchen prepping dinner when the doorbell chimed. NuNu and Mike Frank stood on the porch, looking like young boys with crushes on the teacher. They both blushed when Shy invited them into the house.

"Hi, Miss Shy." NuNu gave his friend's mother a hug with Mike Frank following suit. "We heard Prince was home. We just wanted to check him out, if you don't mind."

"He's in the family room. Prince just woke up a little while ago. I don't mind you visiting but don't stay too long; he's still recovering," Shy stated. She giggled at the obvious discomfort the two boys had when talking to her. Their obvious crush on her was amusing.

Shy returned to her task of preparing dinner. Princess was reenergized from her nap and ready to fulfill her role as mother's helper. "Okay, Mommy, what do we do first?"

Prince was relaxing in his new favorite chair surrounded by teddy bears and baby dolls. Princess left them to watch him while she helped cook. Even Prince had to giggle at the sight when NuNu and Mike Frank entered the room. The new NBA game on PS3 had just come out and Prince was trying to master the game.

"What's up, bro?" Mike Frank gave Prince dap. "You don't want it on the game, bro. We can get one in if you up to it."

Prince was happy to see his friends. Out of all his so-called friends, Mike and NuNu were the only two who cared enough about him to show support. They'd both visited him in the hospital on a number of occasions. Prince appreciated their loyalty to him and Jayden.

"It's all good, bro. We can get it in," Prince replied arrogantly. He felt his skills were honed enough to win the challenge.

Three hours later, Shy and Princess had fed everyone, including Mike Frank and NuNu, put Quincy a healthy-sized plate up, and finished cleaning the kitchen. It was almost time for Shy to go back to the hospital. Brianna had been sitting with Jayden for hours and Shy wanted to go relieve her. Prince enjoyed the company of his friends but was feeling worn out. All he wanted was another dose of pain medicine and to crawl back into his mother's bed. The stress on his body and mind was exhausting for Prince.

"A'ight, man, good lookin' out for chilling with ya nigga. I gotta go grab a nap fo' real. What are y'all 'bout to do?" Prince asked in a tired voice.

"Time to stomp da block. You already know what it is," NuNu replied.

"I can dig it," Prince said.

"We gotta holler before we rise up," NuNu informed Prince.

Prince used the remote to turn off all the electronics before focusing his attention on his boys.

"What it do?" Prince asked.

"Man, ya boy is living foul. He out spittin' hate on you, Jay, and ya pops. That dude running it down to anybody that he's really a McGee and the new king of the streets," Mike revealed.

Prince wasn't surprised by the news. After the surgery, Prince had more pressing things to focus on but he knew Raequan was problematic and not going away. Raequan had done too much for their friendship to heal. The discovery of him being a McGee made no sense to Prince. Sharing a bloodline was of no consequence for Prince; he had to lay Raequan down.

"Word is that Rae hired some young kid fresh outta juvie to drive the car that rained down on you but it was dat nigga Dwayne rolling with ya boy that day." NuNu paused to let the information sink in. Prince and Raequan had been tight all of their lives. Hearing the news had to be overwhelming for Prince. NuNu felt bad for the timing of the information but he knew it had to be told. "Prince, man, it was Rae firing on you, Jay, and Q. Rae was aiming for you but hit Jayden by mistake."

Shy walked into the room just in time to hear that her suspicions were true. Raequan tried to kill her boys. She was furious. How could a boy she had practically raised as her own turn on the only people he loved? Shy knew it was all a charade for Raequan and Cherise to be tested as donors. Looking at Prince, Shy knew her feelings would have to wait. Prince was in so much emotional pain, it showed on his face. Shy rushed into the half bathroom and grabbed the trash can. It was obvious that Prince was going to be sick.

Prince felt like he'd been hit in the chest by a jackhammer. His mind had trouble processing the information. Prince and Raequan had been like brothers their entire lives. They had done dirt, got girls, stolen, rang shots out on other people, and committed countless other crimes together. None of that mattered anymore. Raequan had abandoned camp and latched on to treachery at the speed of lightning. The pain was too much for Prince. His body ached from the surgery and thanks to Raequan, he was experiencing a setback. Shy made it back just in time. Prince leaned over the arm of the chair and vomited into the trash can. Tears escaped his eyes as his heart broke into pieces. Having to vomit after eating solid food was torture. It felt as if his insides were tearing apart. Blood soon mixed with the regurgitation, frightening Prince and Shy.

"Mommy," Prince cried out. He was doubled over in excruciating pain.

"Call nine-one-one for an ambulance, hurry," Shy demanded.

Shy grabbed her son and held on for dear life. She'd tried giving him two of his prescribed pain pills but they came right back up. Prince now lay on the floor being gently rocked back and forth by his mother. Princess kneeled down and stroked her brother's head. She remembered he liked when she played with the waves in his head.

Shy felt helpless to take away her child's pain. It was a horrible feeling for any mother. She kept her arms around Prince until the paramedics arrived. Prince had grabbed Shy's hand as he was wheeled out of the house.

"Mommy, stay with me, please," Prince sobbed. The medics had started an IV and gave him a shot of morphine for the pain. Prince was in less physical pain but the drugs did nothing for his broken heart. Shy gripped Prince's hand with Princess hanging from her other arm.

"You listen to me, baby," Shy began. "You let Mommy handle Cherise and Raequan. I promise on my soul that retributions will be made."

Chapter 32

Can't Make It Home

Prince had blood in his stomach when the medical tech wheeled him into the emergency room. He was immediately whisked off to surgery. The strain of him vomiting resulted in a burst suture. Dr. Fitzgerald was able to stop the hemorrhage and discover another vessel that would have eventually bled. Unfortunately, Jayden and Prince lay beside each other again. He was going to be fine but his recovery had taken a huge setback. Prince received a number of antibiotics intravenously to prevent any infections. The doctor's prognosis was positive. He was going to be fine. Jayden was sorry to see his brother back in the hospital. The twins worried about each other like an old married couple. Shy was relieved to know the twins would be released from the hospital in a matter of days.

Brianna and Monica took shifts with Shy so the twins were never at the hospital alone. Their bedside manners made Prince and Jayden fall in love all over again. Quincy was off on a college tour with a group of classmates or he'd be helping his cousins too. Shy would reward the girls handsomely once the twins were at home in their own beds. Until that day came, Shy had detailed plans to work out. It was time for her enemies to settle their tab.

Shy had called C-Lok and Bossy to the hospital once both of the twins were resting. She had to get to her targets before they tried to flee the city. C-Lok had additional news to share with Shy. The streets were talking. Raequan had been out playing as if he ran the streets. All of the street soldiers and generals wanted his head on a stick but C-Lok had put the word out: Raequan was his, he was off-limits.

"We all knew Raequan's stupid ass didn't come up with this shit on his own," Bossy stated.

"I've been thinking about beating his momma to death, literally. Her deception is an entirely different degree of crime. We'll come back to her felony later. Tell me what's up with Raequan. I'm sure Cherise didn't talk him into turning on Prince, not enough to try to kill him," Shy said, agitated.

"No, she didn't, but you're not going to like the answer. That little nigga's been working with Roberts all this time," C-Lok announced.

"Yea, I know. What the fuck was that about?" Shy fumed.

"That bitch nigga Roberts has been breathing for too long. When I heard Roberts had Raequan fuckin' with nephew while they did their bids I knew it was time to check that niggas ticket. One of those idiots should've realized how loud the streets talk. They plan was flawed from the jump but payback's a bitch," C-Lok fumed at the thought.

With everything that happened, Shy had given little thought to her former best friend and her bastard offspring. She couldn't understand why Cherise and Raequan had moved so far to the left. Cherise had betrayed her and acted as if their friendship never mattered. If anyone had the right to be hurt and out for revenge, Shy did. As far as Shy was concerned, Cherise had spit

in her face every day that she pretended she wasn't
sleeping with Melvin. Cherise was aware of the possible punishment Shy would hand her just for involving her kids. That was totally unjustifiable. Shy sat at
the top of the pyramid next to C-Lok and Bossy. It was
understood that Shy was a silent partner. She never got
her hands dirty. Melvin and C-Lok wanted it that way
but Shy was supposed to be financially stable and the
second powerful woman in Youngstown, second only
to Bossy. She was the third member of the board of
directors and for the first time since Melvin was killed,
Shy was ready to make an executive decision.

"How do you want to handle this?" Bossy inquired.

"Ultimate crimes call for the ultimate punishment.
Get at the peons first; hit up Raequan before the bitch.
I'm doing her and Roberts myself," Shy announced
before walking away. The official order had been given;
there was nothing more to be said.

Roberts paced the worn carpet, feeling a mixed bag
of emotions. He was angry, frustrated, and scared simultaneously. His two partners in crime had turned
out to be mere hired peons. Both Raequan and Dwayne
had failed to deliver the desired results of their assign-
ments. Relying on boys to do a man's job had been
Roberts's mistake but his hands were tied. The entire
plan had blown up in his face.

Raequan was already in with the McGee family. Roberts had played on Raequan's shortcomings and insecuri-
ties in order to manipulate him into betraying his loved
ones. Had Raequan gotten the job done, Prince would be
dead. Getting rid of a seventeen-year-old hustler wasn't
difficult, not in Roberts's mind. Dwayne had been assigned to getting close with Shy and failed miserably.

Pacing the floor had done nothing to help clear Roberts's head. Roberts decided he needed a drink to calm his nerves. He was down to his last twenty dollars until payday. His beat-up Chrysler was running on less than a quarter of a tank of gas so Roberts had a decision to make. Give his last few dollars to the gas station attendant so he could get back and forth to work, or hand it over to the barmaid working at the corner hole in the wall.

Roberts sat on the barstool, wallowing in the hell he'd created. Life had treated him unfairly for far too long. Working as an undercover narcotics officer was a dangerous job but the benefits had proven addictive for the ex-cop. He missed the days of financial comfort and power he held behind the badge. Roberts caught a glance of himself in the mirror behind the bar and found a stranger looking back. His dark chocolate complexion looked ashy and rough. The dark eyes women used to describe as sexy were cold and sunken. It had been weeks since he stepped foot in a barbershop and he was in dire need of a haircut and shave. His appearance was a testament to the way he felt on the inside.

"Hey, baby, you want a refill?"

The young, sexy barmaid interrupted Roberts and his pity party. He looked the pretty woman up and down. She was blessed with natural green eyes and sandy brown hair. Her body was full in all the right places; her creamy mocha skin looked smooth and soft. She was easily as close to perfect as any woman Roberts had ever seen. This woman was no older than thirty and had probably worked as a stripper at some point in her life. Roberts was sure she banked large dollar amounts in tips every night.

"Did you hear me, suga'? You ready for another one? It's dollar night, so drink up." She smiled at Roberts, causing his penis to jump to attention.

"My bad, Miss Lady. Yeah, keep 'em coming," Roberts flirted.

"Don't worry, daddy, Vanilla will take care of you," she said and brushed her hair off her left shoulder.

"Did you just start working here? Because I haven't seen you before."

"So, that makes you a regular customer. This is my first week here. My name is Vanilla so you holler for me when your glass is empty," Vanilla instructed. She winked her eye before moving on to another bar patron.

She had agreed to do a favor for a close friend who always rewarded her generously. Everything her friend asked of her was outside of legal parameters but Vanilla Cream Johnson was up for the task. Men had always melted in her hands. Vanilla held a Master's in hustling men and was proud to be titled a gold digger. There was no shame in her game. Many men had run through Vanilla's legs but never for free. Rent, utility bills, car notes, shopping sprees, expensive hair weaves: it all defined who she was. Vanilla used older men for her necessities and the younger ones to satisfy her healthy sexual appetite.

Vanilla was not tending bar for the money; she was on assignment. She had her target in sight and was well prepared to fulfill the contract. By the end of the night, Roberts wouldn't be able to recover from what Vanilla would put on him.

Roberts mindlessly tossed back drink after drink. He watched Vanilla's hips sway from side to side all night. The more he drank the more attention she gave the washed-up detective. Alcohol to Roberts was like crack to a dope fiend. The more he consumed, the more his body craved it.

"You look like you're past your limit. You're two sheets to the wind, suga'. I'm cutting you off," Vanilla said in her sexiest voice. It was last call at the bar and time to execute her plan.

Roberts opened his mouth to respond but nothing came out. He was unable to converse with the object of his desire. Something was not right. The number of drinks he'd tossed back was routine. Roberts shook his head in attempt to clear his mind but it only made things worse. He was dizzy, nauseated, and embarrassed.

"Hey, are you all right, suga'? You're not looking too good." Vanilla faked concern. She reached out and grabbed his hand.

Roberts felt the warmth of her skin on top of his own. He was elated. The simple gesture was the only human contact he'd had in months. Even then it was with a prostitute. His head was having brief moments of clarity in which he wanted to beg Vanilla to go home with him. After multiple attempts, Roberts found his voice.

"I'm straight." Roberts gave an uncomfortable laugh. "I must have tossed back one drink too many." Roberts cleared his throat and tried to steady himself on the barstool.

"Here, drink some water to bring your high down," Vanilla instructed. She opened the bottle of water for her mark. It was late and she needed to speed up the process. Being in his company was uncomfortable. Vanilla found Roberts to be creepy. "I know you're not trying to drive home." Vanilla faked concern.

"My house is down the block. I walked." Roberts slurred each word. The cold water felt refreshing going down the back of his throat. After two big gulps, Roberts set the bottle of water on the bar and stood on his feet using the bar to steady himself.

"You look shaky to me. I don't have to help close the bar. Why don't I help you home?" Vanilla smirked. Knowing no man would turn down her offer, Vanilla retrieved her purse and bag from their hiding place. She walked around the bar to join Roberts.

His eyesight was blurry but a blind man would appreciate the body on Vanilla. Roberts's drunken mind raced with thought of putting Vanilla is various sexual positions. He wondered if she was flexible.

Vanilla put her arm around Roberts's waist and led him out the door. Out on the street Roberts felt a small measure of clarity as the wind blew in his face. He glanced over at the woman on his arm and again became mesmerized by her beauty. The logical question would've been what a woman of her caliber was doing with a loser like him. With no money, no car, and a lack of personal grooming, he was clearly beneath a confident, strong woman like Vanilla. Alcohol was a confidence builder pulling him right into her spider web of deceit. Roberts was like a puppy dog on a leash being yanked around by its abusive owner. He was oblivious to the effect the woman he lusted after would have on his very short future.

"This is my place. You're going to help me inside aren't you?" Roberts forced his crooked mouth into a smile. There were so many things he wanted to do to Vanilla. He needed to get to his little blue pills before moving things forward. Vanilla smiled and helped Roberts ascend the rickety steps leading to his front door.

Vanilla frowned at the foul order that smacked her in the face upon entering the run-down apartment. She was outdone by the sight. *Why would he invite people in here? He should be embarrassed and ashamed. Let me get this fool out of his misery and get the hell out of here. C-Lok gonna pay me double for this shit.*

"I know it needs cleaning but it's a place to lay my head," Roberts offered as a weak explanation for the way he lived. He pushed some dirty clothes off the old, dusty couch to make room for his company to have a seat. "Have a seat and I'll get us a drink." Vanilla remained standing.

"Don't you think that's a bad idea? You've had plenty of alcohol tonight," Vanilla reminded her host. She frowned at the thought of drinking or eating in her current environment.

Roberts ran his rough hands over Vanilla's hips and behind. He took in all the contours of her body and became excited.

"You're probably right. I don't have anything else to offer you," Roberts said apologetically. His mind was still reeling from the alcohol but it had done nothing to stop his sexual desires. Vanilla did not protest or move when Roberts continued to molest her body with his hands. That gave him the green light to continue. He had to take a Viagra before going in for the kill. "Go on and chill for a minute while I go in the back. It won't take me long."

Vanilla dug through her purse in search of the murder weapon. She'd found it just in time. "Look at what I found." Vanilla held up a bag of cocaine.

Roberts was excited Vanilla got down the way he liked. He responded like a kid in a candy store. A good hit trumped a stiff drink every time. Obviously an addict, Roberts pushed the old newspapers, food, and mail from the coffee table. Vanilla poured half an ounce of coke on a magazine cover. Roberts was now on bended knee in front of the table. It didn't matter that his guest had not joined him on the floor. Nothing could make Vanilla touch anything in the filthy domicile. She used her long nail to form three lines. Roberts had his nose running along the magazine cover before Vanilla pulled her hand back. His left nostril took in the drug as if it were a vacuum. Seconds later, Roberts lifted his head back and pinched his nose. "That's some good shit," Roberts said before it hit him. He wiped his bloody nose with his shirt sleeve as his eyes began to water. Something was wrong. The inside of his nose and throat felt like they were being shredded.

"What da fuck?" Roberts began to panic.

"Do you feel that shit? It's off the hook and it'll be the last hit you ever take," Vanilla said with a huge grin.

Blood started gushing from his nose onto the floor. Roberts looked into Vanilla's eyes, pleading for help. Vanilla laughed at him.

"I have a message for you, Keith Roberts. The McGee family says you should tell Silk they sent their love. I'm also supposed to tell you that Melvin wins from the grave again." Vanilla exited through the back door, leaving Roberts to suffer his excruciating death alone.

The cocaine was mixed with finely ground shards of glass and gun powder. Once Roberts introduced the mix into his body his fate was set. Everything in its path was cut by the glass as the fatal mix entered his system. It was a slow and painful way to die. Just the way Shy felt her husband's killer and son's tormentor deserved to leave the earth, on a slow ride to hell.

Shy watched the twins sleep in their hospital beds as she walked Princess to sleep when she received the text she'd been waiting to receive: One-way departure left on time. She slept in the same position all night. It was her best full night's rest in seven years.

Chapter 33

Worst Day Ever

Cherise listened intently to Raequan's phone conversation. From what she could gather, payback had finally caught up with Melvin's killer. If anyone deserved a painful demise, Cherise felt Roberts topped the list. Raequan made a statement that gave Cherise cause to pause. She wondered if Prince was behind Roberts's untimely death or if Shy had finally found the balls to take care of him herself. Seven years to wait for retribution was ridiculous in Cherise's opinion, especially when the resources were at your fingertips. If C-Lok were her brother, Roberts would've been six feet under the day after he pulled the trigger on Melvin. One of the things that aggravated Cherise about Shy was her habit of overthinking every move she made. Cherise lived by the "just do it" mantra.

Raequan had left his mother in the dark about his continued affiliation with Roberts. She was clueless to the fact that he had remained involved with Roberts even after his release from juvenile hall. Cherise reached for her laptop and searched for details about Roberts's death. Her search netted multiple results. There it was in black and white, confirmation of the cause of death: a drug overdose. Roberts was an arrogant, holier-than-thou alcoholic drug addict who'd earned the type of death he suffered, in Cherise's opinion.

"That fool is weak as hell." Raequan laughed as he got up from the table.

"Did he say what happened?" Cherise asked as if she didn't already know the answer.

"That asshole Roberts got a hit of some pure white girl and it took him out. Fuck him, dat nigga had it comin'," Raequan spat.

Raequan and Cherise had yet to discuss his true paternity. Cherise was ashamed about the situation and couldn't find the right words to explain the situation to her son. She knew she had to tell Raequan her side of the story before B-Boy did. He would make sure she came out looking like a whore in the habit of taking on two men at a time. There was much more to the story that Cherise wanted her son to understand. How does that conversation get started?

"Yeah, he did, and such is life." Cherise squirmed in her seat.

"Whatever, man, I got some runs to make so I'll get up with you later."

"Rae, we need to talk."

"No, we don't, man. Ain't shit to talk about," Raequan said, annoyed.

"I know you have some questions about Boy not being your real dad. We have to talk about it," Cherise said with a shaky voice.

Raequan turned to face Cherise with a scowl on his face. By the look in his eyes, Cherise could see the weight of the hate and anger he carried in his heart. She wanted so bad to reach out and hold her son in her arms. They faced each other as if in a standoff. Her eyes welled with tears; his scowl became more pronounced.

"No, we don't," Raequan responded and slammed the door behind him, leaving Cherise alone with her quilt and shame.

Cherise knew Raequan wasn't the only person she owed an explanation. She had stayed away from Shy to give her time to calm down. Truth be told, Cherise was scared as hell of Shy. Cherise already knew what it was. Whenever Shy grew quiet about circumstances that called for an emotion other than anger, it was best to pull back and give her all the time she needed to deal. Shy had every right to feel betrayed, hurt, angry, and vengeful. Cherise was scared of how those feelings would manifest themselves. Cherise had been trying to figure out an explanation Shy would understand. How could she possibly justify bearing a child fathered by her best friend's husband? The secret was never meant to be uncovered. It was a shame Cherise intended to carry to her grave. How could she have been so stupid? Letting Raequan be tested as a possible donor was reckless on her part. Not once did Cherise think about DNA being part of the process.

In spite of their feelings about each other, Cherise loved Shy's kids, including Prince. Jayden was always excited to be around her and that made Cherise feel special and loved. Jayden was the child she'd hoped Raequan would emulate. The environment in which his parents had raised him pushed Raequan out to the streets in search of approval and attention. Maybe things would've turned out differently had Cherise been honest about his paternity at the time of his birth. Cherise shook her head of more thoughts of shoulda-woulda-coulda's. There was no point wishing for a different past. Chasing after the impossible had filled her life with chaos.

From the beginning of their teenage love affairs, Cherise envied the way Melvin loved and respected Shy. He opened doors for her, bought her gifts, and let the streets know he had love for her in his heart. Melvin did everything Shy wanted and anything he had to do when it meant keeping her happy. She had done the same for him, even when Melvin's flaws surfaced. His love for Shy didn't keep him from breaking her heart a handful of times. Even during those heart-wrenching times, Melvin and Shy never stopped loving each other. When their relationship was good, they kept falling in love. The two of them had an unbreakable connection, even in death. There were times when Cherise hated them both for having what she'd never possess. B-Boy had shown his love by beating her half to death. Believing it was all she deserved, Cherise settled with his selfish and brutal love.

In reality, Cherise slept with Melvin wanting a taste of Shy's life. The ménages à trois had gone down three times in a ten-year span. Melvin was a willing participant only one of those times. Cherise was in on getting Melvin so high that he'd black out. After the night of high school graduation, Melvin vowed it would never happen again. He knew sleeping with his girlfriend's best friend had crossed a few lines. Shy would have every right to never forgive him if she found out. That's what Cherise had to let Shy know. Shy could hate her but she owed it to Melvin to set things straight. He never knew Raequan was his or that the possibility even existed.

Running late, Cherise drove as fast as she could to make her meeting on time. Cherise was relieved to find the parking lot empty when she arrived. She was meeting with her drug connection to negotiate new prices and re-up. Prince had snatched a lot of customers from her when he defected. Cherise was forced to lower the amount of weight she usually copped. Her supplier was not happy. Neither was she; her wallet was feeling the pain and that affected her livelihood.

Cherise turned on her car alarm and headed to the café's back door. What she saw caused her to pause as she went to put the key in the deadbolt lock. Something wasn't right. The door was off its hinges and the frame was busted. Her heart began to race. Cherise pushed the door out of the way and entered the kitchen area of the establishment. She'd been robbed. All of her equipment had been vandalized. It would cost her a small fortune to replace the industrial-sized stove, refrigerator, and small appliances. Cherise was speechless. Her mind went blank. She couldn't figure out how anyone got in; the alarm system should have stopped them in their tracks. As she looked at the clutter, Cherise walked slowly toward her office. There was no way anyone could've found her safe or stash spot. When she reached the room, Cherise quickly discovered that she was wrong. Files were scattered about, her desk and cabinets turned over. The room was almost unrecognizable. A chill rushed up her spine as she covered her mouth to prevent the scream from echoing throughout the room. The safe was standing wide open and empty. The trap door leading to the basement was standing open. She rushed down the stairs to find her stash was gone. Whoever was behind the robbery had taken her out with one shot. They had gotten away with thirty kilos of pure heroin and seventeen packages of cocaine. Cherise had made the mistake of storing all of her money in one place. There had been over $200,000 in the safe. She felt like a victim. Tears streamed down her face. Her entire life had spun out of control. The business was out of commission, her best friend wanted her dead, and she'd been thrust into debt with her connect.

"Damn, Cherise, it looks like somebody got you."

Cherise nearly jumped out of her skin. She'd forgotten all about the meeting. Now she had to figure out how to explain that his money and product were gone along with her own. She had no means to recover the loss. *Life is a miserable bitch,* thought Cherise.

That morning when Cherise climbed out of bed, she was ill prepared for the day ahead. She was in financial ruins and had nowhere to turn. Every dime to her name was in that thief-proof safe. There was insurance on the business but the payout would only be a small percentage of what Cherise owed her connect. Cherise was stuck. By the time she finally made it home Cherise was emotionally drained. Unable to muster up the energy to walk into her house from the garage, Cherise sat in her car and cried. Her entire life had rolled downhill at lightning speed. There was no point asking why it had happened to her because she already knew the answer: karma was a bitch. She had done a lot of wrong in her life and it had all come back around 360 degrees.

She grabbed her purse from the back seat and walked into her home. Her eyes were bloodshot and puffy from all the crying. There had been a few times when Cherise caught herself picking up her cell to call Shy. If ever she needed a friend, it was at that time. Since the truth about Raequan's paternity was revealed Cherise had become a pariah. Bossy, Aisha, and even Terry had abandoned her. Cherise could hardly blame them. If the tides were reversed, she wouldn't trust her either.

Cherise threw her purse on the kitchen counter and was startled by a loud noise in the front room. "Rae, is that you?" Cherise went to the sink and splashed cold water on her face. She hadn't bothered to call her son about the break-in and robbery. There was nothing he could do and she needed time to figure out her next move before involving him. Cherise called out to Raequan a second time when she got no response the first time. "Raequan, come here, I need to tell you something."

"We ain't Raequan, bitch," said a masked man.

For the second time that day, Cherise felt frightened.

"Oh my God! What do you want?" Cherise cried out.

The masked intruder stormed toward Cherise and began brutally beating her where she stood. Blood gushed from her mouth and nose. Cherise was thrown to the floor and stomped on. There was nothing she could do to defend herself. The .25 revolver she carried was in her purse on the counter. She didn't have a chance. The assault seemed to go on forever. At a point, the pain was so unbearable that she prayed for death. Whoever the man was robbing her of the security everyone should have in their own home, he was careful not to take her life. Cherise was supposed to suffer. By the time it was over, Cherise couldn't move or scream for help. She lay on the kitchen floor while her house was ransacked and trashed. A mix of tears and blood pooled beneath her head.

Cherise's vision was blurred by an overhead light. Someone had turned on the kitchen light, finally discovering Cherise's battered body. It was a neighbor who saw her front door standing wide open. The police and ambulance soon followed. Even with help and medical attention, Cherise continued to pray for death.

Chapter 34

Before I Let Go

Quincy returned home from his college visits with mixed feelings. For as long as he could remember, he and Jayden had planned on attending college together. With the current circumstances, Jayden would not be leaving home anytime in the near future. The bullet that seared through his body altered their plans. Quincy felt survivor's guilt. The realization that he could have easily been laid up in the hospital next to his cousin was overwhelming. He found it difficult to keep the shooting off his mind.

Though his mother's reaction would be over the top, Quincy knew once he shared his intentions with her, she was going to explode. Tara was sitting alone in the family room reading a book. Things between mother and son had been tense since Quincy overheard her telephone conversation bashing Shy. Tara had tried to move past it but Quincy seemed reluctant to do so. Tara had no idea how bad things were with her son, but she was about to find out.

"Ma, we need to talk," Quincy announced as he sat across the room from his mother.

Tara could see the seriousness in Quincy's eyes. She inhaled deeply and braced herself for the conversation.

"Sure, how's your shoulder feeling?" Tara asked nervously.

He ignored her question and got right to the point.

"I want to put off going to college until the twins are well enough for Jayden to leave with me," Quincy explained.

"What? You can't be serious. Why would you put your future on hold for anyone?"

"It was always my intent to attend school with Jayden, you know that. He just had major surgery and is going to need time to heal. Prince isn't strong enough to help Aunt Shy take care of Jayden so I'm going to do it." Quincy frowned.

"Look, I know you love your cousins but there's no way your dad and I will back you on this," Tara said loud and dismissively.

Quincy wasn't surprised by his mother's reaction. He expected her to yell and go off the deep end.

"Jayden would do the same for me. I'm not saying that college is out the picture. I can enroll in Kent State and take classes online or at their local campus. After a year, I can transfer to a university but for now, I'm staying."

"You'll do what I say you're going to do. You keep in mind that being with your cousins is what got you shot. I can't believe you still want to associate with them," Tara said, frustrated.

"Ma, the twins aren't some childhood friends. They're my family and I'd never turn my back on them."

Quincy was outdone by his mother's attitude. It was as if she had no loyalty to anyone but herself. He doubted that keeping him away from the twins had anything to do with the shooting. Quincy was convinced it was all about his mother's relationship with her sister.

"You haven't thought this through. As long as you're living in this house and dependent on us, you will be sticking with your original plans whether Jayden is with you or not," Tara threatened with attitude. "He's not your responsibility."

"I'm going to live with Aunt Shy," Quincy jabbed effortlessly.

Tara was sure she'd heard her son wrong. Did he just say he was going to live with Shy? Would he really leave home to be with Shy? She was hurt and angry simultaneously. Quincy had been acting different since the shooting. He was withdrawn and despondent. Tara had spoken with her husband about sending Quincy to a psychologist. Bruce thought it might've been a good idea but wanted Quincy to make the decision on what happened in his life. He knew Quincy was mature enough to know that asking for help was not a sign of weakness but one of strength. Tara knew she should have taken Quincy but like always, she'd relented to Bruce's decision. This desire to live with Shy had to be a sign of post-traumatic stress.

"No, you are not," Tara said and stood up from the rocking chair.

"Yeah, Ma, I am. Aunt Shy's going to need help and I want to be there for her. As far as depending on you to help with school, I'm good." Quincy also stood up.

"What do you mean, you're good?"

"I know there's not enough money in my college fund to pay for school. If the money is available I wouldn't be applying for grants and loans. I'm not stupid, Ma."

"I never said you were, Quincy, but you're about to cross the line."

"Uncle C said he'll pay for me to go to college. He's going to take care of tuition, housing, and anything else I need. Unc said all I have to do is concentrate on school and making it out of here. There's nothing you can say to keep me from helping out with the twins, either," Quincy said defiantly. He was ready to counter every excuse. His mother was right; he was already on the verge of disrespecting Tara if she pushed things too far.

"Just who do my brother and sister think they are? You're my son, not theirs. They have no right to interfere with what goes on in my house. I'm sick of them both," Tara fumed. She was jealous that C-Lok had the means to pay for Quincy to go to a top HBCU and angry that Quincy would rather be with Shy than with her. From Tara's point of view, her siblings' lives were easy. They didn't worry about money but she did daily. Melvin had spoiled Shy with material items, support, friendship, and love consistently. Tara so desperately wanted that in her own marriage. Tara resented Shy for having had the life she should've been living. Her union had been drained of its love years ago. All she had was her son and now he was trying to walk away.

"They're family and are looking out for me. It doesn't matter because I'm going to stay with Aunt Shy for a year or so until Jayden can leave. I already have my own room over there anyway. Aunt Shy said it was okay."

"Shy should've found out if this plan is okay with me. She's been trying to keep you from me all your life and I'm sick of it," Tara said, throwing her hands up. "This is my fault. I let you spend too much time with them."

Quincy struggled to understand his mother. He had substituted the twins for the brothers he never had. They were the same age and got along well. Shy often joked that she'd had triplets not twins. She never kept Quincy away from his cousins. The McGee family enjoyed having Quincy around, that's why he had his own room in their home. Tara had allowed him to spend his time at Shy's house. That's why her attitude left him bewildered.

There was far too much going on around him and Quincy needed a break. He also needed to do something for Jayden. The questions of "what if" and "why not" played in Quincy's mind like a scratched compact disk. Quincy believed he could quiet the haunting questions by being instrumental in Jayden's recovery. He was determined to do as much as he could to get the twins healthy. His parents had to understand his plight. Quincy had approached his dad about the idea three days ago. With very little hesitation, Bruce gave Quincy his okay. He saw the helplessness in his son's eyes. Bruce hoped Quincy would be able to heal by taking care of Prince and Jayden. The only stipulation was for Quincy to get his mother to go along with his plan.

Quincy was torn. His mind was made up; he would be moved by the end of the day. There wasn't a thing Tara could do or say to change Quincy's mind. While he loved his parents, Quincy just wasn't happy with their life. He saw less of his father, who was hardly ever home. Quincy use to be embarrassed by the outward signs of affection between his parents. Lately, they barely spoke and never touched. Instead of waiting on her husband hand and foot, Tara's time was passed by phone conversations or playing online poker. The way his parents interacted had deteriorated so that Quincy could see the breakup looming in the near future. Quincy wondered if they'd stayed together for his sake. If that were the case, Quincy didn't want the weight on his shoulders.

"This argument is futile because your father will never approve of you living with Shy," Tara said, feeling victorious.

"Dad gave me his permission three days ago," Quincy countered, standing firm with his position.

She was shocked. Bruce hadn't said anything to her about Quincy wanting to leave home. She was angry with his failure to discuss this serious issue with her. He was added to Tara's list of untrustworthy people.

Tara wanted to embrace her son and tell him how much love she held in her heart for him. The only time she showed affection was during the honeymoon period with her husband. It was difficult to give hugs and express her love. Quincy hadn't received many hugs, positive reinforcements, or affirmation from his mother. He'd received those things from Shy and for that, Tara was resentful. She hadn't meant to be cold-hearted; it was a defense mechanism from childhood.

"Look, Ma, Aunt Shy has always been good to me. You know how I feel about Jayden and Prince," Quincy said.

"Why doesn't Jayden move in here with us? I'll take care of him and Shy can take care of Prince. That will take a huge load off Shy and you can stay here. This way, everybody will be happy," Tara said excitedly.

Tara took pause. For a fleeting second, she was excited to believe Shy would see the logic in Jayden convalescing with her. He would be well taken care of by someone who loved him and Shy could focus on Prince. That's the way it should've always been, according to Tara.

"My mind is made up. After the way you've treated her Aunt Shy's not going for that. What do you have against her?"

"It's going to work as long as Shy listens to reason. Anyway, she can't play nursemaid to two sick kids, take care of a little girl, and work a full-time job," Tara mindlessly uttered.

"Ma, you aren't even speaking. Did you forget about what happened at the hospital? Aunt Shy's not going with that. Look, Ma, I'm moving in with her so she won't be alone."

Quincy was tired of going back and forth on the topic. It was getting them nowhere. He picked up his over-packed duffle bag and put it on his good shoulder.

"My sister is not your responsibility. Why does everybody take care of Shy? I'm so sick of that shit. Shy is not helpless," Tara said with aggravation in her voice.

Emotionally exasperated, Tara dropped down onto the warm leather sofa. She stared out the window into her own backyard. Tara was in tune with her thoughts and emotions. Something was wrong. One by one her loved ones had pulled away from her. She was the common denominator, she was the issue. Her mood swings and bad attitude had become more relevant. For years, Tara refused to seek help to deal with the trauma she suffered as a child. Time was up. Tara admitted to herself that it was time to let go of past pains.

At the age of ten, Tara walked into her sister's bedroom and caught the son of a family friend with his hands between Shy's legs. Shy was five at the time and didn't know how to react. Tara's job was to take care of her baby sister. Sometimes that responsibility was too much for a child to handle. *Hold your sister's hand walking to the bus stop, help sissy take a bath, and watch out for Shy on the playground.* Those duties were just the tip of the iceberg. It was only natural that Tara took care of Shy when she saw what the teenager was doing to her sister. The boy was startled when Tara walked into the room. He smiled at her and pushed Shy away. "I'll let her go if you let me feel you up." The boy smirked. Tara wanted to grab Shy and run away screaming but he had her by the arm. Tara agreed to do what he wanted. Before he let Shy go, the boy gave Tara a menacing look and threatened to shoot up their family if they ever told. Over the years, Shy had forgotten about the sexual abuse while Tara carried it with her like an expensive purse.

Tara felt as if Shy was worth saving but she wasn't important enough to receive that same protection. No one came to save her when she needed it most. The world stopped on its axis if Shy stubbed a toe. She never told anyone about what happened. Tara knew it wasn't Shy's fault for not telling anyone what happened to them. She was older and should have known better. Her anger ruled everything. Tara unconsciously believed Shy was stealing the blessings meant for her. The husband, the twins, the daughter, the house, the confidence, the independence was rightfully hers. By not getting help for what happened to her as a child, resentment buried itself in Tara's heart like a tumor. The negativity had taken control of Tara's life without her realizing it.

A butterfly hovered over a bushel of yellow roses as Tara sat daydreaming. There it was before her, a symbol of beauty, freedom, and happiness. Tara focused on the butterfly and decided to give up the fight against the tears welled behind her eyes. Tara's heart remained full of hate, envy, and petty anger. The fight between good and evil was rigged from the start. Negativity had become a huge part of who Tara had become. Tara felt at ease with blaming others for her unhappiness because pointing fingers meant she didn't have to face the truth.

In that quietness Tara heard God speak to her. It was time to let go and let God work in her life and heal her heart. Tara was more than happy to release her grip on the past. For the first time since giving birth to Quincy, Tara felt a flash of an emotional peace inside of her soul. Within seconds, away went the quiet peace deep inside. Shy chose Melvin as her life partner. He was a better caliber of a man than Bruce. Tara resented Bruce for not being strong enough to give their family a better standard of living. He kept a roof over their heads, food on the table, clothes on their backs, and supplied every essential Tara cried out for. Tara always wanted more. She was never satisfied with the blessings her family received so nothing was ever good enough. Her selfish ways had worn Bruce down. Bruce had fallen out of love with Tara years ago. She refused to see her role in holding their family's progress back. Instead of supporting him as head of their household, Tara kept a tight grip on the rope she'd looped around him and eventually, Bruce ran out of strength to fight back against the beast. Quincy was what kept both Tara and Bruce from walking away. They loved their son immensely. Tara and Bruce would give him anything except a healthy home life. The hate they shared for each other outweighed their love for their son.

Chapter 35

My Brother's Keeper

Jayden lay in his hospital bed listening to his brother update him on everything that went on after his accident. He couldn't believe what he was hearing. Prince felt Jayden had a right to know. Their mother would probably be mad but Prince had no problem taking that chance. Jayden needed know who had betrayed their family.

"Raequan shot me? Are you sure about that information? You know the streets get it wrong sometimes," Jayden asked with much skepticism.

"Bro, that nigga pulled the trigger on us. He's a bitch nigga fo' sho. Ain't no more Rae as far as I'm concerned. That's my word," Prince said.

"Raequan was always foul and jealous of us but this is out there. Did Roberts put him up to it?" Jayden quizzed.

"Man, I ain't a hundred percent sure but it all adds up. He flipped the script on me behind bars then dat nigga shot my shit up. Rae had to know I'd come after him for opening fire on us. He doesn't have it in him to even come up with a plot against me. Roberts had to be pumping dat nigga head up with false dreams," Prince replied.

"Did he know he's our brother all along? How could Cherise do that to Mommy and still be smiling in her face?" Jayden asked but was really making a statement.

"Oh, she's gon' get it, too. True dat. Mommy been acting like it ain't bothering her because of us being down but she's going through it," Prince sympathetically explained.

"You know how Mommy is. She won't let us see it but her heart has to be broken. How can she deal with the hurt and pain Daddy caused her and he's dead? There's more to it than just Daddy getting with Cherise. I bet any money there's a story behind it all."

"Whatever, it was fucked up fo' him to do Mommy like that. I don't give a fuck, Raequan ain't nothin' ta me no more. Let that bitch eat shit and live," Prince said angrily.

The twins both sat in deep thought. They both had questions for their father that would forever go unanswered. Their father was bigger than life to Prince. Jayden had equated his father to every superhero rolled into one. Finding out that he played their mother was difficult. Neither of them knew how to deal with the pain, but for now, it didn't matter. Getting their mother through it was mandatory.

Brianna and Monica walked in smelling like flowers. Their arrival interrupted the twins' conversation. It was a welcomed distraction for the sorrow they were feeling.

"Good morning, Prince, how are you feeling this morning?" Brianna spoke as she passed his bed.

"What up," Prince replied and turned his attention to Monica. "Girl, you better come give me one before I go off," Prince joked with Monica. She had been by his side almost as much as his mother had. He loved her for that. Monica gave Prince the sloppy kiss he wanted.

"Hi Prince! Hey Jayden!" Princess sang. She was in a playful mood and excited to see the twins.

"Hey, Baby Girl!" Prince and Jayden responded simultaneously with surprise.

Princess climbed onto Prince's bed and planted a kiss on his cheek. In a split second, Jayden received the same show of affection. The caffeine from the Pepsi she'd talked Monica into letting her drink had Princess jittery and hyper. Princess raced over to the chair she and her mother had slept in, and began playing with the television remote and experimenting with the various positions on the La-Z-Boy. Brianna stood between the huge window and Jayden's bed. She stroked the top of his head and laughed at his need for a haircut.

"How's my baby feeling?" Brianna asked in a playful voice.

"I'm good now. It's about time you got here. Me and Prince were shocked when we woke up and found nobody here. Where's our mother?" Jayden reached for Brianna's hand.

"She's at home fussing over everything. Princess was helping her so she asked us to come in her place and bring Baby Girl with us," Brianna explained.

"What's there to fuss over? The house is always spotless so she can't be cleaning." Prince joined Jayden and Brianna's conversation.

"Y'all know everything has to be perfect for your homecoming," Monica added.

"How does she know when that will be?" Jayden asked.

"Yeah, doc ain't said shit 'bout us gettin' up out of here," Prince spoke.

"Until now." Dr. Fitzgerald made his presence known. "How do you boys feel about going home today?" He made his way to the middle of the room. His attention was focused on the charts hanging on the foot of the hospital beds.

"Are you serious?" the twins said excitedly

"I think you both will do fine at home. You'll probably heal faster being in your own environment. There's one condition: take it easy. Don't do anything strenuous, eat right, and make every doctor's appointment. I'm letting you go home but that doesn't mean you're healed. You both had major surgeries and your bodies need rest," Dr. Fitzgerald explained.

"Yes, sir. We hear you," Jayden said happily.

"You got dat, doc. My momma's gon' be a drill sergeant, trust dat," Prince joked.

"I know she will. That's the only reason I'm releasing you guys. I've witnessed your mother in action myself. You'll be in good hands." Dr. Fitzgerald laughed.

Dr. Fitzgerald said his good-byes to the twins and left the room. By the time Brianna and Monica helped Jayden and Prince get dressed, Nurse Gordon was reading off their aftercare instructions. Brianna and Monica followed every word while Jayden and Prince only heard half of what she said. All they cared about was going home.

For the past few weeks, the only thing on Dwayne's mind was death. Fear that someone was out to end his life had him operating on fumes. Every bump in the night had him horrified. His nerves were frayed. It was all too much for him. Dwayne had a gut feeling that Roberts's death was no accidental overdose. If his suspicions were right, he and Raequan were living on borrowed time. Dwayne had tried to warn Raequan only to be dismissed as being paranoid. Raequan thought Dwayne was being insensible. He failed to recognize his own acts as destructible. Raequan continued to live on the edge as if he didn't have a care in the world.

Dwayne found it impossible to do the same. That's why he'd been casing out the McGee household for three weeks.

Dwayne knew Prince had been hospitalized but he figured they had to release him sooner or later. When that day came, Dwayne would be ready to attack. He was tired of waiting for the bogeyman to find him in the middle of the night. The plan was to do what Roberts had been afraid to do. Kill Prince. Prince was going to find out how it felt being a sitting duck. Shy was a good woman and under different circumstances, Dwayne would've tried to build a life with her. She had been married to the villain who ended his brother's life. Unlike Roberts, he had no desire to avenge his brother's death by punishing Melvin's offspring. He did, however, want to preserve his own. The twins had humiliated him and for that, Dwayne wanted payback. Being beaten and left for dead was humiliating. Roberts and Raequan took every opportunity to remind him of the beat down the McGee boys had put on him. Their taunting made it impossible for Dwayne to let it go. Instead, Dwayne's manhood had been reduced to rubble. He felt the only way to get it back was by retaliation. That's why Dwayne took pleasure in driving the car when Raequan pulled the drive-by on the twins. Dwayne pumped his chest at his involvement but continued to be belittled by Raequan and Roberts. Just the thought of it all made Dwayne's chest tight.

He left his painful thought behind when he noticed two teenage girls exit the house with little Princess tagging along. They were carrying duffle bags and smiling from ear to ear. Dwayne's gut told him they would lead him to his prey. Dwayne watched as they practically skipped to Prince's newly renovated candy-apple painted '83 Bonneville. *This is it. They're going to get that punk-ass Prince from the hospital. Why else would they drive his car? It ain't moved in weeks,* thought Dwayne. He followed them at a safe distance, trying not to be noticed. Dwayne was so excited that his substandard-sized penis became erect.

Both Prince and Jayden were wheeled out of the hospital. Dwayne felt like a kid on Christmas morning when he saw confirmation that his instincts were correct. They were assisted into the car by the nurses. From Dwayne's view, they looked healthy. Unfortunately, they also looked exactly alike. Dwayne had no way to tell Prince from Jayden. "Fuck it. I'll just have to put them both down. Prince is dying today. I like breathing," Dwayne said aloud as if he weren't alone. He kept close watch on his prey. One twin got into the front passenger seat's the other was assisted into the rear driver side. Princess hopped into the back, with the girls filling the remaining seats. Dwayne figured it was Prince in the front since they were riding in his car. He assumed the girls had to be the twins' girlfriends. His need for self-preservation prevented Dwayne from calling off his plan until a time when his target was alone. It was now or never. Should a bullet find Jayden or one of the girls, they would be considered casualties of war.

Dwayne had driven Raequan's hoopty for a couple of weeks. Raequan was clueless to Dwayne's plan. He assumed Dwayne needed wheels to get around. Since he'd just bought a new ride, Raequan told Dwayne he could keep the car for as long as he needed. The Bonneville pulled away from the hospital with a gray 1993 Cavalier on its back bumper. Now that the time had come, Dwayne started sweating profusely. His heart felt like it was going to pump out of his chest. Fear was sinking in but Dwayne didn't care. Nothing would stop him from seeing another day. Dwayne picked up the 9 mm automatic from the passenger seat and prepared to take aim.

Princess sat next to her big brother with her head rested on his right arm. She was surrounded by all of her favorite people. If her mother were with them, her birthday would've been perfect. Shy and Princess had spent the better part of their morning getting the twins' bedrooms ready. When Princess heard that her big brothers were finally coming home, she insisted on riding with Brianna and Monica to pick them up. She was in heaven.

Prince and Jayden matched their baby sister's excitement about going home. Per Prince's instructions, Monica kept both hands on the steering wheel, sure not to go over the speed limit. She drove through downtown to the bridge that led to the south side of town. Monica thought Market Street would have been the better choice but Prince wanted to see who was out hustling on the strip.

"Girl, be careful rounding up this hill. People can't drive and be swerving in dis lane speeding down this steep-ass street," Prince said like the typical backseat driver.

"I got it, baby, just relax," Monica responded, trying not to sound annoyed.

Monica looked into the rearview mirror and noticed the same car had been following them since leaving the hospital. She hadn't given it any thought until the driver sped up trying to pass them.

"This dude is tripping. He been behind us all this time and is just now trying to pass us," Monica told Prince.

Prince reached under his seat for the .38 he kept for emergencies.

"Hit the gas, babe. Keep your eye on the road. Jay, y'all duck and cover Baby Girl," Prince ordered.

His opponent had gotten the drop on them and was able to get off the first shots but Dwayne was no match for a professional. Anybody could hit a stable target but connecting with precision while on the move was something totally different. Prince let off bullet after bullet. Monica sped past the assailant and Prince kept shooting. Prince realized Dwayne was driving Rae-quan's car.

The screams from the girls only fueled Prince's anger. Dwayne was a true pussy to do some foul shit with a little girl in the car. Monica held her breath and drove as fast as she could up the hill toward the intersection, where a mother stood at the bus stop with her two young children. Dwayne wasn't experienced enough to shoot and drive at the same time. Dwayne knew that if Prince got away, he and C-Lok would make him suffer a horrible death. Prince and C-Lok would torture him before they'd just put a bullet in his head. Dwayne hit the back of Prince's car. Shots continued to fly his way. Dwayne swerved. A bullet hit his left shoulder, immediately followed by one to the neck. Dwayne immediately bled out. The car hit a curb and went airborne. It crashed into the bus stop instantly killing the innocent family where they stood.

Jayden did his best to protect his baby sister and girlfriend, who were screaming and crying. Brianna and Princess lay in the fetal position on the floor as Jayden covered them with his own body. He maintained his position until Prince said it was safe to move. Prince cautiously directed Monica to slow down and drive home. With his back window blown out and bullet holes on the driver side of the car, they would certainly call attention to themselves.

"Jay, stay down 'til I say it's cool. Monica, babe, are you good?" Prince was out of breath. He felt responsible for everyone in the car. He knew those bullets were meant for him and his loved ones unfortunately would've been considered casualties of war had they been hurt.

Monica pulled into the driveway and stopped short of the garage. "A'ight Jay, get the girls in the house," Prince instructed.

Jayden pulled himself up slowly. His body hurt from the sudden movements but nothing could have kept him from protecting Brianna and Princess. He'd have given his own life to save theirs.

"It's okay, Brianna. You and Princess come on," Jayden coaxed.

Brianna and Princess remained curled up, not moving. Monica had gotten out of the front seat and opened the back door for her sister.

"Oh my God, no!" Monica cried.

"What's wrong?" Prince demanded. His heart sank when he saw what had Jayden frozen and Monica panicked. "No, no, no!" Prince cried out from somewhere deep inside his soul.

Brianna and Princess hadn't moved. Princess was terrified and Brianna was in shock. The voices sounded like white noise to them. Brianna tried to sit up but her body ignored her brain's directions.

"Brianna, Brianna, baby, come on. You have to sit up," Jayden begged.

"Brianna, please move, please," Monica cried.

No movement from them could only mean death. Everyone began crying and begging Brianna to let Princess up. Still with no response.

Shy heard the screams and raced to the back door with Karl on her heels. She swung the door open, ready to fuss at the kids for making so much noise. Instead, Shy rushed to the car. When she saw Brianna holding her daughter, both covered in blood, Shy inhaled deeply and grabbed her chest to calm herself.

"Brianna, baby, it's okay. Come on and let me help you." Shy spoke slow and soft. "Princess, sweetie, come to Mommy." Shy fought back tears. She knew her daughter was alive. Her heart told her so. "Come on girls, it's safe. I'm right here."

Brianna burst into tears when Shy began to stroke her back. Her body shook uncontrollably. Karl stepped past Shy and gently pulled Brianna upright. He carried her into the house with Jayden and Monica in tow.

"Mommy!" Princess screamed.

She was alive. Tears of pain became those of joy and relief. Seven-year-old Princess was the glue that held them all together. Without her, Shy knew Prince and Jayden would be forever lost. It was a miracle. God knew the McGee family couldn't survive another tragedy.

Chapter 36

Meanwhile . . . Across Town

Raequan pushed his old school, gold-toned Bonneville up McGuffey Road feeling as cocky as ever. Since discovering his true birth right, Raequan had made it be known that he was the oldest son of Legend a.k.a. Melvin McGee. He told every street hustler, hood rat, friend, and enemy alike that he, not Prince, was in line to take over the family empire. The reins were his for the taking.

His entire life, Raequan had tried to emulate someone. All he knew how to do was stand in someone else's shadow and mirror the way they moved. As B-Boy's son, Raequan became a liar and a thief. He took advantage of every situation and relationship that presented an opportunity for him to get over. He had no identity of his own. All of their lives, Raequan had schemed to be exactly like Prince. To Raequan, Prince's life, in comparison, was better than his own. Prince's mom was more attentive, affectionate, and loving. Prince's looks outshined his own. Raequan was no match for Prince whatsoever. Being jealous-hearted came natural to Raequan; he got it from his momma. Receiving confirmation that he was a McGee was equivalent to being crowned king of the prom. The title was his; it didn't matter that he got it by default.

One Way's classic hit song "Cutie Pie" bumped from the Bonneville's speakers as Raequan approached his destination. He purposely arrived to the meeting an hour late. Raequan figured Sam, Rex, and Tyrell could wait. They needed him more than he needed them. Arrogance was the reason behind Raequan's disrespect for the game. He didn't understand that a man's word was important. Not too many people would deal with Raequan anymore. He didn't have a friend left after word leaked about him trying to shoot down Prince. Any respect he had left in the game dwindled when rumor on the street was that Raequan set his own mother up to be robbed and beaten. The streets wanted him gone. There was no room in the game for snakes. Raequan thought respect and fear went together like cake and ice cream. He was wrong.

"This is trippin'. He got the game fucked up if he thinks somebody's kissing his ass," Sam barked.

"Here that bitch-ass nigga come now," Rex reported while looking out of the front room window.

"A'ight, let's be 'bout it and get this shit under our belts. Play ya role," Tyrell instructed.

The three street hustlers had distain for Raequan. They'd all gone to school together and had never liked Raequan. He was tolerated because of Prince. After being in juvenile detention with Raequan and Prince, the three-man team came to hate Raequan even more. Tyrell knew how loyal Prince had always been to Raequan. The way he'd played Prince was unforgivable. Unbeknownst to Raequan, he would soon find out just how much he meant to the streets.

"What up, niggas," Raequan's words dripped with arrogance as he walked in the house.

"Yo, dude, we ain't that cool. You ain't gon' be just walkin' up in my crib," Sam fumed.

"My bad, nigga. No disrespect." Raequan gave a fake apology. He took a seat on the black leather sectional and got right down to business. "I trust we're good on that?" Raequan sought confirmation that the cocaine was within arm's reach.

"Yeah, my man, we good," Sam replied.

Sam was a natural-born criminal. He never made a move without analyzing the potential cons and pros of every situation. He didn't have to dissect his dealings with Raequan. The contract to take care of Raequan was like a dream come true. Sam knew Raequan's greed would make it easy to get next to him and, as expected, Sam was right.

"I don't see no bundles. You ready, nigga?" Rex smirked in reference to the additional money Raequan owed the crew.

"Don't even disrespect me like that. I always got mine," Raequan said, cocky.

"Word."

Rex opened the black suitcase to show Raequan his cut of the product they'd stolen from Cherise. Raequan tried not to show his excitement. When he'd hired Tyree, Sam, and Rex to rob his mother, Raequan knew they could handle the job. Raequan had lost what little respect he had for his mother when the paternity results were revealed. He held a lot of animosity about the entire situation toward his mother, which only fueled him to be on top. It was time for him to be the boss, his time to take over. His black heart made it comfortable for Raequan to step on his own mother's back to climb to the top.

"Good job, niggas. Let me get what's mine and y'all got the rest. Job well done." Raequan gave a light-hearted laugh. He'd given the crew instructions to steal Cherise's stash of money and product. It was a simple task with the keys and lock combinations having been provided. Raequan assured his hired hands that there was very little risk of being caught. They too figured Cherise would never suspect her son of such betrayal.

Time ticked by and Rex and Sam had become anguished. They had business to take care of and wanted to get it popping. Raequan was beneath them and did not deserve to continue breathing their air.

"Where's the bread, my man?" Tyrell quizzed. He too was ready to get work started.

Raequan went out to his car and returned with a duffle bag full of money. He felt like a kid on Christmas morning. The dope and money were his ticket to becoming somebody on the streets. It was time for Prince to fall off, as far as Raequan was concerned. His life had been hell because of the parents he was cursed with but no more. Raequan was determined to leave them both behind while he rose in the ranks.

"It was nice doing business wit' you, dude. 'Til next time." Raequan grabbed the suitcase and turned toward the door.

"My man, I'ma need you to do me a favor before you dip," Sam said through an evil smirk.

"What up?" Raequan answered.

"Put that case back down and empty ya pockets," Sam instructed.

Tyrell and Rex pulled out their guns and aimed at Raequan's head.

"Fuck is dis?" Raequan asked in total surprise.

"You know what this is, nigga. We decided to keep all of the dope and ya money. Now, do like my man said and empty ya pockets," Rex said before patting Raequan down. He knew if Raequan had any sense about him, he came through the door strapped. Rex was wrong.

"You need to be jacked. What true nigga comes into a deal without his shit on his hip?" Tyrell laughed.

"Y'all niggas fuckin' up fo' sho. You think I ain't comin' for y'all head behind this bitch-ass shit? Fuck's up?" Raequan thought it might've been a joke. He emptied his pockets of their contents and threw his hands above his head. Rex and Tyrell each grabbed an arm and twisted it behind his back. Raequan's hands were immediately duct taped.

"Take this nigga in the bathroom and make him strip," Sam instructed his cohorts.

Rex and Tyrell pushed their victim down the small hallway and into the bathroom. Raequan knew his time was up. There was no way he would walk out of the house. Even with all of the dirt he'd done to people, Raequan felt he hadn't earned such a fate.

"Ty, go take care of his ride. We'll be right behind you. Rex, take his shit out back and burn it in that pit like we planned. I got dis one alone," said Sam.

"Repent now, nigga, you're done." Rex pushed Raequan into the shower stall.

"Come on, Sam, we cool, dude. We came up together; how you gon' play me like dis?" Raequan cried.

"It's how the game's played. Your deal was good but not good enough. Anyway, I ain't ever liked ya bitch ass."

Raequan was so frightened, he pissed his pants.

"See, bitch-ass nigga," Sam said in response to Raequan's bladder releasing. He grabbed Raequan roughly by the neck and slammed him against the tiled wall.

"Sam, man, don't do this. Please, man, listen, we cool, just let me go." Raequan continued to cry and beg for his life. His words landed on deaf ears. Sam was having fun. He'd accepted the job with no hesitation. The money was great but Sam would've done Raequan for free.

"Fuck you, nigga," Sam responded. He took hold of Raequan's shirt and spun him around. With Raequan's back to him, Sam put the 9 mm to his neck and pulled the trigger.

Raequan's body fell to the floor with a thud. Sam kicked Raequan in the face for one final insult and left the bathroom. He had no remorse or second thoughts about taking a man's life. Sam was a natural-born criminal and would forever live like one.

Rex had the car running and in drive. Fire from the back of the house was already creating gray smoke when Sam hopped into the car.

"We good?"

"We great, nigga. Let's ride." Sam smiled.

"I hope that fire don't backfire on us," Rex said, looking in the rearview mirror.

"They need to find his body. We need this all over the news for two reasons," Sam began.

"So the hit will be confirmed is number one. What's the second reason?" Rex asked, perplexed.

"To let the streets know it's less one parasite." Sam laughed.

Sam and Rex picked Tyrell up from the junkyard where the owner had instructions to crush the car immediately. The old man had already paid him handsomely to do so. Unfortunately, the next morning it was reported that Raequan Jackson had been found bound and shot in the neck. He was alive and in critical condition. If Raequan lived, he'd be paralyzed from the neck down for the rest of his life. Even if Raequan pulled through, he wouldn't have much of a life to live.

Cherise was shocked when the doctor released her so soon after being admitted. A nurse explained that it was standard procedure to send home patients who underwent a mastectomy, hysterectomy, and various other procedures. Early release is very hard on patients who have no one to take care of them at home. The day she was released from the hospital, Cherise was surprised to see Tara and Nyla. They were a godsend. They'd cleaned her house after the police released the crime scene. At one time, Cherise had been like a little sister to Tara. Despite anything Cherise had done, she did not deserve to be the victim of a home invasion. Tara had enlisted Nyla to help get the house together for Cherise. Cherise was grateful. Tara and Nyla's help made a bad situation easier to handle.

Cherise lay in her queen-sized bed, crying. Her physical body was still recovering from the beating it took, and emotionally, Cherise was on the verge of a nervous breakdown. The depth of depression Cherise had sunken into destroyed any thoughts of climbing out. She'd been in the bed for over a week. Life outside of her bedroom was too overwhelming. Fear kept Cherise from descending on to the first floor of her house. Every inch of it caused quick flashes of the brutal attack to invade her mind. Cherise refused to put herself through more emotional pain.

"I can't do this. I have to get out of here," cried Cherise.

She wiped her eyes, blew her nose, and climbed out of bed. The walls were closing in on her inch by inch. Cherise needed a place to take refuge until she pulled it together. There was no way she could recover living in her house.

"I'm going to get a suite somewhere. Come on Cherise and think."

Cherise continued talking to herself from the time she got in the shower until a hotel manager finished up the paperwork needed for her to move into an extended-stay hotel. She only had two suitcases to unpack. It didn't take long for Cherise to get settle. Her cell phone had been ringing all morning. The phone displayed a number but no name so Cherise chose not to answer. After sending the call to voice mail a couple of times, Cherise answered with attitude.

"This is Northside Hospital calling for Miss Cherise Peters-Jackson," said a woman.

"This is she speaking." Cherise tried to sound proper.

"I'm sorry to inform you that your son Raequan Jackson was brought in last night with a single gunshot."

Cherise gasped and grabbed the wall to keep from falling on the floor.

"What happened? Is my son okay?"

"No, ma'am, he isn't. He's already undergone emergency surgery. There are many forms to be completed that allow us to give him the best care possible. Please get to the hospital as soon as possible. He's in the ICU. We will be looking for you." The woman spoke with compassion.

Cherise's heart raced and her breath became short. She felt a panic attack coming on. Cherise fought against it. Her son needed her. She would have to grieve for herself later.

A short, middle-aged nurse called for the surgeon when Cherise arrived. All Cherise could do was look at her baby through the thick glass window. What she saw scared her to no end. There were tubes, machines, and various other medical equipment attached to Raequan's frail body. Raequan was unrecognizable. His face was swollen to twice its size and had turned black and blue. A machine breathed for him. Cherise felt both hopeless and helpless.

The doctor explained Raequan's dire condition to Cherise as best he could.

"Raequan has very little brain activity. The bullet severed his spine. We're doing everything possible to save him. He's in critical condition and if by miracle he pulls through, your son will be paralyzed from the neck down for the rest of his life. Raequan will need twenty-four-hour care should he live. At this time, he requires more specialized care than what we can offer. With your permission, he will be airlifted to Cleveland Clinic. They have specialists with years of experience to take over his care. The nurse will give you all of the information you need. You can meet him there but we cannot allow you to ride with him in the helicopter. Good luck to you and your son."

It was as if the doctor just shared a movie synopsis with Cherise. All she heard was "little brain activity" and "paralyzed." Cherise was overwhelmed. There was no fighting off the panic attack that time. Luckily for her, the nurses knew how to get her through it. She didn't know what to do next. Her world had crumbled and she was alone. There was too much weigh on her shoulders. Cherise's soul was shattered.

"What am I supposed to do now?" Cherise asked toward the sky.

Three months later, life at the McGee house had slowly returned to normal. The boys' health had returned, Princess was being a brat to her big brothers, and Shy had returned to work on a part-time schedule. Prince and Jayden still had doctor appointments and Shy didn't like to be away from her children for too long.

Shy and Karl lay cuddled up on the couch watching a movie together. He had become a constant and consistent support system for Shy. Karl was happy to have such a strong, independent, and loving woman in his life. Until they met, neither realized just how lonely life had become. It was love for them both. Shy tried not to fall in love but her heart had other plans. Karl was comfortable and genuine. With the support of her children and after long talks with Bossy, Shy believed that Melvin would be happy for her. She believed her late husband could rest peacefully knowing his family was in good hands. For Karl, Shy had been sent from the heavens. Happiness for him had also been elusive. After his son was murdered and the failure of his marriage, he'd been a lost soul. His life had consisted of nothing but work and home. Meeting a woman like Shy had been a long time coming. There was nothing he would not do to make her happy.

"Stop playing around, boy. I can't hear the movie." Shy giggled.

"I thought you liked when I kissed on your neck," Karl said softly between wet kisses.

"Oh, yeah? I thought we were supposed to be watching this movie. You know what that does to me, especially with those strong hands of yours rubbing my back." Shy complained but her body language signaled differently. Shy loved that Karl was affectionate. His touch always calmed and relaxed both her body and mind. "We're going upstairs if you don't control those hands."

Karl picked up the remote control and stopped the movie. Shy grabbed the back of his head and pulled him closer. They kissed softly, enjoying the warmth and feel of one another. Without saying a word, Shy stood up and led Karl to her bedroom. All of the kids had gone with Quincy to visit The Ohio State University and Ohio University. It was rare for Shy to have the house to herself and she had been taking full advantage. Inside the bedroom, Shy fell back on her bed and pulled Karl down with her. The couple picked up where they'd left off downstairs.

"Aw damn, who could that be?" Shy asked in response to the ringing doorbell.

"I'll go answer the door and you go fill the tub up. We can make this an evening to remember," Karl said with a smile.

Shy watched the man she loved walk out of her bedroom. Her heart skipped a beat. She loved that man wholeheartedly. With a smile on her face, Shy went into her bathroom to prepare for an intimate evening. The Jacuzzi tub was filling with hot water while Shy lit candles and searched for her Raheem DeVaughn mix CD. His melodic voice would be perfect to help them relax. After pushing play, Shy undressed and slipped into her full-length terry cloth robe. Shy hadn't heard Karl return and was startled when she turned around.

"Boy, you scared the shit out of me. Why do you have that look on your face?"

Shy immediately knew that something was wrong. Her shoulders slumped with thoughts of another dilemma for her to muddle through.

"Promise me you'll stay calm," Karl said with concern.

"Why? Who was at the door?"

"Just stay calm and remember you can't control anything if anger has control of you." Karl spoke with great concern.

"You're starting to piss me off, Karl. Who's at my door?" Shy had become impatient.

"Cherise."

Shy thought she'd heard wrong. *Did he just say Cherise?* She stood with a look of anger on her face. If

Cherise had drummed up the courage to make a random visit to her house, the beat down of the century was about to pop off.

"Did you say Cherise?"

"She just wants to talk with you. I know how you feel about her but this may be a good thing."

Shy looked at Karl as if he'd sprouted a second head. There was no way Cherise being within striking distance could be a good thing, at least not for Cherise.

"I only say that because you must have questions that you need the answers to. You've been so busy taking care of your kids that the paternity issue with Raequan has been lingering. This is your opportunity to get the answers you need."

Shy thought for a minute. Karl was right. She did have a few questions for Cherise. The problem was getting the truth out of Cherise would be an issue within itself.

"Where is she?" Shy relented.

Karl and Shy walked into the dining room hand in hand. It was the closest room to the front door. Karl wanted Cherise to have a clear exit in case the meeting went horribly wrong. Shy was shocked by what she saw. Cherise looked awful. There were dark circles under her weary eyes, causing her to look aged. Her hair needed to be combed and the clothes she wore looked two sizes too big. She looked so miserable, Shy almost felt sorry for her former best friend.

"Shy, I know you don't want to see me but I have nowhere else to go. No one understands what I'm going through but you. I started to call but I knew you wouldn't have answered. It won't take long, I promise. Can we please talk?" Cherise pleaded with watery eyes.

Shy didn't answer. She took a seat opposite the woman who'd betrayed her. There was sincerity in Cherise's eyes offering Shy hope that she would get the truth about what happened all of those years ago.

"You probably heard but Raequan was shot a few months ago. He's in Cleveland Clinic Hospital. They say he'll never walk again if he makes it. My son is paralyzed and suffering," Cherise cried.

"Yeah, I heard," Shy said dryly.

There was no compassion from Shy. After everything Cherise and Raequan had done to her family, Shy felt karma had come full circle, giving them exactly what they deserved.

"The doctors are telling me that he'll need around-the-clock care for the rest of his life. He can't move from the neck down. He won't be able to use his arms or legs. Raequan is an invalid. He had no health insurance and I have no money to speak of. I was robbed of everything that I had in my safes. Everything has fallen apart. All of my friends have abandoned me, I was beaten and left for dead in my own home, my connect wants his money, and I can't think straight. I don't know what to do," Cherise said through tears. Her every word was drenched in emotional agony.

"What do you want from me?" Shy asked, unmoved.

"I know I don't deserve it but I want your forgiveness. I want my friend back." Cherise sniffed.

Karl saw the anger and hatred Shy was nursing reflected in her eyes. There were far too many unanswered questions for Shy to forgive. Cherise's every sin against Shy had not yet become clear. At that point, forgiveness was out of the question.

"What am I forgiving you for? Fucking my husband and making a baby with him? The fact that you looked me in the face every day knowing the betrayal you'd committed? Am I forgiving you playing me for a fool? What the fuck?" Shy was indignant.

"You don't understand," Cherise stammered.

"Damn right I don't understand!" Shy yelled as she jumped up.

"Shy, calm down," Karl instructed, his hand gripping her wrist.

After a few deep breaths, Shy was able to calm down. She sat back down and looked Cherise in the eye. There was nothing but grief and the reflection of a broken woman. Still, Shy felt no empathy. Her twins underwent multiple surgeries and were living with one kidney each due to Raequan's jealousy. Shy felt Raequan had brought on his own suffering. Cherise had raised him to be a jealous, materialistic thug who disrespected the game at every turn.

"I'm sorry Shy. You've always been a good friend to me. I was stupid and reckless. My life was nothing compared to yours. We were children and I didn't understand the weight of my selfishness. Your family treated me like I belonged from the start. All I wanted was to be like you. You had it all and I had nothing," Cherise rambled on, trying to explain.

"Right, my parents never mistreated you. My sister bought you the same things she did me and I was closer to you than Tara. What have I ever done to you for you to hate me?" Shy was choked up.

"Nothing. That's what I'm trying to tell you. Shy, you didn't do anything. It was about me, not you. I just wanted to be happy and loved. You had a man who loved and respected you; what did I have?

"How long were you sleeping with my husband?" Shy snapped.

"It wasn't like that at all."

"Tell me what it was and, Cherise, I want the truth."

Cherise paused to gather her thoughts. It had been her intention to confess and ask forgiveness for her sins. Though Shy looked angry, Cherise knew the pain she carried had to be overwhelming. She had to set things right by being honest. Cherise had it in her mind that by repenting, she could get on the right path. Her life was a living hell that needed a water hydrant to put out, or at least simmer down.

"The night we celebrated our high school graduation was the first time. You were passed out from drinking too much. Melvin knocked on our door wanting some weed when B-Boy invited him to have a three-way. We'd had an argument and I wanted to show you that you weren't any better than me," Cherise explained in an even monotone.

Shy couldn't believe what she was hearing. She remembered that night vividly. B-Boy had hit Cherise and she tried to help, only to be insulted. It was nothing. The former best friends had fights much more serious. For that pettiness, Cherise betrayed her in the worst way. Shy's heart broke. Cherise went on and Shy listened intently.

"You have to understand that was the only time Melvin willingly betrayed you. He loved you and felt horrible for what we did."

"Don't lie to me, that wasn't when you got pregnant so it didn't stop then," Shy fumed.

"I said willingly. It was a couple of years later when me and B-Boy were living on Sherwood Street. We were smoking, drinking, and playing cards. B-Boy had got his hands on some GHB and slipped it in Melvin's drink. Melvin thought he'd passed out when he woke up on our couch the next morning. I washed him up and we dressed him afterward. You don't know half of the stuff B-Boy made me do. B-Boy felt Melvin was leaving him behind as he rose in the game while he kept pounding the pavement. It's no excuse but B-Boy was as jealous-hearted as I was." Cherise tried to make the situation sound logical. Finally confessing to the rape of a man she truly wanted to be with was long overdue. "That same scenario happened one more time. Melvin had no memory of the threesome. He had no idea that Raequan was his."

The truth gave Shy back the respect she'd lost for her husband. They had been so close with a relationship that should've lasted a lifetime. At the same time, she was furious about the way B-Boy and Cherise had taken advantage of him. Shy didn't know whether to choke the life out of Cherise or thank God. She had been thinking the worst about Melvin and Cherise. Shy worried they had an ongoing affair behind her back. Not knowing the truth led way to multiple possibilities, all of which deeply hurt Shy. The truth sounded like fiction until B-Boy was added to the mix. He was Satan himself. Shy put nothing past him.

"He was a good man, a good person, period. If I recall correctly, my husband was damn near taking care of your dysfunctional family because B-Boy was a worthless provider. Why would you do that to him?"

Shy needed to know what Cherise's motive was behind it all.

"Like I said before, I wanted your life," Cherise said matter-of-factly.

Karl was outdone. He tried to put it all into perspective. A grown couple had drugged and basically raped a man they called a friend. Cherise was a psychopath as far as Karl was concerned. Shy had all the facts, which was the point of it all. If she was satisfied with Cherise's explanation, it was time for her to go. Karl couldn't stand to be around a woman with no soul.

"Are you okay, babe?" Karl asked as he rubbed Shy's back.

"Cherise, everything you've ever done in your life has been self-serving. Your reason for telling me all of this is probably more to benefit yourself than to reconcile our friendship. Don't you see that karma has you by the ass?"

"Shy, I am sorry for everything. I was a coward." Cherise began to cry again.

"Answer my question and tell me why, because it's not just that you wanted my life. There has to be more to it." Shy spoke through clenched teeth.

"I was in love with Melvin and wanted him for myself. Like I said, Shy, I wanted to be you." Tears continued to fall from her sad eyes.

Shy knew it. The idea that Cherise was in love with Melvin used to cross Shy's mind every so often. Shy was not surprised. It was a relief and gave Shy one more reason not to feel guilty for what she was about to say.

"Cherise, I want you to take this information with you when you walk out of my house for the last and final time. Raequan had you beaten in your own house because you never told him about his real father. It was Raequan who set you up to be robbed at the café. He needed your stash to get ahead." Shy paused a few seconds to watch the pain set into Cherise's heart. Finding out that your son hated you so bad that he'd ruin your life had to hurt. That was Shy's intent. "That's between you and him. I know all about Raequan's alliance with Roberts and Dwayne. Did you think he'd face no consequences for fucking with my family? You got me fucked up. They all got what they deserved for trying to kill my boys. Raequan didn't deserve to die. Death would have been too weak and too good of a punishment for his level of betrayal. I want him to suffer with every miserable breath he takes. You know I always get what I want."

Karl felt Shy was being too cruel but he understood where she was coming from. Wanting to hurt the person responsible for hurting your child is only natural. He thought Shy was creative to come up with what she'd put into Cherise's psyche. There was no way Shy was behind the deaths of two men and paralyzing another. *She's lying, right?* Karl thought.

Cherise was devastated. It never occurred to her that Raequan was behind the robbery. Could he really hate her that much? Had Shy's words been a lie? Was she just trying to hurt her by saying she had Raequan shot down? Cherise was stunned. Her soul had been crushed by Shy's words. She wanted to lie down and die. Only death would alleviate her pain.

Feeling satisfied with the outcome of their conversation, Shy stood from her seat and walked away from Cherise. On her way out, Shy turned and said to Karl, "Get that trash out of my house. I'll be waiting for you so we can get back to us."

Chapter 37

Nothing From Nothing Leaves Nothing

Commissioner Martin was under the gun. City leaders and the mayor wanted answers and he wanted the pressure. Someone had to be held accountable for the deaths of a single mother and her children. The family was innocent victims caught in the middle of an all-out gunfight. Most accidents are unpreventable; this tragedy was one of them. The city was a powder keg about to explode. Detectives Iverson and Selma needed to close the open case one way or another.

"I want an arrest made in this case," Commissioner Martin stated firmly.

"Yes, sir. We've been faced with more than a few undisputable facts. After gathering many witness statements and a recreation of the incident, the most we would be able to charge the shooter in the second car with is vehicular homicide at best. The occupants of the second car were not the aggressors. Dwayne Willis, driver of the first car, is responsible for those four deaths and that of his own," Detective Iverson explained clearly.

"There was a shootout with bullets flying around people walking down the streets. Residents need a sense of security. I am ordering you to reinvestigate the case with fresh eyes. Go where the evidence takes you step by step. Keep me abreast of your findings."

"Sir, how should we proceed if our investigation fails to result in bringing charges?" Detective Selma asked. She suspected that Commissioner Martin wanted them to file false charges.

"Like I said, Detective, follow the evidence. If an arrest should be made, do your job. If the case is closed without any arrest, do your job," Commissioner Martin explained.

C-Lok was relieved to see his sister looking well. He'd been worried about Shy. Anyone could easily break under all the stress Shy had going on in her life but she faced every issue like a champ. Bossy had tried to reassure C-Lok that Shy would be fine but he was always skeptical. Now, C-Lok would be able to rest easily knowing his sister had walked through hell and survived.

"This meeting is long overdue," C-Lok said as he rolled a blunt.

"My first priority was the twins. They've both healed well and are out and about so I can tend to my own business now," Shy explained.

"It's no big deal. We just have to get this out of the way," Bossy added.

"I was surprised you went ahead with Rae. I just knew you'd leave that one to me. The results are perfect so I'm not complaining." Shy smiled. She'd wanted to punish Raequan for his sins against her boys. Her disappointment faded away when she found out Raequan was paralyzed. It was exactly what he deserved. Death would have been too kind.

"What are you talking about?" Bossy asked, confused.

"I didn't order that hit," C-Lok assured Shy.

"Yes, you did. I didn't put that order in either. What's going on?" Shy wondered.

"Shy, you had a lot going on these last few months. You could have assigned it and just forgotten about it," C-Lok said.

"I'd remember putting that nigga down, C; don't even play me like that." Shy sounded annoyed.

"Before you two get into an argument, let's figure this out," Bossy calmly suggested. "Since the order didn't come from us, we have to figure out who did it."

Being the bosses, C-Lok, Bossy, and Shy were the only ones powerful enough to order a hit. They were clueless as to who would go over their heads and shoot Raequan. Not that they weren't pleased with the results, but there was a method to their madness and it had to stay in place.

"What about Big Black?"

"Shy, he's been back in North Carolina for a while now. There's business he needed to attend to. Anyway, Black would've come to one of us before he took things into his own hands," Bossy rationalized.

"Somebody's off the beaten path and needs to be pulled back. We need to find out who it is," C-Lok said.

"Maybe it was just a drug deal gone badly. Raequan is known for ripping people off," Shy reasoned. Beside the fact that someone had broken the order of the game, Shy was thankful to whoever put Raequan on his back. That's exactly where she wanted him to be for the rest of his miserable life. She wanted to shake the hand of Raequan's shooter and give him a medal.

"What do you want to do about Cherise?" Bossy inquired.

"I'll take care of that bitch. Cherise is going through it as we speak. I told her about Raequan's betrayal. Her ass is probably going crazy." Shy smiled.

"You are letting her live?" C-Lok was surprised.

"Hell no! I'm letting her live with the pain of know-ing her only child hates her so much that he'd put her life at risk. The same child that needs someone to wipe his ass for him. Having a child deprived of a life and still be alive has to be the second most devastating pain for a mother. Let the bitch marinate for a minute," said Shy with disgust.

Just like the initial witness interviews, people had been clear that Dwayne Willis's car was the aggressor. Had it not been for his actions, the mother and her children would be alive. The final step in putting the matter away was to re-interview Monica, Prince, Bri-anna, and Jayden. Detective Iverson hated to make the kids relive the tragic situation but he had a job to do.

The detectives had called ahead so Shy was expect-ing their visit. Detective Iverson had explained why they needed to talk with the kids again. Shy wasn't hap-py about it but reluctantly agreed to the meeting. To help things move along, she'd made sure Brianna and Monica would be at her house. She wanted the entire situation put to rest. All of the kids had enough to deal with and they wanted to forget about what happened. Prince was the only one who'd been in the car who was accustomed to bullets flying over his head.

"Come on in." Shy welcomed the detectives.

"Thank you again for agreeing to this, we know it's an inconvenience," Detective Selma said.

"My only stipulation is that I sit in on each interview. You can speak to them individually back here in our family room. Who do you want to talk with first?"

"The order doesn't matter," Detective Iverson re-plied.

Brianna looked scared to death. Her facial expression reminded Detective Selma of a child startled awake by a nightmare. That was exactly how Brianna felt. She'd been having nightmares about the incident regularly. Brianna tried relentlessly not to think about that life-threatening day. Having Shy hold her hand during the police interview helped Brianna tremendously. She was pleased when Detective Iverson said they were finished with her.

"Brianna, we're sorry you had to relive that day. I know something like this can be traumatizing, so you may want to consider talking to a professional. It can be very helpful," Detective Selma said sincerely.

Jayden gave Brianna a tight hug. He had done his best to comfort her but nothing seemed to help. Sadness was written all over her face. He understood how she was feeling. Brianna wept on Jayden's shoulder.

"I can't do this again. Jay, I'm tired."

"You won't have to, I promise," Jayden said and followed up his words with a gentle kiss on her forehead.

Prince sat next to his mother with an attitude. He felt bad about the deaths of that lady and her kids but that tragedy did not belong on his shoulders. Dwayne was a bitch-ass nigga who'd committed suicide as far as Prince was concerned.

"By the time Monica noticed that we were being followed, it was too late. That nigga sped up and started blasting. My brother, my girl, his girl, and my baby sister were in the car. I did what had to be done," Prince said without emotion.

"Were you expecting trouble? I mean, why have a gun in the car?"

"Detective Iverson, man, I'd rather the police catch me with it than for some nigga on the street to catch me without it," Prince replied matter-of-factly.

"It's odd to me that you'd have a gun in the car having just been released from the hospital," Detective Iverson responded. He kept his voice at a monotone level. The last thing he wanted was for the interviews to sound like interrogation.

"I used to stay strapped. You know the saying, its better the police catch you with it than for a nigga on the streets to catch me without it? That's a street law I always held strong to," Prince stated honestly. His mother gave him a disapproving look. She demanded her children speak according to the occasion.

Prince had long ago grown tired of the police hanging around. He was itching to get back in the game but their constant presence made his drug delivery too risky. Anyway, he was not responsible for the outcome of that drive-by. His statement was over. Without permission, Prince stood up and left the room. He'd deal with his mother's anger later; as for now, the police could kiss his ass.

The detectives made no qualms about Prince ending his interview. They did have compassion for them all but they had a job to do.

Minutes later, Jayden entered the family room looking upset. He'd left Brianna in his room lying across his bed. The only time she seemed to get any rest was when he held her. Jayden didn't appreciate having to leave his girl alone. His physical appearance and attitude made the detectives think Prince had returned.

"Prince, we get that you want this matter closed but—" Detective Selma was interrupted.

"I'm not Prince," Jayden spat.

Shy felt her son's irritation. She rubbed his back in attempt to calm him down. Jayden was never one to run the streets. He'd never pulled a trigger in his life. His focus had always been school, sports, and video games.

Jayden's interview lasted fifteen minutes. Instead of being asked the same questions as his last interview, Jayden narrated everything he remembered. They were wasting time that he did not have. He had to get back to Brianna. "I'll send Monica in." Jayden left the room but not before being excused.

"Hold off on that for a minute, I need to discuss something with your mother," said Detective Iverson. Having mistaken Jayden for Prince gave him an idea. If Shy agreed to it, the McGee family would be free to move on from this tragedy.

The twins stood in a midsized room with four other teenagers of their same height and build. They all wore simple white T-shirts, dark jeans, and sported Caesar haircuts. A number hung around the necks of everyone in the brightly lit room. An officer stood on the far wall staring at Prince and Jayden. He was trying to figure out who was who. Soon, the five witnesses to what happened that unfortunate day would do the same.

Shy had agreed to the police line on one condition. Their lawyer had to be present. Detective Iverson was certain this issue would result in the case being closed. Shy waited outside the room with Monica by her side. Brianna was still emotionally fragile so Shy asked her to babysit Princess instead of dealing with this process. Brianna was relieved she didn't have to be there.

Tommy Jackson Jr. served as the twins' legal counsel. He was pleased with the lineup. All of the boys resembled one another. The twins were mirror images of each other. He was certain things would go in the McGee family's favor.

Prosecutor Marianne Boyce wanted the case in a courtroom. It was an election year and prosecuting

this high profile case would help her become a judge
for sure. Detective Iverson knew Mrs. Boyce was out
for blood. She didn't care if the defendant was guilty.
Detective Iverson felt the McGee family had already
been through a lifetime of sorrow; he was determined
to close the case.

"All of the witnesses are ready. Let's start," Detective
Selma announced.

The first witness was a senior citizen of Hispanic
descent who'd been walking his dog at the time of the
car chase.

"Okay, Mr. Sanchez, look at the boys and see if you
recognize who was shooting the gun. Take your time."
Detective Iverson coaxed him along.

After intense concentration, Mr. Sanchez was unable
to say with certainty who had returned fire.

"No, sorry, son. I can't point him out. They all look
alike. Two even look like twins. Why are you doing this
anyway? They were only protecting themselves. That
young man in the other car was the aggressor," Mr.
Sanchez said to everyone in the room.

"I suspect the remaining four will have the identical
result." Mr. Jackson smiled.

"Let's just get through this, shall we?" Mrs. Boyce
snidely said.

Witness number two had been driving down in the
opposite direction of the two cars. She feared one of
the speeding vehicles would crash right into her car.
Bianca James was so sure she'd be killed, she confessed
her sins and prayed for a quick death.

"I can't say for sure but it could've been numbers two
and five. There's no way I'll be able to tell those twins
apart but they were both in the second car," Ms. James
said with little emotion.

"Thank you for your time, Ms. James. You're free to go," Detective Selma said as she opened the door for her exit.

David Smith was a nineteen-year-old college student headed for the same bus stop Dwayne crashed into. He did not want to be involved until Detective Iverson made him feel guilty for not speaking up for the kids who were killed. His mother supported his decision either way. David just wanted it all to go away.

"Yeah, the twins were in the second car. Like I've been telling y'all, I cannot tell them apart. I don't know which one returned fire to that man who died. What I can say for sure is they didn't start the chase," David said, irritated.

"Look again and take your time," Mrs. Boyce requested.

"Ma'am, I don't know what you want me to say but for the last time, I do not know." David instructed the detectives not to contact him again. His duty was done.

"This is just a waste of time. We all know what's behind this but you don't have a case against my clients," Mr. Jackson said to Mrs. Boyce.

"Not so fast; we have two more witnesses." Mrs. Boyce tried to save face. She couldn't identify Prince from Jayden but wished for a miracle.

"NaTasha Douglas is next. She drove behind the cars and had a clear view of everything that happened," Detective Selma announced.

NaTasha entered the room popping on a stick of gum. She'd just had blue and yellow hair sewn into her tracks and wanted to go show off the new look. One look at her and Mrs. Boyce knew her case was sinking fast.

"There are some fine-ass men looking at me," NaTasha responded to the lineup with curiosity in her voice.

"They can't see you, Miss Douglas." Detective Iverson laughed at the young woman.

"That's too bad 'cause numbers two, four, and five can get it." NaTasha laughed but was serious. "Can I leave my number for them?"

"Miss Douglas, please focus," Mrs. Boyce said, irritated.

NaTasha looked at Mrs. Boyce as if she were Satan himself. She rolled her eyes at the stuck-up woman and turned back around.

"Yeah, whatever. Number two and five are the fine-ass twins dat that nigga was shooting at. If I was them, I would've shot back too. It's a shame about the lady and her kids but dude got what he deserved. Now is that it? I got get ready for da club tonight."

Prince and Jayden stood behind the glass, irate. In their entire lives, not one stranger had been able to tell them apart. Even when Prince sported braids and Jayden stayed lined up, they were always mistaken for one another so they thought the idea of a line-up was great. After an hour of standing in one spot they had grown tired and needed to rest.

Detective Iverson left the room and quickly returned with the last witness. Carla Austin had been sitting on her porch smoking a cigarette when the crash took place. She lied to the police at her initial interview hours after the accident. Getting involved in a shooting could have put her life in danger. The police knew she was lying. They were relentless in pulling a statement out of her when all she wanted was to be left alone. Here she was again, being bullied into going against her will. Carla wasn't afraid anymore; thanks to the police harassment, she was angry.

"So what? Y'all expect me to identify the shooter or something?" Carla asked, incensed.

"Yes, Miss Austin, take your time and look at each one of their faces. Tell us the number of the person shooting the day of that tragedy." Mrs. Boyce tried to sound polite.

Carla wasn't falling for it. No matter what, her involvement in that mess was coming to an end right there and then.

"He's not there," Carla blurted out.

"Miss Austin, just take a—" Detective Selma began.

"I said he ain't there, but I do know where you can find him," Carla barked snidely.

"Where is the shooter?" Detective Iverson asked, somewhat amused by the witness's demeanor.

"Six feet under," Carla replied.

"Miss Austin, please, you are starting to wear my nerves. We need you to identify the shooter of the Bonneville. This will all be over after your corporation," Mrs. Boyce said demandingly.

"The driver of the other car pulls up on that Bonneville and chased them down. He started shooting and the other car didn't respond for a few seconds. Why are you so bent on fucking up those kids' lives? Go press charges against the dead man and while you're at it, kiss my ass!" Carla blared before walking out of the room.

Everyone in the room was stunned by the witness's outburst. Mrs. Boyce seemed to be alone in her exasperation. Detective Iverson was relieved he would be able to close the case. He knew the right thing needed to be done by the McGee family. They had a right to put the incident behind them and move forward. Life so far had tried them in every emotional way possible.

"It seems we're done here. No eyewitness means no charges can be filed. I'll be taking my clients home and any further harassment by the prosecutor's office will result in the biggest lawsuit in the history of this city. It will become a nationwide news story. Now, you all have a pleasant day." Mr. Jackson bid them farewell as he left the room.

Chapter 38

Oh No, He Didn't

Sunday dinner with the family was perfect. Shy had prepared a meal fit for kings and queens; that's exactly who she was serving. As she looked around the table at her loved ones, Shy felt her heart flutter. Prince's and Jayden's health had improved greatly after the criminal case against them became a nonissue. Princess had started sleeping in her own bed again and the therapist was impressed by the little girl's progress. Quincy started classes at Kent State University and worked part time at a car dealership. Jayden and Brianna were talking about moving in together but Shy wasn't having it. They were too young to be playing house. Shy was concerned by how dependent Brianna had become on her son. It wasn't healthy. Brianna needed to see a therapist to get over the trauma. If Princess was able to overcome it, so could Brianna. Monica seemed to float around, waiting to see what Prince wanted of her. Shy had warned Prince that Monica was infatuated with him, not in love. She'd become possessive and passive. Monica was on the fast track to snapping and pulling a *Fatal Attraction* on Prince.

"If Monica tries to pull some *Fatal Attraction*–type bullshit on you, I'm laying her down. Trust me," warned Shy.

"Ma, that girl ain't got the heart for that type of move. She cool, I got this," Prince said dismissively.

Shy decided to leave it alone. Her instincts were never wrong so she knew a storm was brewing. When it hit, she'd be ready.

After dinner, Shy and Karl left for his house. They wanted some peace and quiet. With teenagers always invading her house, Shy found refuge at Karl's house. For the first time since Melvin's death, Shy was happy. She felt love, protection, and comfort with Karl. They seemed to be exactly what the other needed to get past their personal tragedies.

"Are you straight? Do you need anything?" Karl asked before he got comfortable next to Shy.

"I'm fine. Come on and sit down." Shy smiled.

Karl found a position on the couch that allowed him to hold Shy. She pressed play and the movie played. Like the teenagers they'd run from, Shy and Karl kissed, fondled, and whispered sweet nothings to each other. Just as things got heated up, there was a knock on the door.

"Who could that be?" Karl wondered.

"Whoever it is, get rid of them," Shy said seductively.

Karl was in the midst of fixing his pants as he swung the door open. He was shocked by who he saw. His stomach tightened.

"Hello, Karl."

"What are you doing here?" Karl asked, confused and displeased by her unannounced presence.

It was Vaughn, his ex-wife. She smiled as she walked past Karl and into the house they once shared together.

"How are you, Karl? Judging by the bulge in your pants, it seems this isn't a good time." Vaughn smirked.

"Why are you here? And you're right, this isn't a good time," Karl said angrily.

"Oh, you're entertaining company?" Vaughn looked around as she spoke.

"My girlfriend and I are busy. Maybe you should call next time you want to drop by," Karl suggested with displeasure.

"Yeah, maybe you should," Shy chimed in and began a staring contest with the disrespectful woman.

"I'm sorry, have we met?" Vaughn extended her right arm.

"Trust me, if you'd ever crossed my path, you wouldn't have to ask that question," Shy replied straight faced, leaving Vaughn's arm hanging in the air.

Karl was just as surprised by Vaughn's visit as Shy must have been. He watched the exchange between the two women and a feeling of dread washed over his happy mood. Vaughn needed to leave and Shy had to remain calm.

"Vaughn, this isn't a good time. Call me later in the week and I'll try to meet you for lunch or something." Karl held the door open for his ex-wife.

Vaughn took one last look at Shy before rolling her eyes and walking toward the door. Jealousy had snuck up on her at lightning speed. If she had any chance at getting Karl back, her game had to be stepped up. Shy was going to be a challenge. "Okay Pooches, I'll talk with you soon." Vaughn called Karl by her nickname for him. The peck on the cheek she gave him was purely for Shy's benefit.

Karl closed the door behind Vaughn and inhaled deeply. He could only image Shy's wrath. Her attitude alone could be intimidating. Shy stood with her hands on her hips and fully loaded with questions. She loved Karl with all of her heart but would be damned if any man played her.

"So, why the fuck was she here?"

***

Prince, Jayden, and Quincy sat playing *Mortal Kombat 3* in the family room. All of the food they ate had them feeling lazy. It was like old times. Prince and Jayden argued about nothing and Quincy refereed. There were times when they could all get along.

"Is everything cool with Unc?" Quincy inquired.

"Yeah, he's cool," Prince replied.

"Did he ask you about the hit on Raequan?" Jayden probed.

"And you know it. He didn't come out and ask if I was behind it. He just assumes it was me by process of elimination. Unc understands why it had to happen. Everything is good," Prince promised.

"Good, it can never surface that I was behind Raequan being put down. No one can ever find out that there are two young-minded hustlers in the family." Jayden laughed.

An Afterthought

Cherise had teetered on the edge for months. She'd lost it all. With all of her stash stolen and savings depleted, Cherise was nearly destitute. Chase Bank had taken possession of her house, her car was repossessed, and her business was gone forever. She'd called the extended-stay motel home until her money ran out. The insurance money she received after the break-in went toward Raequan's hospital bills. $50,000-plus was just a drop in the bucket. Having had no taxable income, the state approved Raequan for HCAP health insurance but Cherise still had to contribute money she just did not have. Cherise asked Terry for help when she had nowhere else to turn. Terry opened her home to Cherise with the promise to help as much as possible for as long as needed.

The hospital had to move Raequan into a rehabilitation facility. Cherise had no means to take care of herself, let alone her invalid son. After his diagnosis, Cherise often thought death would have been more humane. She felt bad for thinking that way but seeing her son unable to do anything for himself was pure torture. All he did was lie in bed with blank stares at the ceiling. He had no willpower or any desire to accept his current situation. As she sat watching time tick away on her son's life, it slowly killed Cherise on the inside.

Shy's words continued to play in Cherise. There was no off button for the hurtful and devastating words

Shy had delivered. As Cherise stood alone in Raequan's room, she wondered if she was looking at someone who loved her or an enemy who detested the very space she occupied. It was a mother's nightmare. Cherise lived in a state of deep depression. She felt alone. Since it came out about Melvin being Raequan's father, friends had treated her like a pariah. Though she knew everyone was right about her being solely responsible for the way they felt about her, Cherise needed their forgiveness. Even she couldn't fault her inner circle for not trusting her anymore. Life for Cherise and Raequan was over. Perhaps it was karma. Cherise thought back on all of the lies, tricks, and double-crossing she'd done over the years. Raequan was as ruthless and black-hearted as B-Boy and acted with malice and jealousy in his dealings with others. He had just been mimicking the examples both of his parents had taught their son. Whoever said karma was a bitch had not lied.

She looked down into Raequan and searched his eyes for a soul. As she stood contemplating their futures, Cherise could find no redeeming qualities in her son's dark heart.

Raequan looked over at his mother. He felt contempt for her bringing him into the world and raising him without the tools needed to survive. Mother and son stared into each other's eyes for a short time. For the first time since being shot, Raequan spoke to his mother.

"Is it true, Rae? Did you set me up?"

"You deserved it," Raequan struggled to say. His words were without emotion.

"You're as pointless as B-Boy." A single tear trailed down her face.

"Go to hell," Raequan replied as he maintained eye contact.

"You first," Cherise cried.

Cherise held up the .25-caliber gun she held in her right hand, put it to the left side of her son's head, and pulled the trigger, but not before Raequan gave a final smile. In the split second before feeling the cold steel against his temple and Cherise shooting the gun, Raequan felt relieved that his mother finally did something right.

"Lord, please forgive me," Cherise prayed with her eyes to the heavens.

Another pull of the trigger and Cherise joined her son in eternal hell.

ORDER FORM
URBAN BOOKS, LLC
78 E. Industry Ct
Deer Park, NY 11729

Name:(please print):_____

Address: _____

City/State: _____

Zip: _____

QTY	TITLES	PRICE

Shipping and handling-add $3.50 for 1st book, then $1.75 for each additional book.

Please send a check payable to:

Urban Books, LLC

Please allow 4-6 weeks for delivery

ORDER FORM
URBAN BOOKS, LLC
78 E. Industry Ct
Deer Park, NY 11729

Name: (please print): _____

Address: _____

City/State: _____

Zip: _____

QTY	TITLES	PRICE
	16 On The Block	$14.95
	A Girl From Flint	$14.95
	A Pimp's Life	$14.95
	Baltimore Chronicles	$14.95
	Baltimore Chronicles 2	$14.95
	Betrayal	$14.95
	Black Diamond	$14.95
	Black Diamond 2	$14.95
	Black Friday	$14.95
	Both Sides Of The Fence	$14.95
	Both Sides Of The Fence 2	$14.95
	California Connection	$14.95

Shipping and handling-add $3.50 for 1st book, then $1.75 for each additional book.

Please send a check payable to:

Urban Books, LLC

Please allow 4-6 weeks for delivery

ORDER FORM
URBAN BOOKS, LLC
78 E. Industry Ct
Deer Park, NY 11729

Name: (please print):_____

Address: _____

City/State: _____

Zip: _____

QTY	TITLES	PRICE
	California Connection 2	$14.95
	Cheesecake And Teardrops	$14.95
	Congratulations	$14.95
	Crazy In Love	$14.95
	Cyber Case	$14.95
	Denim Diaries	$14.95
	Diary Of A Mad First Lady	$14.95
	Diary Of A Stalker	$14.95
	Diary Of A Street Diva	$14.95
	Diary Of A Young Girl	$14.95
	Dirty Money	$14.95
	Dirty To The Grave	$14.95

Shipping and handling-add $3.50 for 1st book, then $1.75 for each additional book.
Please send a check payable to:
Urban Books, LLC
Please allow 4-6 weeks for delivery

ORDER FORM
URBAN BOOKS, LLC
78 E. Industry Ct
Deer Park, NY 11729

Name: (please print): _____

Address: _____

City/State: _____

Zip: _____

QTY	TITLES	PRICE
	Gunz And Roses	$14.95
	Happily Ever Now	$14.95
	Hell Has No Fury	$14.95
	Hush	$14.95
	If It Isn't love	$14.95
	Kiss Kiss Bang Bang	$14.95
	Last Breath	$14.95
	Little Black Girl Lost	$14.95
	Little Black Girl Lost 2	$14.95
	Little Black Girl Lost 3	$14.95
	Little Black Girl Lost 4	$14.95
	Little Black Girl Lost 5	$14.95

Shipping and handling-add $3.50 for 1st book, then $1.75 for each additional book.
Please send a check payable to:
Urban Books, LLC
Please allow 4-6 weeks for delivery

ORDER FORM
URBAN BOOKS, LLC
78 E. Industry Ct
Deer Park, NY 11729

Name:(please print):_____

Address: _____

City/State: _____

Zip: _____

QTY	TITLES	PRICE
	Loving Dasia	$14.95
	Material Girl	$14.95
	Moth To A Flame	$14.95
	Mr. High Maintenance	$14.95
	My Little Secret	$14.95
	Naughty	$14.95
	Naughty 2	$14.95
	Naughty 3	$14.95
	Queen Bee	$14.95
	Say It Ain't So	$14.95
	Snapped	$14.95
	Snow White	$14.95

Shipping and handling-add $3.50 for 1st book, then $1.75 for each additional book.
Please send a check payable to:
Urban Books, LLC
Please allow 4-6 weeks for delivery